What the Dark Whispers

M J Lee has worked as a university researcher in history, a social worker with Vietnamese refugees, and as the creative director of an advertising agency. He has spent 25 years of his life working outside the north of England, in London, Hong Kong, Taipei, Singapore, Bangkok and Shanghai.

Also by M J Lee

DI Ridpath Crime Thriller

MJ LEE

WHAT THE DARK WHISPERS

CANELOCRIME

Penguin
Random
House

First published in the United Kingdom in 2025 by

Canelo Crime, an imprint of
Canelo Digital Publishing Limited,
20 Vauxhall Bridge Road,
London SW1V 2SA
United Kingdom

A Penguin Random House Company
The authorised representative in the EEA is Dorling Kindersley Verlag GmbH.
Arnulfstr. 124, 80636 Munich, Germany

A CIP catalogue record for this book is available from the British Library.

Print ISBN 978 1 80436 904 3
Ebook ISBN 978 1 80436 905 0

This book is a work of fiction. Names, characters, businesses, organizations, places and
events are either the product of the author's imagination or are used fictitiously. Any
resemblance to actual persons, living or dead, events or locales is entirely coincidental.

Cover design by Tom Sanderson

Cover images © Arcangel, Shutterstock

Printed and bound in Great Britain by Clays Ltd, Elcograf S.p.A.

Look for more great books at
www.canelo.co | www.dk.com

To the people of Manchester:

We do things differently here.

Monday, October 28.

Chapter ONE

By the time Ridpath arrived, the white tent was already erected next to Pump 8 in the petrol station forecourt and a group of crime scene investigators were milling around, their white Tyvek suits making them look like ungainly Michelin men.

Off to one side, three medics were leaning against a vehicle, their work done. One other was completing the contact sheet on his iPad. On the other side, two fire tenders were packing away their gear, the white-helmeted senior officer taking off his protective clothing and climbing back into the cabin.

The area had already been cordoned off and Ridpath had been forced to show his ID twice to the young coppers guarding the inner sanctum of the petrol station.

Terri Landsman, the scene of crime manager, tapped him on the shoulder. 'Hiya, Ridpath, you're early. You here as a copper or a coroner's officer?'

'The latter today. I got the call just as I was heading home, thought I'd drop in here to check it out. Who's the pathologist?'

'Dr Schofield. He's in the tent at the moment.'

'Has he pronounced death yet?'

'Not yet, but it won't be long. This one isn't getting up and walking away.'

2

'Is he the witness who called it in?' Ridpath pointed to a man sitting on a chair in front of the petrol station's shop. He had a grey blanket over his shoulders and was nursing a plastic cup of tea like it was the last source of warmth in the world. The harsh neon lights on the forecourt made his skin seem alabaster white, as if he had seen the most terrifying ghost. A young woman sat next to him, leaning forward to catch every word he said.

At the moment, he wasn't saying anything.

'Worse, he saw it all.'

'Poor bugger.'

'Rather him than me. A Halloween special. I had to hold the lads and the good doctor back until the fire brigade pronounced the area safe.'

'Who's with him?'

'The young detective? That's Megan Muldowney. Just promoted to DC. Do you two know each other?'

'I don't think so – can't remember meeting her. Don't think we've ever worked together.'

'Well, she knows you. Your reputation precedes you, Ridpath.'

'I suppose I should go and say hello before the doctor comes out from the tent.'

Ridpath wandered slowly across the forecourt. The crowds had dispersed now, but there were still a few interested onlookers, hoping for a bit more action before the end of the evening. The television crews had already packed up their gear and departed to file their stories, but a couple of intrepid reporters were still hanging around hoping for a quote or three.

Ridpath noticed the smell was still hanging in the air; the aroma of petrol mixed with something else. He frowned trying to catch what it was. Sunday dinner, that was it. Not the sort of smell he expected on a petrol station forecourt.

Ridpath studiously avoided looking at the reporters. The last people he needed to deal with at the moment were the people of the press.

Not today.

Not with this case.

As he approached the witness, the detective stared at him. The man didn't move though. He just gazed straight ahead as if in a trance, his eyes focused on somewhere far distant and his fingers still gripping the plastic cup as if it were the Holy Grail.

'Hello, my name is Ridpath. I'm the coroner's officer.'

The woman stood up. She was almost as tall as Ridpath, with soft blonde hair tied up in a ponytail. She was wearing the usual clothes of a newly promoted detective constable: blue woollen suit, white shirt and sensible shoes.

She held out her hand. 'I know who you are, I've heard a lot about you. You've got a bit of a reputation at the training college in Sedgley Park.'

Ridpath raised his eyebrows. 'Good or bad?'

'A bit of both actually.'

'Is this our witness?'

'Mr Paul Dacre.'

On hearing his name, the witness raised his head and acknowledged Ridpath's presence for the first time.

'I'm just about to take his statement.'

'Don't let me get in your way.'

The woman sat back down, taking out her notebook. 'I'm sorry, Mr Dacre, let's continue, shall we? You said you live at 11 Roscrea Road?'

'That's right.' The answer came out as a whisper.

4

'Could you speak up? I'll try to get this done as quickly as possible so you can go home, but it's important we take a statement while the details are still fresh in your mind.'

The man's eyes opened wide as if something had suddenly occurred to him. 'My wife, I haven't rung her. She'll be worried about where I am.'

'It's okay, let us take a statement first and then you can ring your wife. If you're not up to driving, we can give you a lift back home.'

The man nodded once and drank some of the warm tea.

'You came to the petrol station to fill up?'

He nodded again, more slowly this time. 'I'd dropped the wife and kids off at home. We'd been to Elterwater in the Lake District for a long weekend as the school had an inset day after half-term. In the morning I have to drive to Leeds for a meeting, so I thought I'd come and fill up tonight to get an early start on the M62 tomorrow.'

He paused for a moment, staring out across the forecourt. 'Stupid decision, I should have waited, done it in the morning.'

'What time did you get here?'

'A little after eight, I think it was.'

'Could you be more exact?'

'8.05 p.m., around that time. I remember I'd just heard the news on Classic FM.'

The young detective was doing well, thought Ridpath. Drilling down when she needed to but letting the man tell the story in his own words.

'So, what happened when you arrived?'

'Nothing really. I drove into the station and parked at Pump 7. I shut off the engine, popped the cap release. I took my wallet and car keys, went round the back of the car and noticed the price of the 95. Daylight robbery, the price of fuel, isn't it?'

The detective ignored his question. 'Did you see anybody else here? Any other cars?'

He shook his head. 'No.' He stopped for a moment, placing his right forefinger on the area above his lips. 'I tell a lie, there was a red car, a Volkswagen I think. As I parked up, it pulled away from the petrol station back onto the main road.'

'Can you remember the licence plate?'

For the first time, the man looked at the detective. 'Why would I remember that? It was just a red car at a petrol station, why would I remember the number?'

Ridpath decided to jump in. 'So, you were filling up your car, what happened then?'

'I'd preselected fifty quid, so I just put the nozzle in my tank and held the lever. I knew it was going to stop by itself so I was just looking around like you do when you're filling up. It was then I noticed a man coming towards me.'

'A man?' Megan Muldowney was probing correctly, trying to find out the dead man's details. 'How was he dressed?'

'A white T-shirt, jeans, some sort of trainers. I thought he was underdressed for late October in Manchester, but some people don't feel the cold, do they?'

'And what did he look like?'

'Look like? Ordinary, I suppose. Dark hair, medium build, mid-to-late thirties, normal face. Just an average person really, not somebody who would stand out in a crowd.'

'Then why did you notice him in particular?' asked Ridpath.

The man frowned again. 'I don't know exactly why. I think it was because he was so focused on what he was doing.'

'Focused?' asked Megan.

'He didn't look left or right, just walked straight up to Pump 8.'

'This was the pump behind your car, is that correct?'

'That's right.'

'What happened next?'

'That was the weird part. He stood in front of the pump as if seeing one for the first time…'

'How long did he stand there?'

Another long swallow of his tea, finishing the last dregs. Paul Dacre stared into his empty cup for a long time then placed it on the ground next to his chair leg. 'Not long, maybe twenty seconds. The nozzle I was holding clicked quite loudly and so I looked down at it. When I looked up again, the man was inserting a credit card into the reader. I thought that was a bit weird, but I was busy putting my nozzle back on its hook on the pump and sorting out the petrol cap.'

Paul Dacre leant forward burying his face in his hands. 'I can't tell you about it. I can still see it, still smell it.'

'What happened, Mr Dacre?' Megan Muldowney persisted. 'We need to know what happened.'

'He put his credit card back in his pocket and then wrote something with a pen on the pump.'

'What did he write?'

'I dunno, I couldn't see. Then, he lifted the nozzle of the pump above his head and I saw him grip the release. A torrent of petrol washed over him. The smell, the smell, it was so strong…'

He stopped speaking for a second, his hands covering his mouth and his eyes closed. 'I couldn't do anything. I just stood there and watched him.'

'What did he do?'

'It was as if everything was in slow motion, like a scene from a film. He put the nozzle down at his feet and pulled a lighter from his pocket. He looked across at me, I'll never forget that look till the day I die. He smiled slowly, his white teeth gleaming in the neon lights, then he shouted, "I'm doing it to save her" in a loud voice. All the time, he was looking at me, shouting at me, only me.'

A long silence before the detective asked the next question.

'What happened then, Mr Dacre?'

'His thumb moved and a small flame appeared on the wick of the lighter. It was strange, nothing happened for ages and then there was a loud whoosh and he was covered in blue flame.'

'What did you do?'

'Nothing, I did nothing, just stood there as his whole body was covered in flames. He didn't scream though, didn't make a sound. And then I noticed the smell, like barbecue only stronger, much stronger. I can still smell it now…'

He buried his face in his hands once more.

'I close my eyes and I can still see him standing there, the flames engulfing him…'

He started to sob loudly. DC Muldowney put her arm over his shoulders, pulling the blanket tighter around his neck. 'It's okay, Mr Dacre, take your time, tell us what you did next.'

'I ran. I suddenly realised I was in a petrol station, I thought the whole lot was about to go up and I ran away. I ran…'

Megan glanced up at Ridpath to see if he wanted to ask anything else. He responded immediately.

'One question, Mr Dacre, why come to this station? There are others closer to your home.'

Paul Dacre answered without looking up. 'We have a corporate account here. I didn't wasn't to use my own money.'

Then he looked straight at Ridpath, his eyes red and his skin blotchy. 'I could have saved him. If only I'd moved quicker, I could have saved him… but I ran.'

Chapter TWO

From his vantage point on a side street, he watched his victim stride down the street to his destination, focused on what he had ordered him to do.

Good, he was following instructions exactly.

They had met up on the top floor of the multi-storey car park in Sale town centre. It was a place he often visited when he wanted a bit of downtime or a quick ten-minute nap. Not many cars made it up to the top floor when there were plenty of parking spaces on the lower storeys.

He had issued the orders, followed by a gentle reminder of what happened to the family who had disobeyed him. At first, the man was surprised and then he nodded his head knowing he was beaten, knowing that nothing different could be done.

He'd left him shortly afterwards, whistling as he trotted down the stairs to find his own car.

Of course, the victim could have gone back on his word, not done as he was told. Or he could have screwed up at the last moment like the last one, the woman. A long time ago he had decided to ensure his plans were always adaptable so he could make last-minute changes. Always fluid to take account of the stupidity, and treachery, of the human animal. Whatever happened, there was always a Plan B.

Just like the family.

Just like on Saturday.

Just in case.

He had an alternative plan for this victim too, but he had been easier to manage than the others. Almost as if he had lost the will to live.

What a pity.

He imagined the man sitting there all alone in his car after he had left him, going through the possibilities once more, his eyes flickering left and right, trying to think of a way out. His mind may have presented him with a list of options, each worse than the last, before realising he had none.

All he could possibly do was obey orders. It was the only way.

Exactly as he had designed it: a horrible end for a horrible man.

He'd driven the short distance from the car park to the quiet side street, leaving the car on a double yellow line. Nobody would notice it or disturb it here. He locked the door and crept to his vantage point. From there, he had a clear view over the petrol station, ready to spring into action in case the man backed out at the last minute.

Later, he would blend in with the others. Just another one of the many people watching a disturbance on a Monday evening.

Following his instructions precisely, the victim strode up to the pump. A motorist, filling up his car at the next pump, was staring in the man's direction.

'Don't move, don't get involved, leave him be...' he whispered.

At the next pump along, the driver did nothing, just looked idly in the man's direction, his hand on the fuel nozzle.

'Good, stay where you are, wait for the show.'

His victim stood in front of the pump for a long time before finally making up his mind, inserting his credit card into the machine, then writing what he had been told to write.

He'd taken the man's wallet earlier, leaving him with just a single credit card to pay for the petrol and a black pen to write his message. He was sure both would melt in the extreme heat. He didn't want the police to discover who the man was.

Not yet.

Not until he had prepared his next victim properly.

The use of the hooks was his idea, getting the man to put them on before he left his home. He'd complained that they were causing him too much pain. If anything, they made him suffer too little. Anyway, they were just a sideshow to confuse the police, make them think that this death had sadomasochistic undertones. Slow the investigation down, waste time in areas they didn't need to go.

He was nearly finished now, just one more to go. Shame about that family, but the father should have obeyed his instructions. When he didn't, they had to pay the price. It made dealing with the others easier. They listened to him now.

But he needed time to complete his plan. Not much time, but enough. Halloween was approaching fast and he wanted to finish on October 31.

It would be a fitting memorial.

Tomorrow was a day off from work as the shifts changed. A day of rest for his colleagues, but for him it was a day to spend out on the hills. Walking for him was a time to pore over his plans, work out alternative actions, revel in what was to come.

They had to pay for what they had done. He'd made a promise.

To himself.

To his mother.

To his father.

To his brother.

To his memories.

They would all pay.

In front of him, the victim was dousing himself with petrol.

It was showtime.

Chapter THREE

Ridpath pulled Megan Muldowney to one side as the witness called his wife. 'Right, Megan, I don't want to step on your toes, this is your investigation, but what are you doing next?'

'I've secured the scene and taken a statement. To me it looks like an open-and-shut suicide with an unusual but extremely effective method.'

'I agree, but you'll still have to conduct an investigation, your boss and the coroner will expect you to have all the details and the timings buttoned up. What are your next steps?'

She thought for a moment, looking around the fore-court and back at the petrol station's shop. 'Interview the cashier; she was the person who called the police. Check if the CCTV is working and find footage of the event.'

'Good, then what do you do?'

'I talk to the medical examiner, check what he has to say and then find out who the victim was, see if he had any ID on him.'

'Your witness said he paid for the petrol using a credit card. It may have survived the fire, so ask the doctor if he's found any ID when he comes out of the tent.'

'Right, will do. I'll brief the scene of crime manager to check the scene for fingerprints and get them to bag any evidence they find.'

'Good, you may find fingerprints, but thousands of people use these pumps every day,' he glanced over his shoulder at Pump 8, 'and that looks scorched by the fire. It's a wonder it didn't go up in flames, too. Right, what's the final thing you do?'

'Final thing?' Megan wracked her brain, trying to work out what she had forgotten, going through everything she had been taught at the police college about managing crime scenes. Finally, she shook her head. 'I think that's all, I can't think of anything else.'

'You call your boss back at the station and tell him exactly what happened, what you've done, and what you're going to do. Remember the first rule of good police work: always cover your arse.'

For a moment, Ridpath heard the voice of his old mentor, Charlie Whitworth. A man who had guided and helped him in his early days on the beat and as a detective, telling him all the stuff they didn't teach you in police training school.

'Right, I'll do the medical officer. My boss will want to know the details.' She turned to check the scene one last time before turning back. 'Thanks, Ridpath, you're better than your reputation.'

'I hope so. You did well, Megan, these deaths are never easy.'

'As a coroner's officer, you must deal with death every day, how do you handle it?'

'I don't, it handles me.'

Just then, Dr Schofield emerged from inside the tent, stood up straight and stretched. Pulling off his mask, he took a deep breath of the freshest air Manchester had to offer. 'Ridpath, are you the coroner's officer on this one?'

The medical examiner spoke in a high falsetto voice which was totally at odds with his outward appearance. The result, as he had explained many times in the past, of suffering from hypogonadism as a teenager. Some illnesses leave their mark for years.

'I have that luck, Dr Schofield. This is DC Megan Muldowney, she's the senior investigating officer.'

'Good, I can do you both at the same time. I've called this death at –' he checked his watch '– 8.57 p.m. precisely. Cause of death uncertain until I have performed the post-mortem. You will order one in this case?'

It is one of the vagaries of the English system of justice that the police do not order post-mortems. That decision is always taken by the coroner or coroner's officer. In this case, Thomas Ridpath.

'Of course, Doctor, I'll send you the paperwork.'

'Good, I'll get my men to take the body, or what remains of the body, to the morgue. I'm free tomorrow around two p.m. for the post-mortem. I presume you will both be joining me?'

'I'll look forward to it, Doctor. Just what I need, a post-mortem of a badly burnt body just after my lunch.' Ridpath glanced across at Megan. The detective took the hint.

'Any idea who it is, Doctor? He used a credit card.'

'Who it *was*,' he corrected. 'Not at the moment. I checked his clothes, or what remains of his clothes, but they were too badly burnt and I could see no identification. His credit card, if he used one, would have melted in the heat. Plastic does have that property, which you may have learnt in GCSE chemistry. I wouldn't hold out for fingerprints either, not much flesh left on his fingers. Unless you can find somebody who knows him, it's going to be DNA I'm afraid. With a bit of luck, he'll be on the database.'

'Thank you, Doctor. And by the way, I got an A* in chemistry.'

'Good for you. Now, if you don't have any other questions, I'll get my colleagues to remove the body. Make sure the ghouls are kept well away – I wouldn't want any pictures of this man to appear on the internet.' He pointed towards the few remaining onlookers.

Ridpath glanced around. The crowds had thinned now, only a few people remained. Even the straggling reporters had left; gone, no doubt, to file their stories from the nearest pub.

'Go ahead, Doctor, and I'll see you tomorrow.'

Dr Schofield beckoned his attendants forward and all three vanished inside the tent.

'I'll make the call to my boss, now, Ridpath. Thanks once again for your help.'

'I'd make sure he's okay before you call.' He pointed to Paul Dacre. The man was standing all alone, the grey blanket still draped over his shoulder. He was staring at the tent as Dr Schofield and his assistants rolled a gurney out of their van and began to unroll a black body bag. 'He's obviously suffering from shock. I'd get him checked out by a doctor.'

'Got it,' she smiled. 'You're really not the ogre you're painted to be at police college.'

'You've caught me on a good day. Or a bad day, I can't work out which. But I've done everything I need to do here, so good luck with your investigation.'

He started to walk away but she called after him.

'I'll see you at the post-mortem tomorrow.'

He turned back for a second, smiled, nodded his head and then carried on walking.

Chapter FOUR

'I'm home,' Ridpath shouted as he stepped through the front door.

It was a habit he'd acquired since the attack on his daughter nearly ten months ago. He knew Eve became nervous every time she heard somebody at the door. Inevitably, her mind jumped back to that evening when Billy Diamond had forced his way into the house with the intention of killing her. That time, she had managed to fight him off and he was now awaiting trial. The English justice system moved achingly slowly as it suffered from fourteen years of cuts imposed by successive governments.

Even worse, the crisis in the prison system with too many prisoners and too few cells meant he was now out on bail, free to roam the streets during the day but curfewed at five p.m. every evening.

Scant reassurance for an already nervous Eve.

'I'm home,' he repeated when he didn't get a response.

He heard the door to her bedroom slowly open and a face appeared around the top of the stairs. 'You're late,' were the only words she said.

'Sorry, I was on my way home then got a phone call telling me to attend an incident in Sale. I finally managed to get away.'

She came down the stairs wearing her comfort clothes: a black hoodie and black sweatpants which matched her newly dyed jet-black hair.

She reached forward to give him a hug and then stepped back immediately. 'What's that smell? It's like smoke and petrol and Sunday dinner all mixed up together.'

'I told you, I was on a job.'

She walked past him. 'What was it? A barbecue gone wrong?'

He ignored the question, hanging up his coat and placing his bag in its usual place next to the hall stand. 'Have you eaten? I could heat up a pizza?'

'I'm not hungry. I had a snack when I came home from school.'

He looked at her. She was tall, almost as tall as he was, but thin. A 'beanpole', in the words of her grandparents. The hoodie hid how thin she was but he had felt her body as she hugged him and it didn't feel right.

'You've got to eat properly. You're a growing girl, you need your food.'

She shrugged her shoulders. 'I'm just not hungry, Dad.'

He brushed past her and walked into the kitchen. 'I'm going to heat up the pizza anyway, I'm starving, Share it with me.'

She rolled her eyes in the way only a teenager can roll her eyes. 'If you say so, but I really have to get this chemistry homework done. Mr Walters will kill me if I don't hand it in tomorrow.'

'I'll arrest him if he does.'

'What?'

'Kill you.' A long pause as she frowned. 'It was a joke, Eve,' he finally said.

She smiled. 'I can see the headlines now: "Teacher strangles pupil for not doing homework. Is the new tougher education regime beginning to work?"'

He took up the theme. '"Dad arrests teacher, charges him with having a bad haircut."'

She laughed hesitantly. 'That's so true. It looks like a butcher cut his hair.'

'I know, I met him at the last parents' evening, remember?' He took the pizza out of the freezer. 'Twenty-two minutes at gas mark 6.' He removed the packaging and placed it on a tray. 'Pepperoni, your favourite. Have a slice with me?'

'Okay, if you push me.'

'Great.' He bunged the pizza in the oven before she could change her mind. 'There's one thing we need to talk about as this is heating up,' he said tentatively.

'What?'

'The school sent me another message,' he said without looking at her.

'Who was it this time? The PE teacher complaining I wasn't putting enough effort into my badminton?'

'Sit down,' he said gently, pointing to the chair beside the kitchen table.

She stared at it for a long while before finally pulling it out and flopping down onto it. 'It's not about my look is it? The school hates anybody who looks different. It's just a microcosm of society in general.'

She had started speaking like this recently. Sweeping statements she had read in half-digested books.

'Actually it was the academic director. They're worried about your latest test results… and a little bit about your look.' He gestured with his hands.

She rolled her eyes again. 'See, I told you.'

The kohl around her eyes and the whiteness of her skin had definitely lessened since the weekend, even though her hair looked blacker than he remembered it. She still had the seven studs arranged neatly around the edges of her ear though.

'Take me through it again. What's the difference between being a goth and being emo?'

She sighed. 'It's simple. Emo stands for emotional core and they believe the world is dark and there's nothing they can do about it. Goths, however, know the world is dark but they find a beauty in the dark parts. Plus, they both listen to different types of music, dress differently, have different emotional attitudes and wear different make-up.'

'So what are you?'

'I'm a bit of both. Screwed up as ever,' she joked.

'Don't say that. Anyway, the academic director is more worried about your declining performance in the tests than your look.'

'Tests, tests, they're always bloody testing. It's like they've run out of stuff to teach us so they just give us more and more exams. Saint-Exupéry said, "And now here is my secret, a very simple secret: It is only with the heart that one can see rightly; what is essential is invisible to the eye." You can't test what the heart sees.'

'Saint-Exupéry? Didn't he play on the wing for United last year?'

She hit him playfully with her hand. '*Dad...*'

'But seriously, you have exams next year and they are worried – *I* am worried.' He took a deep breath and reached out for her hand. 'You always used to do so well at school, it was always so easy.'

She pulled her hand back. 'People change. I'm not your little schoolgirl any more who loved being top of her class. There's more to life than that… a lot more.'

'I know, but you're fifteen. You have the whole world in front of you, a bright future…'

'As long as I knuckle down and pass their tests? Answer me this: when was the last time you used differential calculus in your life? Today, when you were called to that incident you won't tell me about, did you stop and think that organic chemistry and the titration rate of sulphuric acid would be useful to know?'

'I didn't, but I rely on other people who did.' He took a deep breath. 'Let me tell you about today. A man walked into a petrol station, took out his credit card and used it to buy petrol. He then set himself alight as people watched—'

She suddenly looked sick. 'I—'

He held up his finger to stop her interrupting him. 'Now, this man has no ID, no fingerprints, nothing. He will only be identified through his DNA. Some scientist, who has passed all those tests you hate, will use his learning to identify this man for his family. Now do you understand how important these tests are?'

She shook her head and stood up. 'I don't, Dad, and your story only reminds me how screwed up the world is, that a man was so lost he would kill himself like that.'

She looked across at the oven.

'I'm not hungry any more. I'm going to my room.'

She turned, walked out of the kitchen and stomped up the stairs.

Ridpath was left on his own in the kitchen. 'You handled that one well, Ridpath. Five gold stars for being an idiot. Zero stars for parenting skills.'

23

He stood up and switched off the oven. He wasn't
hungry either.

Tuesday, October 29.

Chapter FIVE

The next morning the atmosphere at breakfast was as frosty as the weather outside the kitchen window.

'Shall I make porridge?'

'No.'

'Cornflakes?'

'No.'

'Spaghetti Bolognese?'

'No.' She brushed her hair away from her eyes and pointed down to the small plate in front of her. 'You know I only ever have toast for breakfast, why all the questions?'

'Just seeing if you want anything different. A change can sometimes help increase the appetite.'

She laughed. 'Where did you read that?'

'*Woman & Home*. There was a copy in the doctor's surgery when I went last week to pick up my prescription.'

'You still taking that pill every day?'

'Revlimid. A pill a day keeps the cancer at bay.'

Seven years ago, in the middle of a case, Ridpath had been diagnosed with multiple myeloma, a form of blood cancer that affects the bones and bone marrow. For eighteen months he had been off work, undergoing chemotherapy and driving everybody crazy. Finally, he had been pronounced cancer-free and allowed back to work in the Greater Manchester Police. They wanted to give him a less stressful job so temporarily transferred him from the Major Investigation Team to the East Manchester coroner's office. A 'temporary' transfer that had lasted for six years now.

'Before you say it, I know the doctors who saved your life passed their exams and jumped through all the hoops that were required to become physicians.'

'And because they did, I am still alive.'

'When's your next check-up?'

'Next week, I think. Just one every three months now. According to them, I'm "a shining example of a new treatment protocol". They just mean I'm a guinea pig who survived. But without their work at Christie's, I wouldn't be here.'

She nodded slowly. 'I thought about what you said last night. I promise I'll try harder at school. It's just… I find it so hard to focus now. Everything seems so pointless.'

'Have you spoken with your therapist about your feelings?'

'All the time.'

'What does she say?'

'Time. She says time is the great healer. She gave me some meditations to perform. They help, but…'

'You have to keep using them, Eve, they do help.'

She smiled. 'Yours is imagining yourself on top of Win Hill, overlooking Ladybower Reservoir, the wind blowing in your hair.'

'It's my safe space, Eve, when the job gets too much for me and I feel overwhelmed.'

He didn't ask her what her meditation was and she didn't tell him.

'That reminds me. You have a session this evening with her, don't you? Do you want me to take you there, we could have dinner somewhere in town and you could get your noodles and stuff from Oseyo?'

'No thanks, I prefer to go on my own.' She glanced at the clock. 'You're going to be late for your weekly coroner's meeting, Dad.'

'Shit, is that the time? Do you want a lift to the tram station?'

'It's okay, I'll walk. The exercise will do me good.' She stared at his spreading midriff. 'Looks like you need some, too.'

'Yeah, too many Greggs sausage rolls.'

'Healthy food, Dad.'

'I know, I know, I know.'

'And what did you eat this morning for breakfast?'

'My usual – a mug of black coffee. You know I can't face food first thing.'

She smiled. 'Put these words in order: Kettle. Pot. Calling. The. Black.'

He took a swallow of his now-cold coffee and raised a brow. 'Aren't you going to be late for school?'

She looked at the clock again. 'No, I'll be okay, but *you* are definitely going to be late for your meeting.'

He downed the last mouthful of coffee, dashed into the hallway and grabbed his jacket off the hook. 'Are you sure you don't want a lift to the tram station?'

'Doubly sure.'

'Okay, see you this evening when you get home.' He shouted over his shoulder, picking up his bag from its place next to the hall stand and opening the front door, before rushing back into the kitchen and planting a large kiss on top of his daughter's head.

'Don't forget I love you, Eve. You're the most important person in the world to me.'

28

She shook her head. 'Mrs Challinor is going to be so pissed off at you.'

'Right, I'm off. See you tonight.'

He rushed out of the kitchen, leaving her sitting alone at the table, her half-eaten toast on the plate in front of her.

The door slammed and she heard the sound of his engine as he pulled away from the house.

She whispered, 'I love you too, Dad, but I don't know if I can do this any more.'

Chapter SIX

He was up early, taking the tram to Piccadilly Station. He didn't have a shift until tomorrow and it was his habit to go for a long walk when the change from days to nights happened. After a quick shower to wash away the scent of burning petrol and human being from the night before, he dressed in his cold-weather gear: black beanie, thick jumper, thermal leggings and winter walking trousers. Later, he would place some of the clothes in his backpack as walking uphill brought on a good sweat.

He'd recently decided to re-walk the Greater Manchester Ringway, a two-hundred-mile walk in twenty one-day stages that circled the city. He'd done it once already in the spring, planning exactly what he was going to do as he placed one foot in front of the other.

He loved the way his mind soared freely when he was out walking. But it was also grounded at the same time. A strange juxtaposition, free and tethered, but it worked for him.

It had been in May, in the middle of stage sixteen somewhere south of Wigan in Viridor Wood, when he'd decided to go ahead.

Now, the walks were to remind him of the details of his plans. Almost as if by treading the same territory where they were hatched reminded him of their purpose.

He took the 7.57 a.m. train to Huddersfield, getting off at Greenfield nineteen minutes later. Out of the station and onto the main road, and it was time to open the Go Jauntly app for stage nine. He scrolled through the usual explainers of the route and then, following the instructions on the app, walked around the corner and down onto the towpath for the Huddersfield Narrow Canal.

It was a beautiful, if cold, day, the sun's rays drenching the yellow, maroon and brown leaves still on the trees in a warm light, illuminating those leaves already bathing in the wine-dark waters of the canal. He heard his boots echo on the cobblestones beside the canal. An old boat driven by a young couple putt-putted ahead, a cloud of evil smelling smoke being emitted by the engine. He quickly overtook them, saying good morning as he passed.

They didn't answer. Perhaps the embarrassment of being overtaken by a man walking alone was too much.

He ploughed on past Saddleworth Museum. Memories here, of a time not so long ago.

Sharp, harsh, bloody memories. Smashing the rear window. The dark house. Upstairs, the sound of his shoes smothered by the deep pile of the carpet. Across the landing to the master bedroom. The weight of the shotgun in his hands, her cries for help coming out as frightened squeaks. The knife, gleaming in the dull grey of a Manchester dawn, held against the white neck of the young boy, the bright, oxygenated red of the children's blood across the walls.

So red. So warm. So much blood.

He stopped for a moment, brought back to the present. He reached into his pocket and checked the app on his phone again, confirming his memory of the route was correct.

Taking the path away from the canal on the long trek up to Dobcross Village, his mind went over his plans, checking every detail, working on alternate actions, plotting 'what if' scenarios.

He was happy everything was as it should be.

The i's were dotted and the t's crossed.

Nothing could go wrong.

Nothing would go wrong.

There was a rhythm in his walking now as he climbed ever upwards to Castleshaw and Standedge, checking the app every now and again to make sure he hadn't wandered from the path. The GPS map on his phone showed him as a small blue dot moving inexorably through the landscape, going ever onward.

Past the Roman Fort of Rigodunum and up Standedge. There, he stopped for a moment and looked back at the city of Manchester lying below him, the new skyscrapers standing out like the sore thumbs they were.

Nobody knew what he was doing and only a few people cared. But it was important for him to do it this way. Those people would be given a choice in the same way his parents and brother had no choice.

It was time to go over the details once more as he walked towards Denshaw, across Crompton Moor, skirting below the communication masts at Crow Knoll and then down into Newhey.

A twelve-and-a-half-mile hike to savour the death of a man in every step.

He rehearsed the details once more in his mind.

Nothing could go wrong.

Nothing would go wrong.

Chapter SEVEN

They were all waiting for him in the conference room when he arrived.

'Good to see you could make it, Ridpath.' Mrs Challinor was back in her usual position at the head of the table. Even though she was only working two days a week for the foreseeable future, she insisted that she attend these work-in-progress meetings so she would still know everything that was going on.

But she wasn't the same Mrs Challinor that Ridpath remembered. After her long stint in hospital in a coma, she had visibly aged. Her once tight, peaches and cream complexion now had visible dark spots and wrinkles around the mouth. Her corkscrew hair had now turned completely white and was patchy in some areas where the surgeon had cut into her skull to remove the pressure on her brain. She had taken to wearing bright head scarves to cover up those areas. This morning, the scarf was a vivid blue the colour of the sky in autumn.

But she still had the same authority. An authority that could make even a most recalcitrant government official tell the truth. Or at least not lie too much.

'Well, what are you standing there for? We'd like to get started before hell freezes over.'

He quickly took his seat next to Sophia who passed him a venti latte with a double shot without saying a word.

The usual people were present. Ridpath, his assistant Sophia, now with the new title of Mrs O'Brien, David Smail, the locum coroner from Derbyshire, and Virginia Trelawnay, the new district coroner. She had replaced the previous senior coroner, Helen Moore, who had moved to Somerset last April.

Missing from the table was Jenny Oldfield, the office manager, who had tearfully taken a new job with Manchester council before Mrs Challinor had returned. Her place was taken by a very competent ex-teacher, Olivia Jackson, who had had enough of the politics of her school and wanted a change of career. The fact she had a degree in Computer Sciences immediately endeared her to Mrs Challinor.

'Sophia have you done the stats?'

'Of course, Mrs Challinor.' Ridpath's assistant handed out a spreadsheet of names and actions. 'There were 153 deaths in our area last week. I have indicated those the coroner has already marked for inquests in blue. In addition, I have added five more for the coroner to look at this morning.'

'Thank you, Sophia, I'll let you know my decision before lunch.'

'Can you add one more to the list? On my way home last night I was called to an incident at a petrol station. The victim was unknown but Dr Schofield requested a post-mortem and I have agreed.'

'When will the post-mortem be held?'

'At two p.m. today, Mrs Challinor.'

'And you'll attend?'

'Along with the local detective. I'll give you a report once I've heard what the pathologist has to say.'

Mrs Challinor made a note in her book, ensuring she would follow up with Ridpath. The handwriting was as neat and meticulous as ever, probably more so since the attack.

'Right, what is on the calendar this week, Olivia?'

The woman coughed once before speaking. 'I've kept Tuesday and Wednesday clear of inquests, Mrs Challinor, as I've arranged for the men to give both courts a deep clean. Apparently the last time it was done was before Covid.'

'About time, too,' said Virginia Trelawnay. 'I found a nest of daddy longlegs in one of the drawers last week. Looked like they were having a party.'

'Probably a knees-up,' added Ridpath.

The new office manager ignored the joke. 'It might smell of disinfectant, bleach and industrial cleaner for a few hours so I wouldn't go in there if I were you. On Thursday, Mrs Challinor has four inquests in Court 1 all of which will be postponed pending police investigations and possible court action.'

'I'd like to chat with you about one of them, Ridpath. Normally, I would simply postpone this inquest but I've been reading the documentation from the police so far and I'm not happy, not happy at all.'

'After this meeting, Mrs Challinor?'

'Perfect.'

The office manager continued. 'Virginia has the Camilla Horton case in Court 2.'

'Wasn't that the death of a fourteen-year-old schoolgirl?' asked Mrs Challinor.

Virginia Trelawnay answered immediately. 'It was. There was the usual hand-wringing and fake concern from the tabloids so I asked Ridpath to check the police investigation so far.'

'And what did you find, Ridpath?'

Sophia passed him the file. Luckily he remembered the case well. 'Camilla Horton took her own life in a public park after absconding from school. It seems premeditated as she took the clothes line from the garage of her parents' home. The police investigation has so far found no evidence of bullying at school. In fact, the opposite. She was popular and successful, doing well in all her school subjects, played for the school football team and in the orchestra. Her home life seemed happy and comfortable, she had two younger siblings who adored her.'

'Why did she do it, then?' asked Olivia.

Mrs Challinor stared at him. 'Ridpath?'

'The police investigation hadn't found any reason why she took her own life. The CID in Sale are still investigating as we speak. This is the second suicide they have had in their district in the last couple of weeks.'

'The other was the incident you attended last night?'

'Correct, Coroner.'

'I do hope we are not experiencing another Bridgend.'

'Bridgend?' asked Olivia.

The coroner put down her pen. 'At least twenty-five suicides of young people were reported in Bridgend in South Wales in 2007 and 2008. Reports speculated that a "suicide cult" was to blame, though police found no evidence to link the cases together. Of the suicides, all but one died from hanging. Many of the suicides were teenagers between the ages of thirteen and seventeen. The parents of those who died accused the media of triggering young people and that their reporting "glamourised ways of taking your life". We must make sure the same doesn't happen in our district. How are you going to handle this, Virginia? The father, Charles Horton, is a prominent solicitor.'

'The police still haven't completed their inquiries, so I'll postpone the inquest until they have done so. I'll have a quiet word with the reporters beforehand just to make them aware of the negative aspects of publicity.'

'Will they listen to you?'

'I hope so, I have a pretty good relationship with them.'

'Right, let's move on.'

'Why?' asked Olivia.

'Why what?' answered the coroner.

'Why do these young girls and young men kill them-selves for no reason?'

Mrs Challinor held her hand up. 'I should remind everybody that a coroner's job is not to find out why something happened. It is to ascertain what happened, when it happened and how it happened. And to ensure, in the case of governmental, official or corporate errors, that the same mistakes do not happen again. Our job is to represent the dead in the land of the living, *not* to ascribe blame or guilt. That is the job of the courts and the judicial system.'

'But surely, it is often impossible to separate the how from the why? Surely, understanding why somebody has committed an act will only help in preventing it from occurring again?' asked Olivia.

Ridpath could see Mrs Challinor's face reddening. 'But that is not our job nor is it our remit as coroners,' she added tetchily. 'Please understand what we do, Olivia, if you want to continue working here.'

The table went silent.

'Right, if there is nothing else… Ridpath, I'll see you in my chambers. Now.'

Chapter EIGHT

'Are you okay, Mrs Challinor? You were pretty tough on Olivia.'

The coroner sat behind her desk with her head down, taking deep breaths.

'I'm fine, just a little tired. Did I come on a bit too strong in that meeting?'

'A little. We all know what we're doing and Olivia is new, she has a right to question our approach. It's one of the reasons you brought her in. A fresh pair of eyes, remember?'

She scratched her scalp beneath the head scarf. It was one of the areas where the hair obstinately refused to grow back.

'I know, Ridpath. I'll apologise to her later. It's just...' Her voice petered out as she seemed to lose her thread.

'Perhaps, you came back to work too early, you should have taken longer to recuperate.'

The coroner's head shot up. 'What do you mean by that? You think I'm incapable of doing my job, is that it?'

'Not at all, Mrs Challinor, it's just I wondered if it was all getting too much for you.'

'It's not "too much", as you put it. If anything, it's too little. I only work two days a week at the moment and I was thinking about returning full time. But we're not here to talk about me. You have your meeting with the Major Investigation Team this morning?'

He nodded. 'It starts at noon. Steve Carruthers has started holding lunchtime meetings. They're so swamped at the moment, he's trying to make the best use of everybody's time. It hasn't gone down well. Apparently, eating lunch during a meeting doesn't aid the digestion.'

'A copper's stomach is always a fragile thing at best.'

Ridpath patted the spare tyre hanging over his belt. The same one that Eve had noticed last night. It really was time for him to go to the gym. 'Don't I know it.'

'Anyway, Claire rang me.'

'What did Detective Superintendent Trent want?' Ridpath asked tentatively.

Claire Trent was Ridpath's senior officer on the Major Investigation Team. She controlled policy and manpower while his direct supervisor, Detective Chief Inspector Carruthers, handled operations.

'They're short of manpower again, apparently some of their detectives have been diverted to look at footage from the recent riots and compile cases for the Crown Prosecution Service.'

'That could take years. There must be hundreds of hours of footage from news organisations and online.'

'Plus, they have the home invasion and murder of the Ashton family in Saddleworth.'

'Horrendous, all killed in cold blood for no apparent reason. It's all over the papers. Not our area, luckily.'

'That's why she asked me if you could be spared to work for MIT for a short while.'

'And what did you say?'

'I checked with Olivia and Sophia. You don't have much going on at the moment, having completed your work recently for Victoria's inquest.'

'I know, but I'm still worried about Eve.'

'It's been almost a year since the attack by Billy Diamond...'

'He's out on bail at the moment and, naturally, this has made her more jumpy than usual. Plus, she has her exams coming up next year—'

'I said yes to Claire Trent,' Mrs Challinor interrupted him bluntly. 'I've held her off ever since I returned to work but she pays your salary and I couldn't justify keeping you wrapped in cotton wool any longer.'

Ridpath's salary was paid by GMP while he was seconded to the coroner's office, and he spent time in both offices.

He sucked in his breath. 'It's not me I'm worried about, it's Eve.'

'I know, but they need you working for them again.'

Ridpath closed his eyes. He knew this day was coming but he hadn't wanted it to arrive so quickly.

'How is Eve?'

'Going through a phase at the moment. Or at least I hope it's a phase. She's decided she's a goth. Heavy eye make-up, loud music, dark clothes. I worry that she's hanging out with the wrong people. And her grades have started to suffer at school. She used to be near the top of her class but now she's failing in a lot of subjects, and the teachers are concerned.'

'If she ever needs somebody – a woman – to chat to, I'm always available. I haven't seen her for such a long time. Perhaps I should take her out somewhere at the weekend?'

'She doesn't go out much any more. Spends a lot of time in her room on the internet.'

'Not good. But she's fifteen and at that age young girls are beginning to find themselves, find out who they are. I remember my daughter, Sarah, became obsessed with Kurt Cobain and that whole grunge stuff. I was worried for a while, but it didn't last long. Sometimes, you just have to be there for them.'

'And not be standing over them, worrying.'

'Exactly, Ridpath. Knowing you, you are hovering over her like a kestrel over a field mouse. But do ask her if she'd like to go out at the weekend, I'd love to see her again.'

'Will do. What's the job?'

'What?'

'The job with MIT, what is it?'

'I think it's jobs, one of which coincides with something I want you to look at for me. It's the case of the murder of a mother, Jane Forsyth, by her own fourteen-year-old child.'

'I read about that in the *Evening News* too. Its circulation must be soaring at the moment.'

She pushed a large folder across the desk. 'Here's the file compiled by Sale Criminal Investigation Department so far. It seems rushed and slipshod.'

'In what way?'

'No forensics included in the report. No examination of the girl's social media accounts. No questioning of her friends. No interviews with social workers or health workers. They seem to have performed a superficial investigation, found a culprit and then sat on their hands.'

'Perhaps they did all that work but thought it wasn't relevant to the report?'

'Claire Trent agrees with me in her assessment of the initial investigation.'

Ridpath eyed her. 'So you want to know why she killed her mother?'

Mrs Challinor took off her glasses and stared at him. She answered him sharply. 'No, Ridpath, I want to know if social services, the school or health workers missed anything in this child's behaviour that would indicate she was capable of killing her own mother. Do you understand me? Were any government departments at fault? I can't believe a fourteen-year-old girl would suddenly kill her mother without some sort of prior behavioural indications or personality disorders.'

'Of course, Mrs Challinor, I'll look into it.'

'Here's the file I was sent, but Steve Carruthers will give you more information at the briefing. I want this investigation done properly, Ridpath. Not rushed just because the police have found the perpetrator. I need to have more than this.' She pointed to the file. 'Three pages of nothing.'

'Understood, Mrs Challinor, I'll look into it.'

'Good.' A slight pause as the coroner adjusted the scarf around her head. 'When is Claire leaving?'

'I'm not certain, but she can't have long left now. I think she's under pressure to wrap up investigations before she leaves to work in Birmingham.'

Claire Trent had announced her departure to become assistant chief constable of the West Midlands Police. Ridpath knew she was ambitious and had wanted promotion for a long time, but had been continually stymied in Greater Manchester. The new chief constable had decided to bring in a whole swarm of outsiders in senior positions since the force had been put in special measures in 2019.

Naturally, that meant the existing senior managers would be passed over for promotion.

'I might find out at the lunch briefing,' he added.

'I'll miss her; she was always a staunch ally in the Force.'

'I'll miss her, too.'

'Who is going to replace her?'

Ridpath shrugged his shoulders. 'I don't know. I think Steve Carruthers is going for it but they may want to bring in somebody from outside.'

'I hope he gets it, he's one of the better officers in GMP.' She took a deep breath. 'Sorry about foisting this job on you, but we both felt – myself and Claire – that it was time you were fully utilised again.'

'Justifying my existence before the new person decides it's time to change?'

'Claire Trent likes you, Ridpath. She thinks you are a royal pain in the arse but she believes you solve problems for her. And she believes our arrangement has worked for the benefit of the coroner's office, MIT and GMP. I happen to agree with her. The arrangement has meant that we have uncovered crimes that normally may have slipped through the cracks in the system. But to work, it needs you to be 100 per cent operative across both departments.'

He nodded. In many ways he was glad. He missed the focus of the work. Somehow, he would have to manage Eve and his new responsibilities at the same time. He'd done it before and he would do it again.

'Do let Eve know I'd love to see her again.'

'Will do.'

He stood there as she pulled a file from the pile in front of her. 'Don't you have work to do.'

He smiled. 'Thank you for reminding me a policeman's lot is never done.'

He turned and opened the door.

'Don't forget to keep me informed of what you're doing, Ridpath, no surprises this time.'

'No surprises, Mrs Challinor.'

Chapter NINE

Ridpath returned to his room where Sophia was at her desk with a half-eaten chicken McCrispy in front of her.

'How was Mrs Challinor?' she asked through mouthfuls of food.

'Fine, why do you ask? You saw her yourself this morning.'

'She's been a little unpredictable recently, a bit tetchy. I don't remember her ever losing her temper before, but I saw it twice last week. You were out looking into the Horton case so you missed it.'

'Maybe she's finding it difficult adjusting. She was off work for fourteen months after the attack. She needs time to get back into the swing of things. I remember what it was like myself. I suggested that she take more time off.'

'How did that go down?'

He laughed. 'Not too well. I'd forgotten how hard she works.'

'She's only supposed to be in two days a week but she was here four days last week and it's going to be the same this week.'

'Anyway, Mrs Challinor can look after herself. How are you bearing up?'

Sophia sat back and patted her enlarged stomach. 'All well and good, but I am finding a ridiculous craving for fried chicken burgers. There's a new crispy chicken place in Chorlton, I think Conor has a standing order there.'

'When Polly was pregnant with Eve, it was pizza. I had Domino's on speed dial. How's your mum?'

'Over the moon. She can't wait for a new grandchild to fuss over. Wants me to stop working though, "You can't be a mum and work at the same time."'

Immediately, Ridpath frowned. He'd be lost without Sophia. Since he had hired her straight out of college, she'd handled all the bureaucracy of the job with a competency and professionalism that had amazed him.

'But don't worry, Conor wants me to come back to work as soon as I've laid this egg. We're saving up for our house and nowadays one salary doesn't go very far.'

Ridpath had no such problems. There was just himself and Eve, while Polly's life insurance had paid off the mortgage on the house.

'There is one thing I'm looking forward to though.'

'What's that?'

'Conor's mum is coming over from Ireland for the birth and she's a lovely woman.'

'Two grans fighting over the same baby could be a problem?'

'That's the whole thing. Despite coming from two different cultures and religions – Pakistani Muslim and Irish Catholic – those two get on really well when they're together. Myself and Conor don't understand it. Don't get me wrong, we love it, but we don't get it.'

'You're so lucky. My relatives didn't speak to each other all the time I was growing up. Some long-forgotten feud buried in the mists of time.'

Sophia glanced at the clock. 'Don't you have a meeting at Police HQ at noon?'

'Shit, I lost track of time. I'd better get a move on.'

She reached for a Post-it note stuck on her computer. 'Before you rush off, a Megan Muldowney rang for you. She asked if you were going to be at the post-mortem this afternoon. She sounded very nice but a little young. Is that where you take your dates these days? Personally, I'd prefer a cosy restaurant with a chicken burger special, but there's no accounting for taste.'

'She's not a "date", she's a DC with GMP.' He glanced at the clock again.

For the second time that morning, he grabbed his bag and his jacket and rushed out of the door before returning. 'Don't worry about Mrs Challinor, but if you want me to have a word with her about working too hard, I will do.'

'Thanks, Ridpath. But I do worry, we're all worried.'

Chapter TEN

He returned home after his Ringway walk slightly tired but strangely happy. As usual, he checked the street outside his door for any unusual cars or people watching the house.

There was nobody.

His family had owned this house since the early 1900s. Back then, it had been in the middle of the quiet suburb of Chorlton, surrounded by homes occupied by the merchants and managers of the cotton mills of Manchester. Nowadays, it was at the edge of one of the trendiest areas of the city.

He could never understand why it was so attractive. For him, the place had gone vastly downhill since he was a child. Gone were the independent butchers, the food shops, the clothing shops, even the old Woolworths was now a bloody bar. All there were now were chicken shops, half-arsed pubs, broken pavements and litter floating around in the autumn breeze, but still people were desperate to live here.

His great-grandfather had moved them into the house when it was newly built. The man had started on the floor of a mill, twisting the ends of the cotton as they broke on the looms to keep the machines operating. Gradually he had worked himself up to foreman and then assistant manager. Mr Groom, the owner, had appointed his son as the manager, but it was his great-grandfather who actually ran the place.

Of course, the son had spent all the family money on wine, women and song, squandering the rest. When the old man died, the son was happy to take a pittance for the factory and its machines. A year later, the First World War broke out and the cavalry twill they specialised in manufacturing was in high demand by the armies of Europe. His great-grandfather had made a fortune, buying this house with just a small part of the profits. One of his nearby neighbours had been the famous aviator Sir Arthur Whitten Brown, and the families knew each other well.

Since then, the area had gone to the dogs. All the old merchants' houses had first been converted into students' digs in the Sixties and Seventies and then later gentrified by professionals, with their yuppified one-bedroom bijou flats, in the creative renaissance of Manchester in the 2000s.

Through all that, this house had remained untouched, its Edwardian features still intact – stained glass windows, tiled floors, elaborate wooden entrance, dado rails, high ceilings and plaster cornices.

He'd never sell it, never let it change, never change it.

Of course, he had been made offers, especially when his parents and brother died, from greasy men in cheap grey suits, all desperate to make a quick buck, converting the old mansion into tiny flats.

He'd told them to piss off and shoved a knife in their faces.

They didn't come back.

Checking the road once more – you couldn't be too careful – he inserted keys in all four locks on the front door, opening each one in the correct sequence that would release the alarm. It was another precaution he had taken to protect himself.

He stepped into the dark hallway, hanging his waterproof coat on the hook and taking off his muddy boots. Growing up, this place used to be bright and cheerful, dressed with flowers grown by his mother in the garden, but he didn't have time any more. Nor did he care. The house wasn't a home, it was far more than that.

He went into the kitchen and made two cheese and onion sandwiches. Always butter, never that spreadable stuff; it was so full of seed oils, emulsifiers and stabilisers, it was more likely to kill you rather than feed you. The bread was a sourdough from the Barbakan Deli. Twice a week he went there to get half a loaf which would last him exactly three and a half days. The cheese was Cheshire from Morrisons, none of that posh stuff from the cheesemonger. Why would he spend twice as much for half the cheese? It made no sense. Lastly, a layer of red onions on top for a little sweetness.

He ate cheese and onion sandwiches for lunch and for tea: there was no point in eating anything else. Anyway, if they had worked for his mum and dad, they would work for him. A fresh pot of tea to swill them down and he was ready to face the world. Or, in his case, the wall in the attic.

Taking a tray, he placed the sandwiches and the pot of tea on it, and climbed the stairs to the top floor. The runners were getting a little threadbare now. He should really replace them but there was no point. He would be finished with his work soon. After that, who knew, he might leave Manchester completely or he might take his own life, stopping the dreams and the pain.

But that was the future. He never thought further than the day when his work would end, then he could rest.

Perhaps for good.

He reached the door to the attic, placing the tray down on the floor and unlocking it from the bunch of keys he carried at his waist.

Inside, along one wall, six pictures had red tape crosses pasted over them. He looked at each of their faces. They all deserved to die, he felt no guilt or shame.

This was his place, his sanctum, where he came to work and outline the deaths after his brainstorming walks. He'd decided to add a few more details after the trek this morning, the final touches to the plan.

Just one more death to go and then he would be finished.

On the table, his two laptops lay unopened. He placed the tray down and poured himself a large mug of tea, instantly feeling at ease.

He stared at the laptops. What was it going to be, death or life? The contradiction always amused him, how he could take away life with one machine and give it with the other.

He decided it was going to be life now, he would save death for later.

He logged onto the chat room he had created on Signal and saw the message immediately.

Iceman123: Is anybody there?

He knew who this was. He had communicated with him at least three times before. He was a friend of Camilla Horton, the girl he had tried to save but could not. Perhaps, there was still a chance with this boy.

He scrolled down and saw another message, sent minutes later.

> **Iceman123:** Is anybody online today? I'm going spare here.

He sounded wired, at the end of his tether.

Perfect.

Now he could be saved. He tapped in a response, keeping it deliberately light and cheerful.

> **Rellik:** Hiya, how's it going today?

The answer came back immediately: he must have been poised over his laptop like a vulture waiting for a wanderer in the desert to die.

> **Iceman123:** I can't go on like this any more. It's all so meaningless.
>
> **Rellik:** You must go on. Look outside your window. See the beauty of nature, go for a walk, feel the ground beneath your feet, smell the scents on the air, hear the rustle of the leaves, drink in the joy of living.

His fingers hovered over the keyboard. He was leading him on nicely to the single conclusion that lay in his future. A conclusion it had taken him three years to reach on his own.

> **Iceman123:** I've been out this morning. But all I saw was ugliness. Ugly people in an ugly city, all scowling at each other as they rushed to their ugly, meaning-less jobs. Each living the rat race like little hamsters on their wheels, scurrying noisily but going nowhere.

> **Rellik:** Life isn't like that. It's full of joy.
>
> **Iceman123:** Mine isn't. It's meaningless. I go to school, I listen but don't hear anything. They're teaching me things that I'm never going to use in my life. I mean what's the point of calculus?
>
> **Rellik:** The point is to keep going. It will get better, it will always get better.
>
> **Iceman123:** No, it won't. What's the point of living?

Now was the time to start leading him to the inevitable conclusion. *But be subtle now, you don't want to scare or panic him.*

> **Rellik:** What's your real name, Iceman123?
>
> **Iceman123:** Why?
>
> **Rellik:** I like to know people's real names, it makes my work with them more personal.
>
> **Iceman123:** So I'm work?
>
> **Rellik:** No, you're not, but your feelings are. Don't they feel like hard work to you?
>
> **Iceman123:** They do. Far too hard.

He waited, not replying. His question about the boy's real name was not about being personal but it was about surrender. The boy had to surrender a part of himself if he was to help him.

The answer came a minute later.

> **Iceman123:** It's Chris. A pointless, meaningless name.
>
> **Rellik:** No, it's not. It's your name.
>
> **Iceman123:** A pointless name for a meaningless person.

Rellik: If you feel like that, what are you going to do about it?

Iceman123: I don't know.

Rellik: You need to do something. You must find out the meaning of life for yourself.

Iceman123: What if there is no meaning? What if there is no point?

Rellik: You must find your purpose in life. That is the key to giving life meaning. Do you understand?

Iceman123: Sort of, but how do you find your purpose in life?

Rellik: I'll explain tomorrow. Can you promise you'll go for a walk in a park before we chat again? Enjoy nature and look for its purpose even as we approach winter?

Iceman123: Okay.

Rellik: We will talk tomorrow, I promise.

Iceman123: Okay.

Then he logged off, sat back and smiled. He took a bite of the cheese and onion sandwich, enjoying the nuttiness of the cheeses blended with the sweetness of the onion.

Chris was alone now, lonelier than he had ever been. All that surrounded him was darkness, the dark of endless night whispering its song in his ear.

What had Churchill called it? His black dog.

Chris's black dog was sitting at his feet, ready to bite. He was the only person who could save him.

He hoped he had done enough.

The only way to save somebody was to give them a purpose in life, a goal to keep them going. He had found his purpose a year ago and it had saved him. He relished the contradiction he lived every day. Giving life with one hand and taking it away with the other, but it didn't bother him.

'We all live our contradictions, mine is starker than most,' he said out loud.

Robert Wallace, his next victim, was going to die.

But perhaps he could save Chris.

Death and life were in his hands. That was his purpose; to save and to destroy.

He didn't know which gave him more pleasure.

Chapter ELEVEN

When Ridpath walked into the briefing room at Police HQ, most of the detectives were already there with their sorry-looking sandwiches and half-eaten Greggs sausage rolls.

He had decided to avoid lunch, particularly as he had a post-mortem that afternoon and the last thing he wanted to do was bring up some half-digested pasty as Dr Schofield removed the brain from a corpse.

'Hiya, Ridpath, long time no see,' said Chrissy Wright, the team's civilian researcher, as ever, a City scarf wrapped tightly around her neck.

'It's only been a week since the last meeting.'

'Seems like years. I've been on stats again. If I see another column of figures, I'll go doolally.'

'Like the new hair though.'

She patted the side of her head. 'I've decided to go short, I should have done it years ago. No more faffing about in the morning. Run a comb through it and I'm done. I was tempted to dye it light blue but Carruthers would have conniptions if I did.' She put on a broad Glaswegian accent. '*You're nae havin' that scalpit in ma department.*'

He laughed and took the seat next to her, she had the tone of voice and accent exactly right.

He looked around the room. Everybody was seated in a large rectangle with an open area in the middle, so different from previous MIT meetings, which were more like classrooms with the senior detective dispensing wisdom from on high. Steve Carruthers believed in a more collegiate approach to policing with everybody working as a team.

On the other side of the rectangle of desks, Ridpath saw Emily Parkinson and Helen Shipton sitting together. He nodded at both of them. Turning to Chrissy, he whispered, 'I thought those two didn't like each other?'

'So did I, but apparently they had a heart-to-heart, went on a girls' night out in the town centre, got incredibly pissed and have been best friends ever since.'

'Wonders will never cease.'

Just then DCI Steve Carruthers burst into the room. He strode purposefully to the empty chair in the centre of one side, dumped his heavy load of files down on the table and clapped his hands. 'Right, people, let's get started.'

Ridpath always had to listen closely to his words because his Glasgow accent seemed to have become even stronger during his time in Manchester.

The other detectives stopped what they were doing and hurriedly took their seats at the table or had a last bite of their sausage roll.

'We're incredibly busy as you all know. There's just one case which is a priority at the moment for us and for our lords and masters.' He glanced up towards the ceiling and the higher floors. 'The murder of the wee family in Saddleworth. And it doesn't help that we're missing five of the team who've been seconded to Operation Overlord. Given how that's going, we're not going to see them back for at least three months, probably longer.'

Harry Makepeace stuck his hand up. He was one of the longest-serving detectives on the force and had postponed his retirement to help out, but the golf courses were still waiting for him. 'What's the chance of getting in some extra help?'

'Given the budgets, there's nae danger of any coming soon.'

Harry raised his eyebrow. 'Is that a yes or a no?'

'Nae danger. I suppose you'd say bugger all chance of any help. Ya ken, Harry?'

'I understand "bugger all", boss.'

'Gud, so let's not fanny about. Dennis, you're the SIO on the murders, how are we doing?'

Dennis Leahey was another Scot. Carruthers had brought him down from Glasgow six months ago to bolster the resources of MIT. For Ridpath, he was one of the best hires they'd seen in ages: professional, hard-working and diligent. Not the quickest copper but one who never missed a trick in an investigation.

'At some time around two a.m. on October 23, four victims from the Ashton family were murdered in a house in Saddleworth. A father, mother and two children aged thirteen and eleven. The father was a partner in a legal firm—'

'Anything there? OCG involvement?'

'Not that we can see, boss. He was a commercial not a criminal lawyer, property development, stuff like that. He was on the boards of two companies, but they are both kosher and he was a non-executive director.'

'So, no organised crime involvement?'

'Not that we can see. According to the crime scene, the father and mother were both tied up and then killed with a shotgun blast to the back of the head. Not much left of their heads or their faces.'

'Did we get the casings?' asked Carruthers.

'No, boss, the perp must have taken them away with him. We're still trying to work out whether the parents or the children were killed first. My bet is the young boy heard a noise and ran into his sister's bedroom. Both had their throats cut, the walls splattered with blood. Our perp must have been covered in it.'

'Any DNA or fingerprints left at the scene.'

'None that the forensics could find, boss. The only prints in the house were from the family.'

'Only one perp?'

'We think so. There was one bloody footprint found in the girl's bedroom.'

'Any luck with it?'

'A common or garden work boot, the DeWalt Lennox, size ten, sold in their thousands by Screwfix and thousands of other stores. We're checking all stores that sold that size and make in Manchester, but he could have bought them online or anywhere else. Last year, 18,000 pairs of that size were sold in the UK.'

'How did the perp gain entry?' asked another detective.

'Ground floor bathroom window. It was jemmied open.'

'A professional? Could this be a burglary gone wrong?'

'Not as I see it. No burglar goes to a house tooled up with a shotgun. He did bring the rope used to tie up the mother and father though. Again, a common or garden variety used for climbing and camping, this time we think it was from B&Q. We're contacting all their stores as we speak, but given the perp's MO, I'm not hopeful, boss.'

'Keep going, you might get lucky.'

'There's one other thing the CSIs discovered. The words "I am guilty" written in the boy's blood on the bathroom mirror. It looks like the killer went into the kid's bathroom to clean the blood up and then decided to add a little memento of his visit on the mirror.'

'He's a freak, boss,' interrupted Harry Makepeace.

'He may be a freak, Harry, but he's our freak and we need to put him away. Anything else, Dennis?'

'That's all so far, boss. We're currently going through all the vehicles that passed the ANPR cameras near Saddleworth in the twenty-four hours preceding the home invasion and for the same time afterwards.'

'Who's doing it?'

Helen Shipton put her hand up. 'We've logged 27,548 vehicles in the period, but without something to narrow it down, it's like looking for a needle in a whole field of bloody haystacks.'

'Keep going, Helen. Are you working with Jasper on this?'

'Lucky girl,' interrupted Harry again.

Helen pretended to brush her hair off her face, surreptitiously giving the older detective the middle finger. 'I am, boss.'

'Good, keep at it, you never know what might come up.'

'With Jasper, you can be sure what'll come up,' added Harry Makepeace, 'and it isn't a sausage roll in his pocket.'

Steve Carruthers ignored the comment, turning back to Dennis Leahey. 'So let me get this right, we have a family murdered in their beds for no apparent reason. We have no forensics, no clues, no suspects and no motive after a week's work from half of MIT?'

'We'll keep going, boss, it's all in the details. This guy will make a mistake and then we'll pick him up.'

'But the only way he'll make a mistake is if he attacks again.'

The detective held his hands out but didn't say a word.

'Jesus, we can't wait for him to strike again; it could be anywhere in Manchester.'

'The only other thing would be to hold a public appeal,' suggested Dennis, 'maybe somebody saw something.'

'Right, I'll set it up with force communications. Do you want to front it, Dennis, or do you want me to do it?'

'Your call, boss.'

'I'll do it. Don't take this the wrong way, Dennis, but I'm going to be a lot more involved in the case from now. Our lords and masters are all over this like a Sheltie in heat on a sporran. Give me an hour to make it happen. You do realise all the wee nutters are going to come out of the woodwork for this?'

'We don't have anything else, boss.'

'Right, let's do it.' Carruthers emitted a long, slow sigh like a balloon had been punctured, before finally saying, 'Let's go through the rest of the list. And seeing as you've been a talkative wee soul in the last few minutes, Harry, you can go first. But keep it short, just like yourself.'

The detective opened his files to give himself time to consider his response. 'The Ryman case is still ongoing.'

'Ongoing? It's been going on for well over a year now with no apparent result in sight.'

'It's the Home Office and the Border Force – they take ages to make a decision and when we do finally get one, the Ryman brothers have already moved, dumped their phones and changed their operation so we have to start all over again.'

DCI Carruthers checked his notes. 'You said last week an arrest was slated for last Friday, what happened?'

'It was nixed at the last minute by the Home Office. Apparently some minister was making an announcement and they didn't want it to be upstaged by the arrests.'

'The National Crime Agency are going along with all this bullshit?'

'They are politicians, boss, and I've heard they've just asked for an increase in their budgets for next year to combat OCGs and the people smugglers.'

'Meanwhile, we actually have people traffickers operating in Manchester and we can't take them out?'

'That's about the size of it.'

Steve Carruthers shook his head. 'Whatever happened to operational independence?'

'What's that?'

'Exactly, Harry. I blame that Cressida Dick woman. She bent over so far backwards to please her political masters, she ended up compromising the Met. Stupid.'

'Bit her on the arse in the end, though, didn't it, boss?' Alan Butcher, a detective with a soft face and a hard body piped up.

'True. That's the problem. When you sleep with dogs, you end up with fleas. Anyway, enough of our moaning. Our job is to nick the bad people. We don't care about the bastard politicians, we just do our jobs, understood?'

'Yes, boss,' the chorus of people around the table answered.

'Anything else, Harry? What about your stabbing in Didsbury last Saturday night?'

'The victim still can't be interviewed, her doctors won't allow it. We're getting witness statements and checking CCTV, but no ID on the attacker so far. Plus, forensics haven't got back to me yet.'

'What about the victim? Did she know her attacker? Had she any previous? Had she mentioned any concerns to her colleagues or friends? Why are forensics taking so long?'

'We're still collating information, boss.'

'Come on, Harry. You know better than that. The first forty-eight hours are key in any investigation and you're still on the starting line. I want a full summary of all your actions as SIO on my desk by the end of the day. And I want quicker movement.' He stared all round the room. 'Look, people, I know we're all stretched and we're tired but that's no excuse for a sloppy investigation.'

'With all due respect, sir, my investigation has not been "sloppy". I was also dealing with the Home Office and the Border Force. I had to go down to the National Crime Agency in London yesterday for a meeting.'

'I know you're busy but we can't let stuff fall through the cracks, Harry, and the victim deserves better, doesn't she? Make sure you interview her before our meeting at six. I want to know her side of what happened.'

'But the doctors—'

'Doctors gae me the boak. Explain what you want from them and don't take no for an answer. If you only get five minutes with her, it will make all the difference. Do you want me to come with you?'

'No, boss, I'll do it myself.'

'I'll give forensics a call to gee them up for you.'

'Thanks, boss. They got so sick of me calling, they're no longer answering the phone.'

'I'll bet that happens a lot to you, Harry. I'll see you tonight at six. I want movement on this case, understood?'

'Yes, boss.'

'Next up, we have the luckiest woman in the world: DS Ivy Small. Take a bow, Ivy, and tell everybody the story.'

'It's nothing much. We've been looking for this pair of conmen who knock on old people's doors and pretend they're from the council and need to check the gas. While one of them keeps the old biddy talking, the other nips upstairs ostensibly to use the loo. Whilst he's there he nicks anything worth taking from the bedrooms.'

'Bastards,' said one of the detectives.

'Anyway, I don't think our conmen were particularly smart. Stupidly, they went back to the same house six months after they'd turned it over. This old biddy, Mrs Garland, recognised them immediately and pressed the emergency button on her phone. She kept the idiots talking until the plods arrived. They were found with her jewellery, a Teasmade, a few old clocks and, get this, some of the old lady's underwear in one of their tool bags.'

'Underwear?' asked Alan Butcher.

She held her hand up. 'This is where it gets really funny. When we raided one of the conmen's homes, we found a room with a load of old ladies' bloomers hanging up.'

'What?'

'Apparently, he had a fetish for sniffing them. Liked to pretend they were washing on a line, gets off on it apparently. Said it was his hobby.'

They all started laughing.

'Gross,' said Harry.

'And we found a load of other stolen gear they hadn't sold yet. They copped to eighty-three counts of burglary with intent to steal and ninety-seven counts of imperson-ating a local government official. They're looking at four years each at His Majesty's pleasure.'

'Even better, in one arrest, Ivy has cleared up a whole shitload of burglaries. Our stats have never looked better,' said Steve Carruthers.

'They're going to need some good briefs,' said one of the detectives to more laughter.

'Ones they haven't nicked yet,' added another.

'I wonder if they'll be called to the bra?' added a third.

'Okay, calm down, people. We've a lot to get through today. Well done, Ivy. Anything else you've managed to sniff out recently?'

The rest of the meeting went on in a similar vein. It was quickly apparent to Ridpath that the team were horrendously busy and short-staffed. They were all stretched to the limit and beyond. The recent riots hadn't helped at all.

Finally, Carruthers called his name. 'Good afternoon, DI Ridpath, representing our friends in the coroner's office. What do you have for us?'

'Luckily, I have nothing extra to add to your workload. Last week, we had 153 deaths in our area. The coroner has so far referred six of those cases for inquests. All will be postponed until the conclusion of the police investigation in the CID areas concerned. I don't know if any have been referred on to MIT.' Then, Ridpath snapped his fingers as if remembering something. 'Also, last night I was called to an incident at a petrol station. A man set himself on fire. It's being handled by the local nick but the coroner may want to get involved.'

'One of your inquests *has* been referred to us, Ridpath. Apparently, the boss had a chat with your coroner yesterday and we'd like you to take this case on, particularly as the coroner would like it fully investigated.'

'Which is it, boss?'

'I'll tell you in a meeting after this but I think it's right up your street. Plus, your presence at the petrol station has not gone unnoticed. The local inspector rang me this morning thanking you for your help. They are severely under-resourced at the moment. Apparently, there's a new strain of Covid running through their nick. It's not serious but they've got a real problem.'

'Doesn't everyone,' muttered Harry.

Ridpath ignored him. 'They sent a young detective fresh out of police training college to the incident. She did well, but she looked out of her depth.'

'Another reason to talk to you after this meeting.' He stood up and clapped his hands. 'Right then, get hoachin'. And for those of you who don't understand the King's Scottish, that means get your arse in gear and get busy. I want to see cases closed and villains put in jail.' He let his eyes drift across all of the assembled detectives so they understood the importance of his words. 'Be careful out there. Working hard and quick does not mean cutting corners or making stupid mistakes. Understand?'

'Yes, boss,' they chorused once more.

They all began to stand and put away their notepads when Carruthers continued speaking. 'All the details of the Ashton case are to be kept secret, particularly the MO of the crime scene. We'll discuss what you can say at the press conference later, Dennis, we don't want to give the nutters any chance to guess the forensics.'

'Agreed, boss.'

Carruthers deepened his voice, making it more threatening. 'If I find out any of you wee shites are thinking about feathering your nest by talking to the papers, you'll be out quicker than a highlander tosses his caber. And –' he held up a gnarled index finger '– I'll make sure you spend the rest of your careers standing on Leithland Road in Pollok with a sign around your neck saying you are polis. The Neds up there will chib you in less than thirty seconds. Got it?'

'Got it.'

'Ridpath, I'll brief you now. Dennis, come and see me in an hour. Harry, I'll see you at six this evening. Now get grafting, the lot of ye.'

Chapter TWELVE

Ridpath followed Steve Carruthers to his office in the corner of the MIT floor. It's glass walls and rounded shape had earned it the affectionate name of the goldfish bowl.

Carruthers pushed open his door and bustled in, beckoning for Ridpath to sit.

'How's Eve?' he asked almost immediately.

'She's okay, still going to the therapist.'

'Is it any help?'

'She had a bad experience and it doesn't help that Billy Diamond is out on bail.'

Carruthers shook his head. 'Nowhere to keep 'em all. The prisons are so full we're using the holding cells in our nicks to accommodate some prisoners. Not designed for that were they though; they were built to hold somebody for twenty-four hours at most.'

'No help to Eve, though.'

'Aye, I know it isn't. Anyway, I've asked you to come here today to do a couple of jobs for us. You saw how busy we are out there. I'm worried we'll start to make mistakes and I can't add any more work to their caseloads. Dennis is working all the hours God sends but isn't making much progress.'

'Motiveless crimes are always the worst, boss.'

'There must be something there, but we're missing it. You could also see Harry hadn't followed up on the stabbing quickly enough. The man has mince for brains. He should be out on the golf course, not running invest-igations for us.'

'He wanted to retire but you guys asked him to stay on.'

'We had no choice. We're training detectives as quickly as we can or nicking them from other forces but it'll be another six months before we are fully resourced. Mean-while, the crime doesn't stop.'

'It never does otherwise we'd be out of a job.'

'So that's why I've got you here today. Somehow, the work you did at the petrol station yesterday has impressed the local inspector, Ron Pleasance, so he's asked you to come in on two of their outstanding cases. Apparently he's worked with you on some case before.'

'Yeah, he was just a DC then.'

'They get promoted quickly now.'

'Not me though.'

Steve Carruthers coughed twice, ignoring the last remark. He slid a file across the desk. 'I presume the coroner has spoken to you about this case; a woman who was murdered by her child.'

'She mentioned it.'

'Well, you'll find all the case notes in the file. I've looked at them and so has Claire Trent. We're both not surprised the coroner was disturbed. To call it thin is an understatement. If CPS saw this, they'd be on the phone to the deputy chief quicker than a copper clocking off his shift. We want you to look into it, dot the i's and cross the t's. The child may have done it, but the last thing I need right now is a botched investigation.'

'Won't Pleasance be upset that I'm re-investigating one of his team's cases?'

'You are not re-investigating, you are preparing the case for the CPS. To do so, you have to check the investigation thoroughly. It was pointed out to Inspector Pleasance by Claire Trent how thin the report was. The man is smart, a born politician, he knows which side his bread is buttered on.'

'And the quid pro quo is I help him with his incident at the petrol station.'

'It's good to see you're getting better at the politics of policing, Ridpath.'

'Not something I enjoy, boss.'

'But something everybody has to understand. The inspector will brief you himself this afternoon.'

'I have a post-mortem on the man from the petrol station this afternoon.'

'I'd do the briefing afterwards if I were you. Ring him to arrange it. A word of warning, Ridpath: Pleasance is one of the blue-eyed boys of GMP, the chief constable has his eyes on him.'

'In other words, don't go and upset him. I'll be as tactful as a bull in a china shop, boss.'

'Good. You *are* getting the hang of the politics. Now, off you go to your post-mortem. I've got an appeal to organise for Dennis and budgets to fiddle for the next quarter. Creative accounting is my middle name.'

'Boss, you haven't told me if I'll get any resources to help me with the work.'

'By resource you mean your usual team of miscreants: Chrissy Wright, Emily Parkinson and Helen Shipton?'

Ridpath just sat there.

'Well, I haven't told you because you aren't working with them. We're too short-staffed to spare anybody at the moment.'

'So I'm working on my own?'

'Apparently not – Inspector Pleasance has assigned one of his young detectives to work with you...' He checked his notes. 'A DC Megan Muldowney, new out of Edgehill. You two know each other?'

'I met her last night at the petrol station.'

'Well, there you go, you have "resource" as you so elegantly put it.' Carruthers checked the internal telephone list and picked up his phone. 'Don't you have work to do?'

Ridpath stood up. 'Just one more question, boss.'

'What is it, Ridpath?'

'Who is going to be Claire Trent's replacement?'

'I don't know, Ridpath. As you know, I put in for it but didn't get through the first round. Apparently, it's too early in my career to be promoted to superintendent. There are other candidates including officers from other forces but I haven't received any news who has been appointed to the position. As soon as I do, I will let you and the rest of your colleagues know.'

'That sounds like a political answer, boss.'

'It is and is meant to be. Keep me informed on your progress, and don't do anything stupid.'

A look of mock innocence crossed Ridpath's face. 'Me? I wouldn't dream of doing anything like that at all. I'm Mr Go-By-The-Books these days.'

'Aye, and haggis might fly on Burn's Night.'

Chapter THIRTEEN

Outside Police HQ, walking back to his car, Ridpath spotted the group of inveterate smokers huddled around the tall ashtray. Each was wearing a hooded coat with smoke appearing as if by magic from some secret place within.

He walked across to say hello to one person he knew would be standing there. 'Hiya, Emily, still braving the weather for a gasper?'

DS Emily Parkinson was of medium build, had short, cropped hair and a broad Preston accent.

'You know me, Ridpath, can't live with them, can't live without them. Besides, it gets me away from my desk long enough to get some fresh air with my ciggie.'

The person standing next to Emily turned around. Ridpath was surprised to see Helen Shipton's face hidden in the hoodie.

'I didn't know you smoked, Helen.'

'I don't,' she said, blowing a long stream of light blue smoke into the cold air.

Standing downwind, Ridpath could smell the acrid tendrils of tobacco as he inhaled. After promising Eve, he hadn't touched a cigarette for nearly two years but he could still taste the passive smoke as it curled round his head.

'You have anything for us, Ridpath? I saw you go into Carruthers' office; that means you're on a case.'

'I am, but I'm flying solo on this one. Working with somebody from Sale nick, a Megan Muldowney.'

'Her,' snorted Helen Shipton. 'I did a course with her at Edgehill. She's on the fast track, a graduate from Manchester Uni no less. Proper little brown noser, too.'

'Sounds like you're a little bit jealous, Helen.'

'Why would I be jealous? I'm stuck in a dark room with Jasper Early, a man who thinks Lara Croft is real, staring at badly shot ANPR videos, looking for a car but not knowing the make, model or registration number. I'm living the police life, exactly as it said in the brochures. Meanwhile, she's just out of training college and already has her own cases working with you. Me, jealous? Not a bit.' She threw her cigarette on the pavement and ground it into the concrete with her heel.

'What are you doing, Emily?'

'Working with Harry on the stabbing in Didsbury. God, he's slow – it's like watching paint dry. Between you and me, he's getting forgetful these days. I keep having to remind him what to do next.'

'A good DS always covers the SIO's arse. He was hung out to dry today.'

'I know, Ridpath, but I did tell him. He's obsessed about the Ryman brothers' case. I think he sees it as his last big job before he retires, his swansong. Problem is, he's also got the stabbing to work on too. It's like he can't handle two things at once.'

'Harry never was the most flexible of coppers.'

'Now he's just a working stiff. Should have retired a year ago.' She glanced at her watch. 'Shit, is that the time?' She stubbed out half of her cigarette in the ash tray. Ridpath stared at it longingly.

'I need to drive him to the hospital to interview the victim, but the doctors are running rings around him.'

'A good DS—'

'—covers the arse of her superior officer. Got it, Ridpath. See you later, Helen, and wish me luck.'

Emily ran off towards her car, leaving Ridpath and Helen standing around the upright ashtray like refugees waiting for the arrival of a ship. She lit another cigarette, inhaled and expelled a long stream of blue smoke into the air to join the grey clouds blanketing Manchester.

'For somebody who doesn't smoke, you sure know how to, Helen.'

'I'm dying, Ridpath. Ever since I worked with you on the Lardner case, I've been branded as the go-to girl when CCTV needs to be analysed.'

'I remember you did very well.'

'I did, but since then, I've been the CCTV officer on three other investigations. I don't ever leave Police HQ any more. I'm stuck in a room with a randy, bearded, lecherous troll who thinks baked beans are a food group. You know, I watch television in my dreams now. Even my dreams are played on banks of monitors.'

'I wish I could help, Helen. I asked for the usual team but the DCI made it plain that MIT are too stretched at the moment to spare anybody.'

'We'd better get some fresh bodies soon, it's starting to fall apart. Mistakes are going to be made. You heard Emily: Harry is already floundering.'

'He'll get a grip, he always does.'

'What are you working on?'

'Something with Sale nick. I'm going to be briefed this afternoon.'

She leant in closer to him. 'Go on, you can tell me – what is it? A murder?'

Ridpath shook his head. 'You know I never discuss my cases except with my direct colleagues, Helen. Look, if anything comes up, I'll let you know, okay?'

She took another drag from the cigarette. 'You're no fun, Ridpath.'

'That's what my daughter says.'

'I've got to get out of that room. You know the only reason I smoke is to get away from him. Every lunchtime, he consumes his body weight in cheese toasties, afterwards he sweats cheddar. One day, I'm going to lose the plot and strangle him. Then you'll be investigating me.'

Ridpath glanced back towards his car. 'I've got to go, Helen. A post-mortem.'

'You know, even a post-mortem would be more fun than being stuck in a room with him.'

'See ya.' He turned to go and then stopped. 'You've got over 27,000 cars to go through?'

'Tell me about it, an impossible job.'

'It could take you years to check them all.'

'Do you have a better idea?'

'Why don't you see if any car has been in the area more than once? I'm sure the perp must have recced the area before he committed the crime.'

Helen Shipton raised her eyebrows. 'From his MO, he must have done. But there would still be all the cars from the residents of the area. They would appear more than once.'

'Why don't you get HOLMES to eliminate all cars registered to the Saddleworth postcodes?'

Helen Shipton sucked on her cigarette, her eyes narrowing. 'It might work. At least it would reduce the number of cars we need to look at drastically.'

'Anyway, I have to get going. See you, Helen.'

'Yeah, bye, Ridpath. Remember me to the world, won't you?'

'I'm sure you'll find something new to work on.'

'I hope so, Ridpath. But I'm serious, I'd love to work with you again. Last time was the best work I'd done since joining the force.'

'I'll let you know if anything comes up.'

She waved goodbye at him, but still stood there, hood pulled up around her face, puffing away at her cigarette, already pulling another one from the box in her coat pocket.

Ridpath remembered her as an ambitious – too ambitious – young detective, eager to climb her way up the police ladder. Now, she was a chain-smoking wreck spending her time in a darkened room staring at monitors all day long.

Police work. It should come with a health warning.

Chapter FOURTEEN

As Ridpath entered the morgue, the familiar shivers stomped down his backbone. He had been here so many times and yet he still experienced the same reaction every time. He'd worked out long ago that the antiseptic stench of the place combined with the echoes off the white tiles produced a visceral reaction in him.

For a second, he thought about turning away and heading back to the coroner's office. But he recognised the fight-or-flight syndrome and forced himself to step forward to greet the receptionist.

She was different from the last woman who sat behind the desk, he guessed nobody lasted working here long. She was presently engrossed in painting her nails a bright, shocking scarlet.

'Hello,' she said without looking up, 'how can I help you?'

'DI Ridpath for Dr Schofield.'

'The post-mortem?'

'Well, it wouldn't be a church social.'

She briefly glanced up at him and then checked her calendar. 'He's in Lab 3, you can go straight in once you've suited up.'

She extended a long, red nail towards the changing rooms.

'I know where it is,' he answered curtly, before leaving her to paint her left index finger.

He quickly changed into a Tyvek suit, ensuring the plastic coveralls were over his shoes and his mask fitted correctly, before finding Lab 3.

For a moment, he stood in front of the door and took a deep breath. Knocking three times, he entered without waiting to be invited.

Despite the mask, the smell of the corpse hit him immediately. A mixture of burnt toast, roast pork and petrol flooded his nostrils.

Ridpath swallowed, tasting the bitter saliva in his mouth. *Keep it together.*

Dr Schofield was bent over the blackened cadaver in front of him: the chest was open and the white ribs clearly visible. An empty hole lay where the lungs should have been.

For a second, he looked up. 'Good afternoon, Ridpath, glad you could make it. Your colleague, DC Muldowney is over there. As you can see, we've already started. Give me a second to remove this heart and I'll take you through what we've discovered so far.'

'Good afternoon, Doctor.' Ridpath nodded at Schofield's assistant, Miss Wong, who was presently holding a steel bowl waiting for the doctor to place the heart there, before weighing it.

Megan Muldowney stepped out of the shadows and walked towards him. She looked younger than he remembered, her blonde hair now hidden by the hood of her Tyvek suit.

'Hiya, Ridpath,' she whispered leaning close to him, 'I'm so excited – this is my first post-mortem.'

Ridpath glanced towards the corpse lying on the stainless-steel table. The body was blackened, the limbs twisted into impossible angles. Where the fingers and toes should have been, there were only stumps, suggestions of digits. Both arms were raised in the classic pugilist's pose – the effect of the fire on the muscles of the arms. Ridpath couldn't see any eyes or hair. The fire had consumed them.

'You're not repelled by this?' He pointed at the body.

She shook her head. 'It's fascinating, isn't it? I love the detail of the doctor's work.'

'*It* is a person, or was a person; we should always remember that.'

'Of course, but this is science in the raw. You'll be amazed at what the pathologist has already discovered.'

Dr Schofield thanked his assistant and then turned to face the two police officers. 'We made quite a bit of progress, Ridpath. Any luck finding a name for this man?'

Ridpath glanced at Megan. She shook her head.

'Not yet, Doctor.'

'Right, he'll remain as John Doe until we hear otherwise. What we have here is a Caucasian male, approximately forty years old, five feet eleven inches tall and weighing 95.2 kilos, so slightly overweight for his height. He's of medium build with only one distinguishing mark as far as I can see.' He pointed to a section of the chest above the heart. 'There is a tattoo on the skin here. Unfortunately, the fire removed the detail and the image but there is a ghost of it which I can see quite clearly. Miss Wong has taken some photographs under infrared light.'

The assistant pressed a button on a laptop and an image appeared on an overhead screen.

'As you can see, we're uncertain of the colours used but the shape seems to be that of a stylised elephant. Maybe the tattoo was done on holiday in Thailand or somewhere in Southeast Asia? But we'll leave that to your investigations.'

The doctor paused for a moment as if remembering something. 'Oh yes, DC Muldowney tells me, you've been seconded to this case. Are you here as a detective or as a coroner's officer?'

'Both, Doctor.'

'Good, killing two birds with one stone.'

'You could put it like that; I'd probably say GMP is under-resourced.'

'Aren't we all? I'm short of three lab assistants, it's one of the reasons we're having to outsource much of our work these days. Anyway, back to our John Doe. He's relatively healthy if a little overweight, as I said. His heart, which I've just removed, does show some fattening around the arteries suggesting some lifestyle issues. It would have given him problems five or so years from now but at the moment, it functions quite well.' He coughed. 'Or I should say it used to function quite well. We've already taken samples of his DNA and you should get a response within a day, if it hasn't been damaged by the fire.'

'I asked them to make it a priority, I hope that's okay, Ridpath,' said Megan.

'Of course, we need to find out who this man is.'

'Our John Doe had one broken left collarbone which is well healed. My bet is he broke it when he was young. He may have had scarring or other tattoos but I'm afraid we will never know.'

'What was the cause of death?'

'Ah, that is a quite an interesting question, Ridpath. Petrol burns at approximately 1,026 degrees Celsius so the fire is intense. There are three possible ways of dying if a person sets themselves alight. The first is burn shock. The heat from the fire damages the cells in the skin and body by denaturing proteins that are critical to their function. Think of frying an egg and seeing it become solid.'

'Not a very pleasant image, Doctor.'

'But true, nonetheless. The cells would be unable to function as a result and die. Allow this to continue long enough and your organs will cease to be able to maintain their functions. However, this may take a while to reach a lethal stage simply because the internals of the body aren't burning directly, so the heat must be sufficient and the outer layers massively damaged to result in death. It's one of the reasons many people survive severe burns with timely help. The second way of death is through suffocation; the fire robs the surrounding air of oxygen, including the air in the lungs, and produces lots of carbon dioxide and some carbon monoxide, which can result in lethal poisoning by strongly binding to haemoglobin in the blood cells and reducing oxygen transport.'

He walked over to a metal side table where a large dish contained a pair of pinkish human lungs.

'I examined these and found soot particles inside plus the blood had a 21 per cent carboxyhaemoglobin concentration and 0.07 µg/ml of cyanide. That doesn't mean he was poisoned, merely that cyanide is present in the petrol fumes he inhaled. We've sent the blood off for further toxicology to see if he was under the influence of any drugs at the time he committed this action.'

Ridpath found himself drifting away as the pathologist continued his lecture.

'The third way of dying is simply a combination of the previous two. Quite simply, the air becomes hot enough to burn your lungs, preventing gas exchange with the blood and the body goes into toxic shock as a result.

Considering the gasoline is vapourising prior to the burn, this probably happens quickly.'

There was a silence as Dr Schofield stopped speaking. Before Megan Muldowney asked the obvious question.

'So which one was it, Dr Schofield?'

The pathologist shrugged his shoulders. 'By the evidence from the lungs, my hypothesis is he died from asphyxiation. But I can't be certain. The only thing I am sure of is that he is dead. Very dead.'

Ridpath snapped out of his reverie. 'Of course, we'll wait for your final report with the toxicology but from the evidence of the CCTV and witness statements, it seems this man took his own life. Thank you for all your work.'

Ridpath turned quickly to escape the lab and the smell of burnt barbecue.

'But there is one thing that is a little puzzling...'

Slowly and reluctantly, Ridpath turned back. 'What is that, Doctor?'

'He had something tied around his upper thigh.'

'What?'

'Whatever fabric was used burnt away but there were metal hooks embedded in the skin, fused to it because of the heat.'

Ridpath moved closer to the post-mortem table and the blackened corpse lying on it. 'What?'

'A girdle of some sort around his right upper thigh. We X-rayed the area and this is what we saw.'

The doctor pressed a key on his computer and an image came up on the screen. Ridpath could see a vague outline of a thigh and bone. In the centre, in bright white, a row of hooks circled the thigh, their sharp barbs clear as day.

'What are those?' Ridpath asked leaning in to see the screen better.

The doctor pointed at the screen. Ridpath noticed how incredibly small his hands were, almost childlike, but they could still remove a victim's skull or deliver a heart on a plate.

'If I were a gambling man, I'd say they were fishing hooks. To test my theory, I cut one away from his thigh.'

In his small, gloved hands, the doctor held a fishing hook three-quarters of an inch long with a sharp barb at its end.

'On the X-ray, we counted sixteen of these hooks.'

Ridpath shook his head in disbelief. 'Why…? What…? Why tie fish hooks around your leg?'

Megan Muldowney joined him. 'Is this sexual. Was he a masochist?'

The doctor shrugged his shoulders. 'I have no idea but it's probably something you need to find out. The complexity of human existence never ceases to amaze me even now.'

Chapter FIFTEEN

'I heard you were joining us to help out.'

Ridpath and Muldowney were outside the morgue, standing on the pavement. The rain was falling in a soft mizzle. That mixture of mist and drizzle that soaked anybody to the skin before they even realised they were wet.

Ridpath was breathing in lungfuls of the thickest Manchester air, desperately trying to rid his nose and lungs of the aroma of burnt corpse.

'Where's your car?' he asked.

'Over there, I'm using my own as the pool cars are all wrecks. Do you want a lift?'

He shook his head. 'I have my own. Let's chat while we walk back.'

They walked down to the pedestrian crossing where he pressed the button and waited. 'Your boss, Inspector Pleasance, has requested my help for a couple of days. Apparently, you're short-staffed at Sale nick, some flu bug or something. Seems like every department of GMP is short of people.'

'Yeah, I'm one of the few left, but I never get ill. Constitution like an ox. Growing up on a farm must have helped.'

'Where was that?'

'Near Buxton. I'm a Derbyshire girl born and bred.'

'Why join GMP then?'

'I wanted the adventure of the bright lights and big city. The last thing on earth I wanted to be investigating was the disappearance of another cow. Been there, done that, all my life.'

'So instead you're looking into the death of a bloke who walks into a petrol station and sets himself on fire. I think I'd prefer looking for a missing cow.'

The pedestrian crossing beeped and they stepped out from the pavement as the cars stopped.

'I heard you're to help on this case and in the murder of a woman by her daughter.'

'That's not one of yours?'

'No, it's Andy's.'

'Who's Andy?'

'DC Fletcher. He's fresh out of Edgehill, too.'

'Are there any detectives with any experience working in Sale?'

'Don't think so, that's why you're helping, isn't it? At least we can wrap our case up pretty quickly?'

'You think it was suicide?'

'Looks like it. It's all on CCTV.'

'You checked the footage?'

'Last night. It's exactly as the witness said. He walked up to the pump, paid with his credit card and then set himself on fire. Nobody else was involved. Open and shut case, isn't it?'

'A couple of questions...'

'Go on.'

'Why did he do it and who was he?'

'I can't answer either but my guess is he was depressed, maybe he had money or relationship worries.'

'There are far easier ways to end your life than walking into a petrol station and setting yourself on fire. Doesn't it concern you he chose such an unusual method?'

'To paraphrase Dr Schofield: "The complexity of human existence never ceases to amaze me."'

'Not good enough. To wrap this up we need more.'

'Like what?'

'We need to find out who he is and then chat with colleagues, friends or his family to find out why he did it. Then and only then, can we close the file.'

'What do you want me to do?'

Ridpath was beginning to like this young detective. She was always willing to do the work, her enthusiasm and zeal hadn't yet been worn down by the system.

'The DNA is key. Push the lab hard to get the results back as soon as you can. Meanwhile, check missing persons. See if somebody answering his description has been reported missing. Check Manchester first and then expand it out to the rest of the North. My bet, he's from Sale or nearby though…'

'Why?'

'There are thousands of petrol stations all over the country. Why choose that particular one?'

'Because it was close.'

'Exactly.'

'Okay, I'm on it.'

They stopped near her car. A dark grey Range Rover with flashy wheel rims.

'How can you afford one of these on a copper's salary?'

'I can't. It's my mum and dad's. One of the perks of living in the country.'

Ridpath checked his watch. If he left now, he could pick up Eve as she came out of her therapist's office and drive her home. The place wasn't far from there.

'Megan, can you do me a favour?'

'Sure.'

'I'm supposed to meet your boss later this evening, but something has come up. Can you rearrange it with him for tomorrow morning, early. Say nine a.m.? Make sure Andy whatshisname is there too?'

'Fletcher, his name is Andy Fletcher. Ron Pleasance won't be chuffed, he was expecting to meet you today.'

'Like I said, I have something important to do, plus I want to read all the files on the case before meeting him.'

'Okay, I'll arrange it. Do you have a number where I can contact you?'

Ridpath gave her his mobile. 'Thanks for this. To be honest, I want to pick my daughter up from her therapist and have a chat with her. And I do want to read all the notes before meeting your boss.'

'Thanks for the honesty. Family should always come first but it's hard in this job, isn't it? I'll rearrange it for you.'

'One last thing, why do you think our man in the petrol station had fish hooks embedded in his skin?'

'I dunno. Maybe he was into S&M. Being burnt alive is a pretty painful way to die.'

Ridpath sucked in his breath. 'It doesn't make sense, does it? In the old days, some monks and priests used to wear girdles with hooks or sharp points. It was a way of discovering God through pain, a way of reminding themselves that life on earth was painful and only in heaven would they be free.'

She looked at him quizzically.

'I was brought up a Catholic. Guilt ladled down own throats like it was hot soup by the monks at school.'

'Sounds a bit too deep for me, I'm just a country girl.'

Ridpath laughed. 'A country girl who drives a top-of-the-line Range Rover and went to Manchester Uni?'

'How do you know that?'

'Helen Shipton told me. She was on a course with you at Edgehill.'

'I remember her, an ambitious little soul. A tad too ambitious for me. What's she doing now?'

'Working for MIT.'

'I'd love her job. Sale can be a bit suburban if you know what I mean. The sort of place where the serious crimes happen behind closed curtains not out on the streets.'

'Not any more they don't. Our main priority is to discover the man's identity as soon as we can. Understand?'

She made a mock salute towards him. 'On it, Ridpath. By the way, why don't they call you by your Christian name?'

He laughed again. 'My mum called me Thomas and I've hated it all my life. I much prefer Ridpath.'

'I like Thomas as a name, it has a formality about it, an old-world charm.'

'To you I will be known as Ridpath, DC Muldowney. As a senior officer, you can take that as an order.'

She mock-saluted him again. 'Aye, aye, Captain Ridpath.'

'Just Ridpath will do.'

'Aye, aye, sir. I'll confirm the time of the meeting with you this evening by text.'

'If Ron Pleasance is a problem, let me know.'

'He won't be, I can handle him. He's a sweetie is Ron.'

'I don't remember him like that.'

'You two have worked together before?'

'A murder case a few years ago when he was a young DC like you.'

'He's been promoted fast, somebody must be looking after him.'

Ridpath thought about himself, still a detective inspector after all these years and now unlikely to be promoted as long as he worked with the coroner.

He opened his car door. 'Got to go now, don't forget to confirm the meeting with me this evening.'

She saluted him for the third time. 'Aye, aye, Cap'n.'

'Ridpath, just Ridpath, will do.'

He sat in the driver's seat and started the engine, watching her through the mizzle as she walked over to her car.

He'd have to watch himself with this one.

90

Chapter SIXTEEN

'Just one more question and we'll call time on this press conference. Does any member of the press have any more questions concerning the murder of the Ashton family in Saddleworth?'

Steve Carruthers leant forward, his mouth close to the microphone on the table. Behind him, a large poster displayed the GMP logo against dark blue. There was no slogan, just three bullet points: keeping people safe and supporting victims, reducing harm and offending, strengthening communities and place.

Sitting next to Carruthers, the force's male PR officer pointed at a reporter on the second row. 'Todd Simpson from the *Liverpool Echo*.'

'Good morning, Detective Chief Inspector Carruthers. Do you think the killer is local to Manchester or is it possible he could come from further afield, perhaps from Liverpool or somewhere like that? And what preparations have you made in case he is from our area?'

'That's two questions, Todd.'

'No worries, Max, I can answer both. We have run the home invasion at the Ashton family residence through HOLMES, the Home Office's Large Major Enquiry System. Which I'm sure you all know is an information technology system used by UK police forces for the investigation of major incidents such as serial murders or the crime we are investigating in Saddleworth. We are particularly interested in its capacity for crime mapping and geographical profiling.'

'Could you explain that more, Chief Inspector?' the reporter asked.

'Certainly. The theoretical foundation of geographic profiling is in environmental criminology. That is, each criminal, particularly serial offenders, have a pattern to their offending, their MO. This involves considerations such as the journey to the crime, their routine activities, rational choice making and the pattern of the crime. The initial criminal acts are likely to occur close to the offender's home or workplace. As the success rate increases, the criminal's growing confidence will lead them to expand their area of operations. Saddleworth, as you know, is on the other side of Greater Manchester to Liverpool with no direct routes of travel from the city. We therefore expect the perpetrator of this crime to live closer to the incident, i.e. in Manchester itself.'

'You say this is true of serial offenders,' Todd Simpson continued, 'but what if this crime wasn't committed by a serial offender? And if it was, does that mean you are waiting for him to strike again?'

Steve Carruthers coughed twice. 'We are investigating both possibilities and are actively seeking to arrest the perpetrator of this awful crime before he strikes again.'

The reporter was about to ask another follow-up question when the force's PR officer interrupted. 'Thank you, Chief Inspector Carruthers, we have a dictionary available on your way out for those who didn't understand the operational head of MIT's Scots brogue.'

The reporters dutifully laughed, even Carruthers' face reddened.

'Thank you to everybody from the press and the television channels for coming here today. As you can imagine, DCI Carruthers is a busy man and so we must end the press conference here. You can pick up a release and fact sheet on your way out. I will repeat once more that the most important thing we are looking for is that any members of the public who have information should come forward. If you could print the response line number prominently in your reports it would be appreciated. Thank you.'

He covered the mike with his hand and leant across to whisper in Steve Carruthers' ear. 'I think that went rather well, don't you? The lines are manned and we should be getting the calls soon.'

'Aye, it went well until the last question about him striking again. I played it down. We don't want all the householders of Manchester to be scared of a home invader.'

Dennis Leahey walked onto the stage. 'Well done, boss, I understood what you were saying even if nobody else did.'

'Thank you for your ringing endorsement, Dennis. Now let's hope the people of Manchester also understood it and particularly any witnesses who may have seen our perp in the early hours of Wednesday morning or somebody who knows who he is.'

'The phones are manned and waiting, boss. We only hope we don't get too many wee nutters ringing in.'

'I hope so too, Dennis. We don't have the manpower, or womanpower, to track the bastards down if they all call at once.'

Leahey held up his crossed fingers.

'Not nearly enough, Dennis, you need to cross your toes too and any other assorted appendages that may be available. We're gonna need all the luck we can find from the fairies for this one.'

Chapter SEVENTEEN

Ridpath spotted Eve as soon as she came the down the steps from the building that housed a whole host of therapists ready to cure the world of their ills.

Normally he was sceptical of these people but when Polly had been murdered he'd been forced to come here. At first, he had gone along with his therapist because he knew, without her sign-off, he would never be able to go back to work. But despite the misgivings, he found the process useful. Simply talking about his feelings to a stranger had been almost cathartic. He still hadn't overcome his feelings of loss about Polly – he still missed her every day of his life. But at least he now understood the process of grief and his therapist had given him some tangible coping mechanisms.

The door opened and she slid into the car.

'How was it?'

'Okay.'

'Just okay?'

'It was good.'

Ridpath realised that was the only answer he was going to get at this time so he started the engine.

'What do you want to eat?'

'Food. I'm starving. Talking to her always makes me hungry for some reason.'

Ridpath could think of thousands of reasons why that might be but he wasn't going to mention them to Eve. Instead he said, 'Food? Could we be a tad more specific? Could we narrow it down to a continent perhaps? Asia? America? Europe? Antarctica?'

'I know what I want,' she snapped her fingers. 'Deep-fried penguin with a side order of curly fries.'

'Is that like a deep-fried Mars bar without the crunchy bits?'

'Sort of. But if one of those is not available, I'd love a Rudy's Margherita with extra cheese. I'm in a gooey, cheesy mood.'

'I know the feeling. Let me just order one and we'll pick it up on the way home. Garlic bread on the side?'

'You can read my mind, Kimosabe.'

He had the pizza house on speed dial and rang through the order, confirming he would pick it up in twenty minutes.

He started the car and pulled out into the middle of the traffic.

After he'd driven for five minutes in silence, she asked him a question. 'Dad, do you still miss Mum?'

'Funny, I was thinking about that while I was waiting for you. Truth is, I miss her every day.'

'Me too, but I'm worried she's starting to vanish in my head. I can't remember what she looked like any more and it feels so wrong I can't remember her face. Occasionally, it comes back to me. Like when I clocked Billy with her lamp. Before your lot came in, he was groaning on the floor, and all I could smell was Mum's perfume. And it was like she was there with me in the bedroom, protecting me. Weird, huh?'

'I don't think it's weird at all. Smells always make us think of people or places all the time. It's one of the reasons I want to be sick when I smell red cabbage. It always reminds me of my mum's cooking.'

'It was that bad?'

'It wasn't great and she'd put this pickled red cabbage straight from the jar with everything. Fish and chips and pickled red cabbage. Irish stew and pickled red cabbage...'

'Apple crumble and pickled cabbage?'

'Don't laugh, I'm sure I ate that at least once in my childhood. It was better than her custard though.'

'I won't ask.'

'Don't. The local painter and decorator used it for wallpaper paste. Stuck far better than anything he could buy in the shops, according to him.'

'I dread to think what it was doing to your insides.'

'Oh, I never ate it. The dog loved it though.'

'Dad, you didn't feed it to your dog?'

'Not all of it.' Ridpath laughed at the memories. 'He used to have these lumps of yellow custard glue stuck to the end of his nose. He always tried to lick them off but they used to stay there for days.'

'Didn't your mum notice?'

'Not really, she didn't notice much my mother. Not after dad left, anyway.'

'I wish I had met her.'

'No, you don't.'

'Why?'

'She would have made you eat pickled red cabbage and custard. And we don't have a dog to give it to.'

'I could use it to stick my posters on the walls – they keep falling off.'

'Wish she'd given me the recipe. Not.'

She laughed again in a way Ridpath hadn't heard her laugh since the attack. She was back to being the Eve he knew and loved.

'Dad, I'm glad you came to pick me up tonight.'

'So am I, Eve, so am I.'

Chapter EIGHTEEN

The clock in the attic struck seven p.m. It was an old-fashioned mantle clock that played the Westminster chimes, followed by striking the hour. But for some reason, the bells always played two hours less than the real time. He'd tried to fix it but finally gave up, exasperated.

Over the long afternoon, he had slowly taken the plans and the timelines down from their walls, neatly folding them up and placing them on his father's desk next to the rulers, pens, Sellotape, markers, scissors and scalpel. Each had its own place on the table as his father had decreed.

'A tidy desk is the sign of a tidy mind. Too many people waste their lives looking for stationery they have mislaid. If you know exactly where it is, you will always be able to find it.' A sharp click from his tongue. 'A little to the left. The highlighters must be exactly three inches away from the edge of the desk, perpendicular to the ruler. Understand?'

'Yes, Father.'

He understood. He always understood.

To this day, he still followed the same rules and he had never wasted time looking for anything. Not a second. He always knew where everything was. They called him Mr Tidy at work simply because of how organised he was.

Another of his father's dictums: a place for everything where everything has its place.

When he had folded the plans neatly and filed them correctly in the right drawer, he slowly turned to the final wall.

The final plan.

Here, the picture was bigger than on the other wall, the man's face larger to emphasise his importance. The anniversary was on October 31 at 12.02 p.m. All Hallows' Eve, so fitting.

He had chosen that time to carry out the final execution: the time, the place and the method. A suitable one, he thought, to honour both his parents' memories and the manner of their deaths.

He checked his calendar. It would be exactly forty-one hours from now. Time enough for him to go for another walk and play all the details through in his head again and again.

He had read somewhere of athletes visualising the races they were going to run before they even approached the stadium.

Tomorrow, on his walk, he would visualise every detail of the man's death. What would happen, how it would feel, the smell of fear, the trembling of his hands, the last tentative steps to oblivion.

He'd rehearse the plans, going over every single detail, every nuance, every word he would say. Then afterwards, he would send the man his final instructions.

He stared at the man's face on his wall and a shiver of pleasure ran down his body. Should he shorten the deadline?

No. Let him suffer. Let him taste fear.

It was time to get started, the man would be expecting his message.

He logged on to the group chat Signal. He had chosen this app because of its strong security features and the ability to disappear messages when he wanted. It was far better than the basic service offered by Snapchat.

The man was already waiting for him.

> **PropMan76:** Are you there? You said to log on at six p.m.
>
> **Rellik:** I am sending through your instructions, Robert. The date you have been given is October 31 when you will leave the house at exactly 10.45 a.m. You will no doubt recognise it. I thought it was rather apt. You will read the instructions and comply. Your final orders will be given later.
>
> **PropMan76:** Why are you doing this to us?
>
> **Rellik:** You know why. I have explained why.
>
> **PropMan76:** But you don't have to hurt anyone. We can talk about it, work it all out.
>
> **Rellik:** It's too late, Mr Wallace.

He sent the file to the man's email address then logged off, but the account remained connected to Signal, as he waited for the man to click on the file.

Turning the man's computer into an observation and listening device was a simple programme he had bought on the dark web. He had embedded the code in the instructions he had sent. Once the man clicked the link, it would download onto his computer, creating an unblinking eye so he could watch and listen any time he wanted. The whole code was voice activated, so if the man spoke, the camera on his computer would begin filming and recording.

Of course, he had planted other bugs in the house already, but he would allow the man to find them later. It was all part of the game.

He watched as the picture flickered into life as the man scanned the orders he had been given, seeing the final instruction at the end.

The look on the man's face was perfect: a combination of disbelief and horror all at the same time.

Beautiful.

He continued watching the man and his family for the next hour. Robert Wallace and his wife talking when they thought the children weren't listening, whispering to each other, fear in every word they used.

It was magnificent.

He would not talk to them until tomorrow afternoon but he would know exactly what they were doing and what they said until then. They, of course, would be as ignorant of his presence as they were guilty of their crime.

He had a lot to do tomorrow: loose ends to clear up from the last death and preparations for the next one. He would go to bed soon, listening to Robert and his wife discussing their predicament as he drifted off to sleep.

By now, both the man and the woman would understand what was going to happen and were deciding whether they were going to comply or not.

Either way, the man would die. Or his wife and family.

Or everybody.

It was their decision.

Chapter NINETEEN

Ridpath settled into his armchair, a pot of tea and some chocolate biscuits by his side. Eve had gone to her room twenty minutes earlier to do her homework. It was good to know she was finally back on track. He'd been worried about her since the incident with Billy Diamond. Perhaps the therapist was right: time was the great healer.

He picked up the file given to him by Steve Carruthers. Perhaps he should have gone to meet Inspector Pleasance earlier, but he didn't regret his decision to pick up Eve instead. Sometimes family had to come first.

He opened the file. Inside were the notes from the investigation, a disk with the interview with the young girl, a thumb drive of the initial 999 call and statements from the first responders, both police and medics.

'Best start at the beginning,' he said aloud, inserting the thumb drive into the port of his laptop.

He was about to press start on the audio file when his phone pinged with a message.

> Briefing arranged for nine a.m. tomorrow morning with Inspector Pleasance. Not a happy bunny that it wasn't tonight, but he never is.

> Okay, I'll be there. Can you make sure Andy Fletcher attends too?

> We'll see you afterwards. Pleasance wants a one-on-one with you first.

> Okay.

> See ya tomorrow.

Ridpath put down his phone. He was tempted to rebuke Megan for her flippant response. If he'd sent the same sort of message to his old boss, Charlie Whitworth, he would have been bawled out within seconds. 'Respect the rank, Ridpath.'

Maybe he would have a quiet word with her tomorrow.

He returned to the case of the daughter who had murdered her mother, pressing play on the audio file and listening carefully.

> **Call operator:** Hello, emergency service operator. Which service do you require? Fire, police or ambulance?
> **Girl:** I don't know, ambulance... and the police. My mum, she's not breathing.
> **Call operator:** I'll connect you to the ambulance service.
> **Call handler:** Ambulance service, what's the address of the emergency?
> **Girl:** My mum, she's not breathing.

Ridpath paused the playback. The girl's voice was calm and collected. She wasn't upset or frantic in any way, which was strange if her mum was no longer breathing.

He pressed play again.

> **Call handler:** Can you give me your full address?
> **Girl:** 26 Handley Road, Sale.
> **Call handler:** Can you tell me again just to confirm?
> **Girl:** It's 26 Handley Road, Sale.
> **Call handler:** We'll be there as quick as we can. Can I take a name and a contact telephone number please?
> **Girl:** My name is Anita Forsyth. I'm using my mum's phone. The number is 07894278817.
> **Call handler:** Are you calling about yourself or someone else?
> **Girl:** My mum, she's not breathing.
> **Call handler:** Are they male or female?
> **Girl:** It's my mum.
> **Call handler:** What's happened today?
> **Girl:** My mum's not breathing. [A long pause.] I think I killed her.
> **Call handler:** What? What was that?

Ridpath could hear the disbelief in the call handler's voice.

> **Girl:** My mum, I think I killed her.

Another long pause.

> **Call handler:** Is she responsive?
> **Girl:** No – like I said, she's not moving, just lying there on the bed.
> **Call handler:** Is she breathing at all?

Girl: I don't know.

Call handler: The ambulance is being organised for you now. I have also alerted the police. So the address we will be sending the ambulance to is: 26 Handley Road, Sale. Can you confirm that's correct again?

Girl: That's my address.

Call handler: Is there any further information that will help the crew find the address?

Girl: I don't think so.

Call handler: Is the scene safe?

Girl: What do you mean?

Call handler: Is it safe for the ambulance crew to enter the premises?

Girl: Yes.

Call handler: The ambulance is on its way right now, but I just need to ask you a few more questions. This won't delay the ambulance and police reaching you. Okay?

Girl: Yes.

Call handler: How do you know your mum isn't breathing?

Girl: Because I killed her. She hasn't moved for a long time.

Call handler: How long is it since she moved?

Girl: About thirty minutes.

Call handler: Did you try to resuscitate your mum, give her CPR?

Girl: No, why would I do that? I'm doing it to save her.

Ridpath frowned. *What was that?*

He rewound the playback twenty seconds.

Call handler: How do you know your mum isn't breathing?

Girl: Because I killed her. She hasn't moved for a long time.

Call handler: How long is it since she moved?

Girl: About thirty minutes.

Call handler: Did you try to resuscitate your mum, give her CPR?

Girl: No, why would I do that? I'm doing it to save her.

Weren't they the same words used by the man who took his life in the petrol station? The witness was very clear, the man shouted those words as he set himself alight.

Ridpath rewound the machine again and again, hearing the words spoken by the girl.

I'm doing it to save her.

Why would two people use exactly the same words? And why use the present tense? Why not use the past tense, 'I did it to save her?'

It didn't make sense.

Chapter TWENTY

She sat in front of her laptop in a place she knew so well, staring at the empty wall in front of her. The marks where she had stuck her BTS posters still visible against the white of the walls. It seemed so long ago when she was young and innocent and her mum was still alive.

She found the correct address and logged onto the chat room. Her friend at school had given it to her a few weeks ago, saying, 'If you're down or depressed, this site is really helpful. The guy seems to understand what it's like and he doesn't judge.'

'You spoke with him?'

'You never hear his voice, you just chat with him.'

'How do you know it's safe? He's not some sort of perv?'

'Well, he doesn't ask for anything. He just listens and tells it like it is. He helped me through some bad times with my mum. You don't have to use him but I know you've been down recently.'

So that night, she'd logged onto the page she'd been given. He was already there waiting. He didn't say much but he was very good at responding to her when she told him how she was feeling. It was like having a therapist on call without leaving your home. She hoped he would be on again tonight.

For some reason, she always thought of him as a he even though she had no idea of their gender. Perhaps, it was the way they phrased their sentences, or the way their typed words appeared on the page.

She thought back to one of her study textbooks. Hadn't some academic run the play *Doctor Faustus* by Christopher Marlowe through the Collocations and N-Grams electronic database to find some parts had been written by Henry Porter? Perhaps she should do the same with this guy's sentences, look for connections, for repetitions. It might give a clue to what sort of man he was.

She closed her eyes. Why did she always take the emotion away from everything, replacing it with an academic distance. *Disassociation*, that's what her therapist called it. She could never tell people how she really felt. Why did she do it?

Was it all meaningless, the shrill screaming of a frightened girl in an empty room when nobody was listening?

She glanced at all her notes arranged alphabetically on the bookshelf beside her.

A life wasted.

A life that was senseless in all meanings of the word.

Hadn't Sartre said that hell was other people? He was wrong, hell was herself and her life. She typed in a message.

HalfHalf: Are you there?

Silence. Nothing. Nada. Emptiness.

Her soul in the machine.

Rellik: Hiya, HalfHalf.

He was on. A strange flutter tingled in her body. Even though he wasn't speaking, she could hear his voice, recognise the strong Manchester accent; an Oasis twang through a machine. She imagined he typed how he spoke. None of this BBC received pronunciation crap, but his voice, his authentic voice. She had no intention to ever meet him, not after last time, but she did like chatting to him on this forum. It was like chatting to a friend, but one that understood what she was going through.

> **Rellik:** How ya doin?
> **HalfHalf:** Same old, same old.

She thought for a moment. Should she be bold?

> **HalfHalf:** I can't go on like this any more. It's all so senseless.

A long pause.

> **Rellik:** But you must. Struggle is the point of life, to keep going when all about you is lost. To rage against the dying of the light.

She smiled, she recognised the quote. He had remembered she was studying Dylan Thomas in English.

> **HalfHalf:** Dylan Thomas. Have you been reading it? The poem is a villanelle, turning on itself, advancing and retiring to finally come to a conclusion. Some people have likened it to King Lear's speech on the heath or Sonnet 18...

She stopped typing and stared at the screen. Why did she do this? Turn every idea, every thought into a class. Her therapist was right. It was her way of distancing herself from everyday life – from avoiding the banality of it all?

His new words interrupted her thoughts.

> **Rellik:** You must keep going. We all must keep going.
> **HalfHalf:** I'm tired.

She closed her eyes again and spoke the words out loud. 'So very tired.'

> **Rellik:** But we *have* to fight.
> **HalfHalf:** Why are you doing this? Why do you care? Why are you helping me and my friends?
> **Rellik:** I'm doing it to save them.

Eve didn't know how to answer.

Wednesday, October 30.

Chapter TWENTY-ONE

Ridpath had a restless night. The words from the young girl had played themselves again and again in his dreams. He woke up early at five thirty a.m. and went downstairs to make himself a pot of coffee, pausing for a moment at Eve's door, listening to the gentle sounds of her sleep.

Outside the window, a classic late autumn morning in Manchester played out; dark skies without a glimmer of a dawn, the wind was howling and the rain sleeting down. One of those days where the best decision was to spend it in bed huddled beneath the duvet.

Instead, he sat in the kitchen staring into the void. How could a young girl kill her own mother and have no feelings of guilt? Throughout the telephone call, she had betrayed not an ounce of remorse, not a sprinkling of regret. It was as if she felt nothing.

He couldn't understand it. One question kept reverberating around his brain.

Why?

He went to the sitting room and retrieved the file, bringing it back into the warm kitchen. He opened it up and went through the first responders' statements again.

The first witness statement was from PC 9614, Alan Sagfield. Glancing through it, Ridpath saw immediately the copper had remembered his Advocate training well.

They had all been taught to write their witness statements in the same way.

GREATER MANCHESTER POLICE
INCIDENT LOG

Incident #: 90064651M

Date and Time reported: October 26, 11.32 a.m.

Date and Time occurred: October 26, approx. 11.00 a.m.

Incident Type/Offence: Suspicious Death

Reporting Officer: PC Alan Sagfield 9614

Approving Officer: Inspector Ronald Pleasance

Report Entered: October 26, 4.25 p.m.

Narrative:

On October 26 at 11.32 a.m., myself, PC 9614, Alan Sagfield, and PC 10024, Ellen Townley, were dispatched to 26 Handley Road, Sale, in response to a 999 call from a young girl, Ms Anita Forsyth. We were in rapid response vehicle PO 14.

On arrival at the said address, a semi-detached house in a quiet residential street, we knocked on the door, which was immediately answered by Anita, a young girl aged around fourteen. She seemed calm and in control. Her first words were: 'My mum, she's not breathing. I think I killed her.'

I asked if she was the person who had made the 999 call and she responded in the affirmative.

While PC Townley stayed with Ms Forsyth, I went upstairs to a front bedroom to check on the mother and found her lying on top of the bed, still dressed in her nightgown, but not moving. I immediately tilted the woman's head back and blew five times into her mouth before performing CPR in accordance with operational procedures.

As I was doing this, I was joined by an emergency medical technician who asked me to stop while he took over. The EMT continued with CPR and attached some machines to the woman to monitor her status. We both realised after a few more minutes that the situation was hopeless. The EMT then pointed out to me the marks on the woman's neck and asked if they were caused by my efforts at CPR. I replied that I didn't think they were.

I returned to the downstairs sitting room where the young girl was sitting quietly with PC Townley. I told her that her mother had not responded to CPR and was no longer breathing.

For the first time, the young girl became agitated. 'What? I just gave her some sleeping tablets, I didn't mean to kill her.'

The girl then kept repeating, 'I didn't mean to kill her, I didn't mean to kill her.' Together with PC Townley, I restrained her.

I then called for backup and a senior officer, Inspector Ron Pleasance, 6542, arrived within ten minutes. After checking the marks on the woman's neck, he decided we should take Ms Anita Forsyth back to the station and call for a pathologist and a forensic team to come to the house.

I was ordered to take Ms Forsyth to Sale Police Station to question her further. This was performed by myself and PC Townley at 12.08 p.m. During the journey to the station, Ms Forsyth did not speak at all but sat quietly in the rear of our car sobbing.

At Sale Police Station, we handed over Ms Forsyth to the custody officer, Sergeant Paul Turngoose, and he took her into custody at 12.14 p.m.

I wore bodycam and it was switched on at all times during this incident.

Signed,

Alan Sagfield PC 9614

He put the statement down and made a note to check the bodycam footage, but he was sure it would corroborate PC Sagfield's account of the incident. Had the young girl said the exact words stated by the police? She seemed confused, one moment saying that she thought she had killed her mum, the next denying being involved.

Next he decided to re-read the statement of the medical technician called to the incident, David Grayson.

STATEMENT OF WITNESS
(Criminal Procedure Rules, r. 16.2;
Criminal Justice Act 1967, s. 9)

STATEMENT OF David Grayson, Emergency Medical Technician employed by the Greater Manchester Ambulance Service

Age of witness (if over 18, enter "over 18"): Over 18

This statement (consisting of 2 pages) is true to the best of my knowledge and belief and I make it knowing that, if it is tendered in evidence, I shall be liable to prosecution if I have wilfully stated in it anything which I know to be false, or do not believe to be true.

I responded to a call from the dispatcher at 11.10 a.m. on October 26 to 26 Handley Road, Sale where a woman was posted as not breathing. I was driving BMW E1 Emergency Response Vehicle number ERV 26.

Two police officers were already at the scene when I arrived. I found out later that these police officers were PC 9614, Alan Sagfield, and PC 10024, Ellen Townley.

On entering the house, I found PC Townley downstairs with a young girl who I presumed was the daughter of the woman. PC Townley told me her colleague was upstairs. As per protocol, I put on my Nitrile gloves and went upstairs.

In the front bedroom, I found PC Sagfield attempting emergency CPR on an obese woman aged in her early thirties. The woman was not responding to his efforts. I asked him to stop and quickly performed an assessment to determine the patient's level of consciousness and breathing status. The woman was unconsciousness and not responsive. I checked the patient's airway to see if there was an obstruction but found none present. The airway was open and clear.

The woman was still not breathing so I attempted to provide rescue breaths using a bag-valve mask, whilst at the same time checking the carotid artery for a pulse. None was detected. I then began cardiopulmonary resuscitation with chest compresses and rescue breaths.

When there was no response, I attached three ECG leads and an oximeter checking for any cardiac activity and oxygen levels in the blood.

No cardiac activity was recorded and oxygen levels were disastrously low and falling. I then noticed the marks around the woman's neck and ceased CPR.

A belt was lying next to her on the bed and I pointed this out to PC Sagfield.

At 11.52 a.m. I handed over the scene to Inspector Ron Pleasance from Sale, explaining to him my concerns over the marks on the neck of the woman. He then detained the child, Anita Forsyth, and I waited for the arrival of the pathologist.

Dr Lawson came to the house at 12.36 p.m. and I handed over the scene to him.

I am not certain whether the marks were caused by CPR activity before I arrived or they were made by the belt being placed around the neck.

Signed: David Grayson

Ridpath put down the report and rubbed his eyes. He could imagine the scene in the bedroom; the woman lying there unresponsive and the EMT desperately trying to bring the woman back to life.

He checked the statement one more time. There were some slight discrepancies over the timings and the detail of the actions made by the EMT, but, other than that, the statement was in line with that of the constable. In addition, there was a covering line at the end of the statement. Had the marks on the neck been caused by CPR or had they been caused by the belt?

If it were the latter, then there may be evidence of an attempt at strangulation.

Ridpath poured himself some more coffee. Outside the window, the sky was beginning to lighten in the east. Another day was dawning.

He still had the pathologist's report to read, but he couldn't face going through the whole thing again nor could he look at the pictures of the woman taken during the post-mortem.

Not this morning.

He jumped immediately to the summary provided by the pathologist, a Dr Lawson.

CONCLUSIONS

1. To all intents and purposes, the woman, Jane Forsyth, was relatively healthy despite being obese, in her early thirties, whose

heart, lungs and all other vital organs displayed no signs of deterioration or abnormality.

2. There is evidence of bruising to the woman's chest probably caused by the attempts of the police and emergency medical services to provide CPR.

3. There is extensive bruising to the neck, consistent with ligature strangulation. This bruising would not be caused in CPR efforts by experienced medical technicians. In addition, the hyoid bone appeared to be fractured. The hyoid bone is a horseshoe-shaped bone situated in the anterior midline of the neck between the chin and the thyroid cartilage. At rest, it lies between the base of the mandible and the third cervical vertebra. Such a break would not occur during CPR.

4. On examination of the face of Jane Forsyth, there were several petechial areas, swelling eyelids with ecchymosis more pronounced in the right rather than left eye and subconjunctival haemorrhages.

5. Toxicology shows there was the presence of pentobarbital in the bloodstream, enough to cause drowsiness or coma but not enough to cause death.

6. A belt with traces of the woman's DNA on it was found beside her on the bed.

I would conclude therefore that this is not an accidental death but Jane Forsyth was strangled with a ligature and death came through pressure obstruction of the carotid arteries preventing blood flow to the brain.

Therefore, I give as cause of death:

Category 3: Murder by person or persons unknown.

Signed: M Lawson, Pathologist

There it was. The doctor was unequivocal in his report. Jane Forsyth was murdered. Was her daughter the killer? Had a fourteen-year-old child killed her own mother? And, more importantly, why?

As Ridpath finished reading, he heard the first signs of sentient life stirring upstairs as his daughter rose to face another day.

He stood up and put all the documents and pictures back in a folder, placing them in his briefcase. The last person he wanted to see these was Eve.

He put on the kettle to make himself some more coffee, placing two slices of bread in the toaster, and also put an empty bowl, the packet of Weetabix and a bottle of milk on the table where Eve could help herself if she felt like eating something else. It was a long shot but he could try.

Once more, his mind drifted back to the case.

Only one question remained.

Why had the daughter done it?

Chapter TWENTY-TWO

He parked up well away from the block of flats, making sure the car was hidden out of sight and securely locked. You couldn't take too many chances with the young kids in this area. They'd steal babies out of prams and sell them back to the mothers.

He'd already changed out of his jacket and put on a black hoodie – what passed for sartorial elegance in this corner of Manchester. He pulled the hood up over his head, hunched over his shoulders and plodded on towards the flats, just another Joe Bloggs, blending into the environment. He laughed to himself, just like a cheetah in the African savannah, except around here, it was a hoodie and not a spotted fur coat.

This was his first job of the day, clearing up the evidence from Monday's death before the police discovered who had died. Later, he would prepare for the next death, but that could wait. Now was a time to focus.

He stopped behind a wall near the bins that gave a good view of the caretaker's hut. After waiting five minutes, the man rounded a corner with his mops and brooms, placed the cart into the shed and locked the door.

The caretaker took off his brown overcoat and put on his own jacket before marching across the car park.

He looked at his watch. Nine a.m. on the dot. Right on cue, there he was, off to 6C for his morning cuppa.

The area would be free and there wouldn't be anybody else around for at least the next thirty minutes.

Checking the area for passers-by, he walked quickly to the front door of the flat and entered the code IIII. The caretaker had been good enough to show him the number when he'd posed as a potential tenant a week ago.

He climbed up the stairs to the top floor as quietly as he could. No point in disturbing the cat lady on the second floor. The door would be locked but that would be no problem for him and his credit card. He'd seen they used spring locks on the doors when he'd done his recon, and it should be a simple breaking and entering.

He put on his purple latex gloves and took out the card. Inserting it just above the lock, he felt for where the latch went into the recess in the door jamb. Sliding it down, he heard a slight click and he pushed with his shoulder.

He was inside.

The flat was as neat as ever. For a copper, the man was a bit of a neat freak. Shame about the security though; it was abysmal.

The mobile phone and laptop were placed exactly where he had told him to put them. He walked over to the coffee table and placed both in the haversack brought from the car.

Now it was time to mess with the police. Give them the impression the man had totally lost the plot or somebody had burgled the place. Anything to confuse them, to give him time to finish the job. He could have just nicked the phone and the laptop but then the police would immediately realise they were missing.

He went to work, enjoying himself for the first time in a long time.

After he'd finished, he stepped back, admiring his handiwork.

Perfect.

It was all a delaying tactic. At the moment, he just needed time. He would be finished soon, just one more person left to go.

The biggest one. He had something special planned for this one and his family. Something the man would never forget as long as he lived, which wouldn't be very long at all.

He closed the door behind him and then pushed it open a little.

No point in making life too difficult for the plod, was there?

Chapter TWENTY-THREE

Ridpath walked into Sale Police Station having parked his car round the back of the old building. He'd never worked here before, despite knowing the area well.

The nick was situated right in the centre of Sale behind the new council buildings and close to the Bridge-water Canal. Often as a young man, he had whiled away many happy hours over a pint of snakebite in the King's Ransom, a pub on the other side of the canal. He had often walked back to where he lived along the towpath eating fish and chips and full of ale. It was a wonder he had never fallen in.

He had dropped Eve off that morning at school. For once she was chirpy, almost back to her bright bubbly self, but she still had her black, kohl-ringed eyes.

'You seem chipper this morning,' he'd noted.

She shrugged her shoulders. 'I slept well and thought a few things through.' A long pause. 'Sorry, Dad, I've been a bit self-obsessed lately.'

'You're a teenager, it goes with the territory. Plus, you've had a bad time recently. I wouldn't beat yourself up about it.'

'I won't, but I have realised I want to do more, help people, save them, a bit like Mrs Challinor. She has such a strong direction in her life. Dad, did you remember to ring her last night?'

'Sorry, I forgot, I'll do it after my meeting this morning.'

'Don't forget will you? I'm looking forward to spending Saturday with her.'

'What about your homework?'

'Don't worry, I'll do that at school and at home this evening. It's only history, usually pretty easy for me. Ring her, won't you?'

Eve seemed quite insistent that she wanted to meet Mrs Challinor. Perhaps she needed a woman to talk to, and Ridpath could think of nobody better than his boss.

'I don't think I can pick you up this evening but I'll message if I can.'

'No worries, I can get a lift with Maisie's mum.'

'You two are friends again?'

'Sort of. Maisie's okay, just a little straight. Everything by the book, that's our Maisie.'

'Sometimes it's good to follow the rules.'

He pulled up behind a brand-new BMW X5 outside her school.

'Says the man who's continually being upbraided by his superiors for not following procedures.'

'Ah, there's the difference. I bend the rules, not break them.'

She gathered her bag from the back seat and opened the car door. 'Semantics, Dad. I'm just like you. I like bending the rules.'

And with that, she was gone.

Ridpath watched her blend into the pack of black-jacketed pupils and vanish through the iron gates into the school. Perhaps she was right, she was more like him than he realised.

Putting the car back in gear, he decided to park that thought for later. Was he such a rebel or did he just not let anything get in his way? Was her school just another, younger form of the police? A less regimented place, it was true, but still with its petty rules and regulations which Ridpath, and apparently his daughter, naturally rebelled against.

Too deep for this time in the morning, he thought. Instead, he switched on his music and turned the volume up loud.

'The Jean Genie', with saint David Bowie at his imperious, gender-defying best, blasted out from the speakers. A few of the pupils glanced into Ridpath's car as they walked past. He smiled back at them and pulled away from the kerb. At least, he would now enjoy the drive to Sale, Bowie's collaborator Mick Ronson's power chords bouncing around his brain.

Twenty minutes later and the album only halfway through, Ridpath was parking around the back of Sale Police Station. The sergeant behind the desk at the reception counter was hidden behind layers of thick glass.

Ridpath bent down and spoke through one of those mesh grills. *Why did they make them so low?* 'DI Ridpath to see Inspector Pleasance.'

'Is he expecting you, sir?'

'He is.'

'One moment, sir, I'll ring him.'

Ridpath sat down in one of the plastic chairs that were bolted to the floor. It was as if the powers-that-be expected somebody to nick them in the middle of a police station. Then again, it could be to prevent them being thrown at some unsuspecting copper.

He glanced around the reception area. The usual tattered and stained posters were there: *Clunk click every trip. Don't drink and drive. Watch out! There's a thief about.* All the oldies and goodies they kept reprinting, and some clearly still up from decades past. There were even a few new ones looking for more recruits and one with the catchy headline: *Keep you and your belongings safe.* It must have taken the copywriter in Force Communications all of three seconds to come up with that one.

Somebody appeared at the door to the inner sanctum of the station wearing a uniform but without the jacket and with two pips on his shoulder epaulettes. Ridpath recognised him immediately, it was as if he hadn't aged at all.

He buzzed the door open. 'Ridpath, good to see you.'

'And you, Ron, how long has it been now?'

The man frowned. 'At least five years, back when I was a newly promoted DC.'

Ridpath instantly flinched at the memory. Ridpath had worked with Ron Pleasance when he was assigned to CID and they investigated the deaths of a man in Wythenshawe and a homeless man in the centre of Manchester near Piccadilly. If Ridpath remembered correctly, he did all the work while Pleasance took all the credit.

'It seems like longer, is it only five years? You've been promoted quickly, inspector now.'

'And you haven't. Still working with the coroner and MIT?'

Pleasance knew the answer, so why was he asking?

'Still working across both organisations.'

'Good, well come to my office and we can have a chat.'

'I'd rather get working with your officers. There are a couple of things I'd like to ask them about, a few inconsistencies in the cases.'

'Same old Ridpath, still looking for a conspiracy when there's nothing there. But come to my office first, I'd like to brief you before you work with *my* officers.'

Ridpath heard the stress on the word. Pleasance was just guarding his territory, making sure Ridpath knew who was in charge here. He didn't need to do it, because Ridpath didn't care. He was going to follow the leads on these cases wherever they took him, not where some jumped-up clerk masquerading as a copper told him to go.

They walked up a flight of stairs in silence and entered a small office dominated by an old-fashioned filing cabinet and an extra-large desk, with just one hard chair placed in front of it.

Pleasance slipped behind the desk, sitting in his ergonomically designed executive seat while Ridpath pulled out the hard, government-issue plastic chair and sat down.

'Can I lay my cards on the table, Ridpath?'

'You can lay them anywhere you want, Ron, it's your office.'

'You've been foisted on me by upstairs. The powers-that-be think we have a problem because our two remaining detectives are fresh out of training school.'

'It's not what I was told. They said you requested my help.'

Pleasance smiled. 'I'm perfectly capable of running a station and a few open-and-shut cases on my own.'

'The "powers-that-be", as you describe them, seem to disagree.'

'Well, while you are in my nick, you report to me, understand?'

Why was GMP always so territorial? It was as if giving a copper a small station to look after immediately made him into some medieval warlord.

Ridpath decided to ignore the question. 'I don't think the cases they've asked me to help you with are as open-and-shut as you think they are.'

Pleasance frowned again. 'Look, we've only had a suicide and a murder in the last couple of days. All of the cases are open-and-shut.'

'Not what I was told by my DCI. They're worried about the manner of the suicide, and the murder may not be as straightforward as you think it is.'

'Anita Forsyth admitted it. We have her confession on a body-worn camera by one of the officers. Plus, there's a host of forensic and post-mortem evidence to show she killed her mother. We've remanded her to a secure children's home prior to charging and we're waiting on a psychiatrist's evaluation. All you're supposed to do is help put together the case for CPS before we send it to them.'

'I'll do that but you have to understand that charging somebody that young is fraught with difficulties.'

'She's over ten, she's over the age of criminal responsibility.'

Pleasance seemed to have all the empathy of an amoeba.

'But this case is going to be watched like a hawk by the media. It's perfect clickbait.' For a second, an image of Eve at the same age flashed through Ridpath's mind. 'She's still a child and she needs the protection of the law.'

'She's a murderer who strangled her own mother with a belt. She's a monster and the sooner she's locked up in a secure facility the better. I don't want another Thompson and Venables case here.'

In 1993, two ten-year-old boys, Robert Thompson and Jon Venables had murdered a two-year-old, James Bulger. They took him from the New Strand Shopping Centre in Bootle, after his mother had taken her eyes off him momentarily. His mutilated body was found on a railway line two and a half miles away two days later.

'The two cases are completely different.'

'No, they're not. It's murder, end of story. Look, your job is to put together the evidence for the submission to the CPS, understand?'

'My job is to investigate the case to ensure that all the procedures have been followed and the evidence gathered to ensure a safe conviction. If you have a problem with that I suggest you contact my bosses, Detective Chief Inspector Steve Carruthers or Detective Superintendent Claire Trent, and argue the toss with them.' He stood up. 'Until then, I'm going to do what I've been sent here to do. Understand?'

There was no answer from Pleasance.

'In addition, the coroner has asked me to look into the recent suicide on your patch. The man who set fire to himself in the petrol station on Monday night.'

'The Bunsen? Why do they want you to go there?'

Ridpath flinched at the use of the word. Police slang for somebody who was set on fire, or set themselves on fire.

'I don't know, but that's what I've been ordered to do.'

'But I've read Megan's report and seen the CCTV. The man walked into the petrol station and lit himself up. Why bother looking any further?'

'Because that's what I do. Now, where are your detect-ives waiting for me?'

'They're in the briefing room. But before you go, Ridpath, I want to make it clear that you report to me. I don't want any surprises on these cases. For me they are open-and-shut, understand?'

'Like I said, Ron, I reviewed the files last night and this morning, and there seem to be a few anomalies in one of the cases that I need to look into.'

'A word of warning: don't look for problems where there aren't any. Sale nick has the best stats for clearing cases in the whole of Greater Manchester and I want to keep it that way. We investigate quickly and we close cases, understood?'

'As clear as the canal, Ron.'

Ridpath opened the door, turning back just before he left. 'Hasn't it occurred to you that the reason I'm here is maybe because our bosses think you are clearing cases too quickly? That maybe you are sweeping things under the carpet?'

Pleasance's face fell and Ridpath closed the door.

Well, that little speech put the cat amongst the pigeons, he thought. *My bet is he's going to be on the phone to whoever's mentoring him to find out what the hell is happening.*

Ridpath pressed his ear against the closed door. Sure enough, Pleasance was talking loudly into his phone.

Chapter TWENTY-FOUR

DCs Fletcher and Muldowney were waiting for him when he opened the door to the briefing room. Both stood to attention formally.

'There's no need for that crap. I'm not royalty, I'm here to help.'

Both visibly relaxed, with Andy Fletcher putting his hand out. 'Pleased to meet you, Ridpath, I've heard a lot about you.'

'All of it untrue. Sit down and we'll go through both cases.'

'Both?' said Megan Muldowney. 'I thought we only had one.'

'The coroner and Detective Superintendent Claire Trent have added the man in the petrol station.'

'Good,' said Megan, 'I'm not having much luck finding out who he is. No ID on him and nobody has come forward to report a missing person that matches his description.'

'You've sent the DNA out to the labs?'

She nodded. 'Should get it back soon, I made it a rush job.'

'Until it comes back, let's concentrate on our potential murder.'

'Potential?' said Fletcher. 'I thought we had this one sewn up. The girl admitted to killing her mother, we've got her confession recorded. We cordoned off the area and had a forensic team go through the house with a fine-tooth comb. They found a belt on the bed with the mother's DNA on it. I even interviewed the next-door neighbours to see if they had anything to tell us but they hardly knew her, kept herself to herself apparently.'

'No husband or partner?'

'Not according to the neighbours.'

'Hmm.' Ridpath frowned. 'Let's look at the station interview, shall we?'

'No problem.' Andy Fletcher brought out his laptop and booted it up. 'You know Pleasance is happy with this case, don't you? He only wants you to help us prepare it for the CPS, not re-investigate.'

Ridpath ignored him for a moment, asking a question instead. 'Who attended the interview?'

'Just myself and the on-duty appropriate adult.'

'Nobody else?'

'There was nobody available.'

'Not even a female PC?'

Andy Fletcher shrugged his shoulders. 'What can I say? We were stretched that day with lots of people off sick plus Pleasance gave me the go ahead. He didn't want to wait while we had the girl at the station.'

'It seems to be Inspector Pleasance's method of working.'

Megan Muldowney raised an eyebrow quizzically.

'Rushing everything, not taking his time and thinking it through,' responded Ridpath. 'Was a solicitor present?'

'Anita Forsyth was offered one but she declined.'

'A young girl who's just been through the trauma of losing her mother is not capable of making a rational decision, particularly if that involves her own culpability.'

'I did offer her a solicitor.'

'And the appropriate adult?'

'He was on duty. A James Sturgess, local clergyman.'

'Not a social worker?'

Fletcher shrugged his shoulders.

'Nobody was available who understood the legal ramifications of interviewing a fourteen-year-old girl under caution?'

'Like I said, there wasn't time. Inspector Pleasance wanted her questioned as soon as possible.'

The laptop had finally booted up.

'Here's the video.'

Andy Fletcher pressed a button on his keyboard and a video started. The interview room was small and claustrophobic. The young girl, Anita Forsyth, was sitting opposite the detective across a tiny table. On her right-hand side was a bulky man wearing an overcoat and a dog collar.

'This is Detective Constable Andrew Fletcher interviewing Ms Anita Forsyth. The time is four thirty p.m. on October 26, 2024. Present is Mr James Sturgess, the local appropriate adult. Ms Forsyth—'

'I prefer Anita,' the girl interrupted. The voice was calm but forceful, she seemed totally in control of her emotions.

'Sorry, *Anita*. You have been offered the opportunity of having a solicitor present but you declined, is that correct?'

'Stop it there,' interrupted Ridpath. 'Why are you using reported speech? Why not just offer her the presence of a solicitor again?'

'This was the third time I'd made the offer. I just wanted to make sure it was on tape.'

'And that's what it looks like: a copper covering his arse. Next time, just make the offer on tape. She's four-teen, for Christ's sake. A good brief will pull this apart and say she didn't understand the question.'

'But she did understand the question.'

Ridpath sighed and stared at the young detective constable. For a moment he felt like Charlie Whitworth educating a young copper called Thomas Ridpath on the facts of judicial life. 'Your job is to cover yourself completely against any allegations of impropriety, leading witnesses or breaking any of the interview rules. Particularly when you are interviewing a minor. Straightaway, you've asked her a negative question. What did they teach you at Edgehill?'

Fletcher sighed like a particularly recalcitrant student quizzed on his homework. 'Always ask the suspect or witness open questions.'

'Exactly. In this case, ask her again and let her confirm that she doesn't want a solicitor present. In my opinion, because the duty appropriate adult was not a legal or social work professional, you should have waited for a solicitor. Carry on playing it.'

Fletcher stabbed at the key on his laptop with his index finger and sat back, crossing his arms.

'What happened this morning in your home?'

'What do you mean, what happened?' answered Anita Forsyth. 'I've already told you I think I killed my mum.'

'You have, Anita, but I'd like to understand why it happened. Take me through the events of this morning?'

Ridpath reached forward and paused the laptop. 'Did you caution her?'

'What?'

'It's a simple question, DC Fletcher, did you caution her before this interview?'

'I think the custody sergeant did it when she was booked in or Inspector Pleasance did it at her home.'

'You *think*...' Ridpath's eyes rose in his head. 'You didn't think to caution her on tape again. You do remember the words, don't you? "Ms Anita Forsyth, I am arresting you on suspicion of causing the death of your mother. You do not have to say anything. But it may harm your defence if you do not mention when questioned something which you later rely on in court. Anything you do say may be given in evidence." Did you use a form of those words before you interviewed this girl?'

'Well, no, she had already been cautioned by the custody sergeant, I didn't think it was necessary to do it again.'

Ridpath shook his head. 'Just play the tape.'

Andy Fletcher jabbed the play button with his finger.

'Please take me through what happened, Anita.'

'I woke up as usual at eight thirty. I could sleep late because it wasn't a school day. Mum was already up and in the kitchen. She made me breakfast. Afterwards, I watched TV for a while, I like the cartoons. Mum came into the living room and asked me to switch off the TV, I thought I'd done something wrong. Then she asked me to help save her.'

'Can you play that bit back again.'

Fletcher reversed the recording.

'...thought I'd done something wrong. Then she asked me to help save her.'

Those words again. Ridpath leant in closer to the laptop.

'I didn't understand but she said I needed to help save her. So I said, "Of course, Mum. What do you want me to do?" I thought she wanted me to go down to the shops for something. Then she said, "I want you to take this packet of pills and grind them up into a powder and then put them into some hot milk." I asked her if she had a headache and she said "Yes, a big headache." You see, Mum sometimes had these migraines.'

'Had your mum asked you to help with her headaches before?' asked Fletcher on the tape.

The girl shook her head. 'It was the first time.'

'So what did you do?'

'I counted all the pills in the pack. There were twenty which I thought was too many, so I only ground up five and put the rest in a jar in my pocket.' She paused for a long while before continuing. 'I should have done exactly what Mum told me.'

'So what happened?'

'I ground five tablets into a powder and put them in hot milk, giving it to her to drink. Before she drank it, she asked me if I'd done as she told me. I lied and said I had. Then she said, "I'm doing this to save you.""

For the first time on the playback, Anita began to lose a little of her cool self-assurance. Her voice rose an octave.

'What happened next?'

'She drank it down in one, which was strange because my mum didn't like hot milk, she preferred tea or coffee. Then, Mum gave me a hug, told me she loved me and went upstairs to lie down on the bed.'

'What did you do?'

'I switched on the TV, the cartoon hadn't finished yet.'

'When did you go upstairs to check on your mum?'

'It was after the cartoon had finished. I went upstairs to ask when we were going to the shops. We usually go on a Saturday.'

'And what happened?'

'She was lying on the bed and she looked like she was sleeping. So, I walked over and tried to wake her up but I couldn't. Then I noticed she was hardly breathing…'

'Then what did you do?'

'I was worried when she wouldn't wake up so I rang 999 like they'd taught us at school.'

'You said you thought you'd killed your mum?'

'I thought I hadn't mixed enough tablets with the milk and that's why mum wouldn't wake up.'

'So when did you use the belt?'

'What belt?'

Ridpath stared at Andy Fletcher.

'The belt that was found beside your mum on the bed. The one you used to tie around your mum's neck.'

On the playback, Anita had lost all her previous coolness. 'What? What are you talking about? I didn't use no belt, I don't know anything about no belt.'

The clergyman sitting next to her put his hand down on the table. 'I think this interview has gone far enough, DC Fletcher, this young girl needs legal aid.'

'I just need to ask her a few more questions.'

'No, you won't. This girl needs a solicitor. I am not competent to advise her at this point in time. I am ending this interview.'

The recording ended.

There was silence in the room for a long time. Megan Muldowney simply stared at her young colleague in disbelief. Finally, Ridpath said, 'Thank god the clergyman intervened. What do you think you were doing?'

'I was interviewing somebody who admitted to killing her mother.'

'You were interviewing a fourteen-year-old girl whose mother had just died. What did you do next?'

'I reported to my boss, Ron Pleasance, and arranged for a solicitor and a social worker to come down to the station. They decided to place the girl in a secure children's unit immediately and that was four days ago.'

'You haven't interviewed her since?'

'They won't let me anywhere near her.'

'I'm not surprised. Did you find any relatives?'

'None so far.'

'The father?'

'We don't know who he was.'

'What about the neighbours?'

'I interviewed the ones close to her house, but like I said, they knew nothing about Jane Forsyth.'

'What else have you done?'

'I went to the post-mortem. The pathologist confirmed she had pentobarbital in her bloodstream and her stomach. She had been strangled with a belt, probably the one found on the bed. I've had DNA from the belt analysed and there are two signatures on it. The girl and her mother, nobody else. The forensic lads have been through the house and found no other fingerprints or DNA except for the mother and the girl.'

He sat back in the chair with his arms open wide. 'Look, Ridpath, I don't know why she did it, but my hypothesis is that she was annoyed with her mother so added some sleeping tablets to her milk. The mother must have realised it so Anita got scared and tied the belt around her mother's throat as she lay sleeping. Then she took the belt off and rang 999 to report her mother wasn't breathing.'

'That's it, that's your theory?'

'Nothing else explains it.'

'Why?'

'Why what?'

'Why did she kill her mother?'

Fletcher glanced around, looking for support from Megan Muldowney. She pointedly looked away, apparently finding something interesting happening in the corner of the room.

Finally, he answered. 'I don't know, they won't let me interview the girl.'

'We need to find out why she committed the murder. Or at least have a better hypothesis for the motive than "I don't know."'

'What should we do?'

'Right, the first job is we need to do a house-to-house on the rest of the street, see if any of the neighbours knew Jane Forsyth – she can't have been a complete loner. Next we need to check on Anita's school. See if she has ever displayed any aberrant or aggressive behaviour there. Finally, we need to find out who the biological father was or if any relatives are living; a visit to the register office to check what's on her birth certificate may help.' A smile crossed Ridpath's lips. 'And by *we*, I mean *you*, DC Fletcher.'

He smiled at the young detective. 'One more thing, when she was searched on arrival at the police station, what did they find in her pockets?'

Fletcher frowned. 'What do you mean?'

'It's a simple enough question. What did they find in her pockets?'

'The usual kid stuff: sweet wrappers, a few coins, a hair bobble...'

'Did they find the tablets?'

Fletcher slowly nodded.

'How many?'

'Fifteen.'

Before Ridpath could say any more, he was interrupted by a sharp rap on the door. An older female PC popped her head into the room.

'Is it okay to interrupt? Megan asked me to bring these DNA results in as soon as they arrived.'

'Thanks, Mellissa.'

Megan Muldowney opened the brown envelope and looked at the single typed page inside. Her mouth and eyes opened wide.

'What is it, Megan?' asked Ridpath.

'I asked them to put the DNA results for the man in the petrol station through the database this morning and they came back with nothing, despite having over seven million DNA records on file. So I remembered something they told us to do at training college; I put the results through the elimination database.'

'Elimination database?' asked Fletcher.

'It's the elimination profiles generated from DNA samples provided by police officers, CSIs, those involved in the lab and anybody else who could possibly contaminate a sample from being on the scene.'

'And?' asked Ridpath.

'We've got a hit.'

'You know who the man in the petrol station was?'

She nodded. 'Apparently his name is Tony Abbott and he works for the police.'

Ridpath sighed. 'So, the sample was contaminated. It means we need to get another one.'

'I don't think so, Ridpath. He's an inspector in the road policing division of GMP and none of them were involved in the incident on Monday.'

'What? He's a copper? Why would a copper want to kill himself like that?' asked Andy Fletcher.

Ridpath tapped the table. 'I don't know, DC Fletcher, but we're going to find out. Let's meet back here at six p.m. for a debrief.'

DC Fletcher looked unhappy.

'A problem?' asked Ridpath.

'No, it's just that I have a squash game with Inspector Pleasance then.'

'A pity,' said Ridpath with heavy sarcasm, 'but I'm sure even the inspector realises that a murder investigation comes first.'

Chapter TWENTY-FIVE

'Anything useful, boss?' Dennis asked.

DCI Steve Carruthers was in his office going through the 4x5 file cards collated by the specialist call centre group he'd set up to respond to all the phone lines on the home invasion case.

'Well, so far, we have a Mrs Moira Ingham from Stalybridge who is convinced that alien body snatchers from Mars did it. All we have to do is send a probe to the planet and we'll find the Ashtons living in luxury amongst the Martians.'

'Sounds plausible, boss.'

'Aye, and if you believe that, I have a bridge to sell you and Scotsmen are going to stop drinking whisky to please the English.'

Dennis pointed to the cup on Carruthers' desk. 'So we're going to be *tea*-total from now on?'

'Very funny, but save the comedy for the Edinburgh Fringe Festival from now on, Dennis, I'm in nae mood to laugh.'

He placed the card on a pile of rejects sitting on his desk.

'Here's another from Hilda Ogden in Salford saying her next-door neighbour is the man we want. Apparently he walks in a funny way and returned home last Wednesday at three in the morning.'

'Didn't Hilda Ogden use to be on *Coronation Street*? I have a feeling that could be a fake name.'

'You'll make a fine detective one day, Dennis. We sent a car round to the house to check and the man does have a funny walk. His right leg was amputated from the knee down. Even worse, he has a cast-iron alibi for Wednesday early morning.'

'Anything we can use in those bunch of cards, boss?'

'Just two. A local Saddleworth woman said she saw a van parked in the lane at the bottom of her house when she went to bed at eleven on Tuesday night, but it was gone the next morning. It's a white van apparently. She didn't know the make, model or registration number. Just a normal white van.'

'That narrows it down, boss.'

'Aye, but not much though. How many white vans are there in Manchester? The other is a bit more promising. It's from an ex-copper who lives in the area. Apparently he was driving home at two thirty a.m. on Wednesday morning and saw a man in a black hoodie walking away from the house. He only noticed him because the man walked under a street light as he was passing him.'

'Any description, boss?'

'A tall man, taller than usual, was the only thing the ex-copper could remember about him. Even that is dubious. How easy is it to judge a man's height as you're driving past?'

'But an ex-copper should be better at it than most.'

'True, and the man was walking in the direction of the white van mentioned by the old woman.'

'If it is our man, we know he was alone and at what time he left the house. The timing correlates with the times of death of our victims.'

'It's a big *if*, Dennis. With a bit of luck, we may get more phone calls today. Unfortunately, we still have 521 respondents to visit. One of them might even be sane enough for us to take them seriously. Does Manchester have more than its fair share of absolute bampots who've got nothing better to do than ring up police hotlines?'

Dennis Leahey looked dramatically over his shoulder. 'You ask me and I ask who, boss?'

'The mayor? Perhaps he's researched it. He's looked into everything else.'

There was a knock on the door and Helen Shipton burst into the room without waiting to be invited to enter.

'I think I may have something, gaffer,' she said trying to catch her breath.

'Well, tell us what it is, Helen, we're all ears.'

'Just ran up the stairs from the audio-visual department,' she panted, trying to catch her breath.

'I can see that. What do you have?'

'Well, gaffer, you know I said we were looking at 27,000 cars who were in the Saddleworth area in the day before the home invasion, on the day and the day after?'

'I remember you telling me.' He checked his notes. 'You actually said and I quote, "We've logged 27,548 vehicles in the period, but without something to narrow it down, it's like looking for a needle in a whole field of bloody haystacks."'

'After the meeting I started to think—'

'That's a good start, Helen.'

'What if there was a way of reducing the number of cars?'

'From like 27,548 to one?'

'Exactly, gaffer. So I thought, given the perp's MO, he would have likely recced the area at least once before Wednesday.'

'That's logical, more than once is my bet.'

'And he would have done it on either of the two days before the home invasion. He had to be sure nothing had changed with the family, see, he had to be sure they would be at home.'

Steve Carruthers leant forward. 'Go on…'

'So I concentrated on the two days before and that reduced the number of vehicles down to 19,579. But that number also included the residents of the area and they were obviously going to show up on the ANPR results. So I got HOLMES to exclude all vehicles that were registered to an OL3 or an OL4 postcode.'

'And?'

'The number was then down to 103 vehicles.'

Carruthers shook his head. 'I thought it was going to be fewer, but it's still a lot better than over 27,000.'

'Hang on, gaffer. I had another thought: what if we excluded delivery vehicles, those registered to the Post Office and government departments like the Police, Fire and other official vehicles?'

'And?'

'And we just have three vehicles on the list. Even better, I checked the ANPR pictures and one of those vehicles was logged on the Mossley Road camera at 2.42 a.m. on Wednesday morning travelling in the direction of the city.'

'Would the vehicle just happen to be a white van?'

Helen checked the print-out from the vehicle licensing office in Swansea. 'How did you know, Dennis?'

Carruthers jumped up. 'Brilliant work, Helen, you have an address for the van?'

'It's registered to a Ronnie Rellik in Chorlton, boss. The name sounds Polish or Eastern European.'

'Dennis, get onto the Tactical Unit. I want a team ready in thirty minutes. Organise the cars: I want us to raid the address in the next hour. You could finally have given us the break we need, Helen, brilliant work.'

For a second, Helen was tempted to give Ridpath the credit too then she dismissed the idea as quickly as it had appeared in her head. All was fair in love and careers, wasn't it?

Instead, she asked, 'Can I come on the raid, gaffer? I need to get away from the bloody monitors for five minutes.'

Carruthers grabbed his coat. 'You're in our car, Helen. Dennis, get an office organised and maps of the area printed out. I want to brief the Tactical Unit as soon as they are ready. And get Chrissy Wright to check the address. We need to know everything about the place before we go storming in with our size tens.'

'On it, boss.'

'Come with me, Helen. You're away from Jasper Early on this one, and on the team.'

Chapter TWENTY-SIX

'Anything on him in the force directory, Megan?'

'Just checking now, Ridpath.'

Megan's fingers were a blur across the keyboard. Ridpath wished he had learnt how to type as quickly. It would have saved him years of frustration and countless hours of retyping documents to fulfil the needs of the ever-hungry bureaucracy of a modern police force.

Both Ridpath and Andy Fletcher were reading the man's bio over her shoulder.

'Looks like he's been in the force for fifteen years and an inspector for seven. Classic career really. Worked his way up the ladder, specialising in emergency services on the motorways in the Road Policing Unit. When that was merged with firearms, dogs and the Tactical Aid Unit in 2016 to form the Specialist Operations Branch, he stayed there. Seems to be part of the Serious Collision Investigation Unit based out of Eccles nick.'

'Poor bugger. I met one of those guys once. Not much left of anybody after a crash at ninety miles per hour on the motorway.'

Ridpath ignored Fletcher and spoke directly to Megan. 'Any home address given?'

'Not on this file, Ridpath, I need to contact HR for that sort of information.'

'Do it while I ring his boss and see if I can find out anything more about him.' Ridpath went on to the force directory and found a number for the head of the RPU, a Superintendent Matt Durrow.

He called the number and it was answered curtly, 'Durrow.'

'Good morning, sir, this is Detective Inspector Ridpath of MIT, we're investigating an incident that happened in Sale on Monday.'

'What does that have to do with me?'

The man was abrupt to the point of rudeness. Ridpath ploughed on regardless.

'Do you have an officer working for you, Inspector Tony Abbott?'

'Tony works for me, yes. He's an officer in our Investigation Unit.' A short pause. 'Why are you asking about Tony, and what incident happened on Monday?'

Ridpath ignored the questions. 'Where is Mr Abbott now, sir?'

'He's on administrative leave.'

'Oh, why is that?'

'Listen, I don't have to answer any of your questions, Inspector...'

'Ridpath, sir.'

'Ridpath. I don't have to answer questions until you tell me what is going on and why you are quizzing me about Tony.'

Ridpath took a deep breath. 'It appears that on Monday evening at approximately 8.10 p.m. Mr Abbott took his own life, sir.'

'What? Impossible, Tony would never do that, he's a happy man, a—' The superintendent stopped speaking.

'I'm afraid it appears to be true, sir. DNA recovered from the scene corresponds with that of Inspector Abbott.'

A long silence.

'How did Tony die?'

'I'd rather not divulge those details over the phone until his family have been informed, sir. Was he married?'

'Divorced, once child.'

'Any other next of kin?'

'Not that I know of. He was a bit of a loner, our job attracts people who are comfortable working alone. Since the pandemic many don't even come into the office that often, they work from home.'

'Do you know where he lived, sir?'

'Why do you need that information if you are certain he killed himself?'

Ridpath decided to play the sympathy card. 'I've been ordered by my boss, Chief Superintendent Claire Trent, to look into the incident, sir. I'm sure you can understand I need to make a full report to her.' This was not strictly true but using Claire Trent's name and rank might help open this man up a little.

Unfortunately, it had exactly the opposite effect.

'If Superintendent Trent wants to discover information about one of my officers, I suggest she ask me herself, not get one of her lackeys to do it for her.'

Megan Muldowney leant over Ridpath and placed an address in Stretford written on a piece of paper in front of him.

Ridpath tried a different tack. 'Can I come to see you myself, sir, explain what happened in more detail and perhaps take a look at Inspector Abbott's desk? In cases like this, we need to gather information as quickly as possible to ascertain if there was any force culpability in the officer's death.'

It was a subtle threat which Durrow immediately picked up on. Obviously, the head of the division would be culpable, not just the force. Ridpath heard the turning of pages.

'My diary is full, but I can squeeze you in at two thirty this afternoon.'

'I'll make myself available at that time. One more thing, sir, somebody needs to tell his ex-wife about the death. As the investigating unit it is our responsibility, but some commanding officers prefer to break the bad news themselves.'

'I don't know the woman so I'll leave it to you, as it is your job.' Durrow said it rather too quickly. 'Don't be late, I'll see you at two thirty.' The phone went dead in Ridpath's hands.

He stared at it for a second, saying some rude words in his head, before looking down at the address written on the scrap of paper. 'I know where these flats are. Megan, let's go and see if we can look inside our man's flat.'

'What about his family, Ridpath, aren't we going to tell them first?'

'According to his boss, there are no next of kin. He was divorced from his wife and had one child. But see if you can get her address from HR.'

Ridpath stood up and grabbed his jacket from the back of the chair, while Megan rang them on her mobile.

'What do you want me to do?' asked Fletcher.

'See if you can find out more about Jane Forsyth. Where she was born, what work she did. Go house to house down her street and talk to everybody. Finally, get on to Anita's school and find out all about her. Has she displayed any tendencies towards violence? Has she been disciplined for bullying? Also, check the births and deaths registry, see if you discover who Anita's father was or if she has any living relatives. We need to find out more about her, too.'

'On my own?'

Ridpath pretended to search the room. 'Well, I can't see anybody else here. Of course, on your own. It's time to do the basic police work you should have done before you decided to interrogate a fourteen-year-old in a police station.'

Fletcher's mouth opened wide like a fish out of water. He was about to protest but he stopped and meekly said, 'I'll get on it.'

Megan's phone beeped. 'HR has given me the ex-wife's address, Ridpath.'

'Come on, we have work to do. His flat first and then we need to visit the wife.'

Chapter TWENTY-SEVEN

Thirty minutes later and they were gathered in the designated major incident room in Police HQ for Operation Chancellor, the project name given to the investigation into the home invasion in Saddleworth.

The team was huddled over a table, staring at a map. Carruthers was at the centre, flanked on either side by Sergeant Lance Rivers from the Police Tactical Unit and Dennis Leahey. Helen Shipton and Chrissy Wright, the civilian researcher, were standing on the same side as Leahey while a platoon of black-clad tactical unit officers were arrayed around their sergeant.

'Right, we have a possible lead on the perpetrator of the murders of four people in Saddleworth in the early hours of last Wednesday. We believe the suspect may be armed with a shotgun and could also have additional weaponry. His name is Ronnie Rellik and he is currently holed up in this house, 76 Keppel Road, Chorlton.'

'Isn't that where the Bee Gees used to live back in the Sixties before they became famous?' asked one of the PTU officers.

'I dunno, before my time,' answered Carruthers.

'They did but they lived further up the street at number 51,' answered Chrissy Wright.

'Thank you, Chrissy, but can we focus on the job at hand, people?'

'Do we know if anybody else is in the house?' asked the sergeant.

'Sorry, that information is not available at the moment as we only found out about this address thirty minutes ago. Chrissy, why don't you take us through what you have found so far?'

The civilian researcher tapped the map with her finger. 'I'm afraid it's not much. As the boss says, the house is registered to a Ronnie Rellik. I couldn't find any birth details for him so I checked through the electoral register and he's been registered there for six months. Before that, it seems to have been a variety of tenants who move on after three years.'

'Students?' asked one of the officers.

'Possibly, it is that sort of area. I haven't had time to go back further than twelve years. At the moment, Rellik is the only adult registered to vote at this house.' From a folder, she produced some pictures. 'Here are screenshots of the front of the house taken from Google Street View. As you can see, the vegetation is quite dense in the front garden.'

'Good, that will give us cover as we approach. What about the back?'

'Here's a top shot of the area, I can't get exact shots. The back garden is overgrown as well. I rang the local nick in Didsbury and they said they have had no reports of disturbances at the house. Keppel Road used to be a big student and drugs area but it's been gentrified in the last ten years. Still a bit sketchy but definitely on the up, according to them.'

'The house looks deserted, boss,' said Dennis, staring closely at the pictures.

'Good, I hope there's just him inside. Thanks, Chrissy.' Carruthers checked his watch. 'The time is now ten thirty, I'd like us to effect an entry at exactly noon.'

'Can't we postpone it, sir?' asked the PTU sergeant. 'I'd like more time to reconnoitre the area. At the moment, we don't know who's inside and what we are likely to find once we enter.'

'Sorry, Lance, this job is urgent. We can't miss this chance of catching this bastard.'

The sergeant nodded once before turning to one of his team. 'What's the weather report, Doug?'

'Clear till one with rain coming in after then. It's Manchester, what do you expect?'

Lance Rivers nodded his head, making a decision. 'Okay. This is a smash and grab entry. No point in waiting as we don't know what's inside. We'll use two teams to effect entry. Team A at the front and Team B at the back. We'll assemble here at 11.45 a.m.' He pointed to a supermarket car park nearby on the map. 'We'll jump off at exactly 11.55 a.m. Teams C and D will block entry to Keppel Road using the PTU vehicles on the corners of Warwick Road here, and Brantingham Road, here.' He indicated both corners on the map. 'Nobody is allowed in or out of the area until I give the all clear. Understand?'

'Any reports of activity?' asked one of the PTU officers. A man with tattoos curling up his arms and vanishing beneath a short-sleeved shirt over tight biceps.

'We don't know, Jed. We have no eyes on the house. This is going to be a blind entry so be careful, everybody.'

They all grunted acknowledgement.

'Communications will be on Channel 3 of your Airwaves. No extraneous chatter; people will be listening.'

He nodded at Steve Carruthers, indicating he had finished with his comments.

'I will be Gold Commander for this operation with Dennis, Silver Commander. Sergeant Rivers will have operational control of the entry of the building. Nobody is to go in until he has made it secure and detained whoever is inside. No blues and twos: this is a silent operation. Our objective is to capture this bugger. Okay? The time is now exactly 10:33 a.m. The operation will commence at precisely 12.00 hours. Let's be careful out there.'

A loud rap on the door was followed by the entry of Claire Trent.

'Good morning, ma'am,' said Sergeant Rivers as his men all stood up straighter.

'At ease, gentlemen. Is everything arranged, Steve?'

'It is boss.'

'And on your side, Sergeant Rivers?'

'I'd like more time to reconnoitre, ma'am, but I understand the need for urgency.'

'Good. Are you all finished?'

'We are, ma'am.'

'Well, what are you waiting for? Get the bastard.'

Chapter TWENTY-EIGHT

Tony Abbott's flat was wedged between the canal on one side, an industrial estate on the other, with the third side bounded by a sewage farm.

'Nice place,' said Megan Muldowney, looking up at the five low-rise blocks that formed the small estate. 'Not the sort of place I'd expect an inspector from GMP to be living, though.'

Ridpath breathed in, smelling the aroma from the sewage plant. As he breathed out, clouds of smoke seemed to issue from his mouth and visibly frost in the air. 'Come on, let's see if there is a caretaker around somewhere.'

'Caretaker?' Megan snorted. 'We'll be lucky to find a prison officer.'

Ridpath shrugged his shoulders. 'You never know.' They walked towards the middle block. 'What was the address again?'

'Flat 3B, 16 Ranglement Street.'

Ridpath scanned the buttons, looking for the right number. 'Here it is.' He pressed the doorbell and waited.

No answer.

'Why did you do that? He's divorced, probably living alone in a small one-bed flat in this area.'

'A tip, Megan. Always knock on doors or press doorbells before you enter anywhere. The last thing you want to do is be surprised if somebody is inside.'

'Can I help you?'

An old man had crept up behind them silently.

'Who are you?' asked Megan.

'The caretaker for the flats. I'll ask again, can I help you?'

A quick glance across at Megan before Ridpath reached into his pocket and pulled out his warrant card. 'Police. DI Ridpath and DC Muldowney. Does a Tony Abbott live here?'

'Top flat, left-hand side. What's he done?'

'Nothing, we just want to chat with him.'

'I've heard that one before.'

'Do you have a key to Mr Abbott's flat?'

The old man sucked in air through his two remaining teeth. 'I don't know if I can do that? Aren't you supposed to have a warrant or something?'

'Mr Abbott is dead, we need to check out his flat, see if there are any reasons why he died and check if he left a note. We just want a quick look.'

'He's dead? But I only saw him a couple of days ago, he looked fine.'

'Can you let us into the flat? It would save us all the time of going to a magistrate to get a warrant.'

The man shook his head. 'More'n my jobs worth to let strangers into people's flats.'

'We're not strangers, we're police. If we have to get a warrant, we will, but then you wouldn't have just two coppers in plain clothes, there would be police cars, flashing lights and we'd be disturbing all your tenants, wouldn't we? I bet there's a lot going on in these flats to interest the police. Don't you, DC Muldowney?'

'I'm sure there is, sir.'

'And of course, we'd have to look into your back-ground, Mr...?'

'I didn't give you my name.'

'I'm sure we can find out easily enough. What is it?'

The man looked down. 'Albert Biggs.'

'Can you run the name through the police database, Megan, check if there are any outstanding warrants?'

'No problem, Ridpath.'

'No, no need to do that. I can let you in. I'll have to stand at the door and, if you take anything, I want a signed receipt. Have to protect myself, don't I?'

'Of course, Mr Biggs.'

The caretaker pressed a few buttons on the entry phone and the door clicked.

'The password is 1111, not terribly original,' said Megan.

'Easy to remember, innit? When you get to my age, passwords are a pain.'

'They're a pain at any age,' replied Ridpath.

They entered the reception area of the flats with Albert Biggs stepping back to let the detectives go first. Ridpath was struck by the strong smell of cooked cabbage as soon as he entered. A smell that immediately took him back to his childhood and his mother's cooking once again.

'It's on the top floor. The lifts ain't working, they never are.'

'How long has Tony Abbott lived here?'

'Not long, he moved in a couple of months ago. Nice man, kept himself to himself and he always put his rubbish in the right bin. I liked him.'

They all trudged up the grey lino-covered stairs. The smell of cabbage getting stronger as they reached the second floor where the high note of cat's pee was added to the assault on the nostrils.

'That's Mrs Downey, she keeps taking in stray cats from the neighbourhood. Tried to stop her, but she don't listen. Women, hey?'

Megan ignored the old man.

'Do you know what work Mr Abbott did?'

'No, he didn't tell me and I didn't ask. You don't ask people what they do around here. Not polite. But he was always well dressed going to work. Shirt, tie and jacket. Proper posh, he was.'

'Did he have a car?'

'Never saw him driving one. Took the bus, I think.'

Ridpath thought it was strange that a traffic investigator didn't own a car. Did he only use pool cars to get to his accidents? It was something he would have to ask Superintendent Durrow this afternoon.

They climbed the last flight of stairs, turning left at the top. The old man breathing heavily as they reached the door. He dug deep into his overall pocket and found a single master key.

As he touched the door to put the key in the lock, it swung slowly open. 'Strange, people don't leave their doors open round here. And it wasn't open this morning when I mopped the floors.'

Ridpath pushed him aside and placed himself in front of the door, signalling Megan Muldowney to come around to his right. He pressed the doorbell twice and shouted, 'Police, anybody there. Anybody inside?'

He stopped and listened for an answer. When there was none, he took two steps forward, crossing the threshold, peering inside. 'Police, come out now if you are inside.'

He walked down the hallway, checking an open doorway on his right. 'What the…?'

Chapter TWENTY-NINE

Detective Constable Andy Fletcher was pissed off.

Actually, he was angrier than that and it showed in his driving; accelerating too quickly, taking corners too fast, stamping on his brakes just as the lights changed, shouting at all the other drivers who were too slow, too stupid or just too in his way.

He'd spent the morning being patronised by that old fraud of a detective, Ridpath, a man who was so bad at his job they'd farmed him out to the retirement pastures of the coroner's office. Then, after Megan and Ridpath had gone to see their Bunsen's home, he had been called in by his boss.

'How was the briefing?'

'He's sent me out to interview the area and find out more about Jane Forsyth and her daughter.'

'Why? That case is wrapped up tighter than a Christmas parcel. The daughter admitted giving her mother sleeping tablets in her interview. Then she strangled her with the belt we found at the scene.'

'I know, but his lord and master thinks there are "anomalies" in the case. A confession isn't good enough for him, he wants to find out more.'

'Bollocks. She's locked up in a secure children's home, pending a report from a trick cyclist. Why are you still investigating?'

'Ridpath wants more background before he sends the papers to CPS. Get this, he wants to know *why* she did it.'

'Because she's a bloody nutter, that's why.' Inspector Ron Pleasance shook his head. 'It's time for you to grow a pair of balls if you want to carry on working in this nick, Andy. You need to handle Ridpath, show him who's boss, understand?'

'I'm going to have to waste my time gathering a load of useless background information that nobody's ever going to use just so Ridpath can ease his mind about "anomalies"?'

'Until I sort him out, that's exactly what you will do. Give me a couple of days and I'll cook his goose. I'm putting a plan into action. Ridpath won't know what's hit him. Your job for the next couple of days is to do exactly what you're told, understand?'

'Got it, boss,' was his only answer. So, he had to go out and interview a bunch of old slags just to ease Ridpath's mind. What a load of rubbish.

He accelerated to a space at the top of Handley Street. Gathering his notepad, a few pens and his coat from the front seat, he stepped out of the car. The weather was so bloody freezing a couple of brass monkeys had just ran past looking for a welder. Even worse, he'd forgotten his gloves and already his hands were beginning to go numb.

He looked up to see the clouds were darkening heavily over his head. It looked like an apocalyptic storm was about to break. Just another late October day in Manchester.

Grabbing an umbrella from the back seat, hoping the rain would keep away long enough for him to get the bloody interviews done, he walked up the garden path of number two and knocked on the door. A woman answered wearing a long housecoat and her hair in curlers.

'What do you want?'

Andy Fletcher put his game face on. 'My name is DC Andy Fletcher from Sale Police Station and we're looking into the death of Ms Forsyth at number 26. Did you know Ms Forsyth?'

The woman shook her head. 'Never met her. You don't meet many people round here, everybody keeps themselves to themselves. But I heard what happened, shocking weren't it?'

'You never met her or saw her daughter?'

A child started bawling from inside the house. The woman shouted over her shoulder. 'I'll get your toast in a minute. I'm just dealing with this man at the door.'

The child's crying grew even louder.

The woman turned back to him. 'Nah, never met her. Used to see her walk past here going to the shops but we never talked. Can't help you, sorry.'

The child's crying grew even louder, followed by a loud crash as something was thrown against a wall.

'Sorry, I'd love to help but I didn't know her, sorry. Got to go now before my kid really loses it. She's hungry...'

The door closed and Andy Fletcher was left holding his name card in his hand.

At the next door down, the reception was even worse. The front door was answered by an old woman whose hearing aid wasn't working.

'What did you say?'

'Did you know the woman at number 26, Jane Forsyth?'

'What was that?'

'The woman at number 26,' he shouted louder, 'did you know her?'

'I don't want any today thank you, the council have already been,' she finally said.

After similar reactions at all the doors on the street, he reached number 18, just as a few drops of rain began to splash on his shoulders. He pressed the button on the umbrella, trapping his finger as it shot open.

'Shit, shit, shit.'

One side of the umbrella had come away from the spokes but he couldn't be bothered to fix it. Instead, he opened the gate, marched up the garden path and rapped on the door.

It was answered almost immediately as if the woman were waiting for him. She was a middle-aged woman with a double chin and a thick head of dark curls, which she proceeded to scratch vigorously.

He ran through his usual patter. 'Good morning, madam, my name is Detective Constable Fletcher. I'm sure you've heard about the incident at number 26, I'm just asking her neighbours about Ms Forsyth. Did you know her?'

'Of course I knew Jane, we went to yoga together.'

'Yoga?'

'The exercise. You know downward dog, the warrior, happy baby. Jane was quite good at it even though she was on the chubby side. I have problems touching my toes, and according to the teacher my back muscles are very tight, it's all the sitting, you see. I—'

'When did you first meet Ms Forsyth?' interrupted Fletcher.

'I think it was at the pre-natal class in Trafford General. Oh, it must be fourteen years ago, but we lost touch and then I moved in here with Debs two years ago and met her again. I thought the police would have been around sooner.'

Andy Fletcher blushed, realising right away that he should have started at number 26 and then worked his way outwards.

'She was a lovely woman. Or at least she was until about a month ago.'

'Why do you say that?'

'She suddenly changed. One minute we were the best of friends and then next she was blanking me on the street. I thought I'd done something wrong.'

'Did you ask her why?'

'I never had the chance, and then I heard all the commotion with the ambulances and the police cars at the weekend. Shocking isn't it, her young girl could kill her like that?'

'How do you know what happened?'

'Well, everybody knows, don't they? The man from the *Evening News* is coming round later with a photographer.'

At the mention of the *Evening News*, a shiver ran down Fletcher's spine. The last thing he needed right now was a bloody reporter sniffing around his case.

'Did you know the child, Anita?'

'I used to see her with her mum occasionally and Debs went to school with her.'

'Debs?'

'My daughter. Anita used to come round here sometimes when her mum had to go out.' Her hand flew to cover her mouth. 'Oh god. I've just thought she used to play with our Debs when I went to the bingo. She might have murdered her.'

'But Debs is okay, isn't she?'

The woman nodded.

'Good. Do you know who Anita's father was?'

'I asked Jane one day where the father was, and she just said he was away. I got the impression that he wasn't involved in his child's life at all, just another bloody sperm donor. So many men like that around here; they get the woman pregnant and then run away as far as possible from the responsibility of actually bringing up the kid. Take my sister, she—'

'So you never saw any men visiting the house?' interjected Fletcher impatiently.

'Not a one. She was a nun, was Jane. Between you and me, probably the best way for a woman to live. Men: can't do anything with them, but can't do anything without them. Just like my John, he did a runner after I told him I was pregnant—'

'Is there anything else you can tell me about Jane Forsyth?' interrupted Andy Fletcher again. 'Like what job she did?'

'I don't know what she did before, but when I was going to the yoga with her, she said that it involved computers, she spent an awful lot of time on her laptop. We could sometimes see the blue glow through her window late at night. She was probably getting some work done whilst Anita slept.'

'But you don't know what she actually did for a living?'

The woman shook her head. 'I thought you lot would have found that out by now.'

It was Andy Fletcher's turn to stay silent.

'I will say one thing, though. She loved that child with all her heart. I couldn't imagine why Anita would hurt her. She was a loving and devoted mother to the little girl. I mean it goes against nature, don't it? A child hurting her own mother. What's the world coming too, hey.' Then she leant in conspiratorially. 'But I'll tell you, when our Debs is crying sometimes, I could strangle her.'

'I wouldn't do that if I were you, Mrs…?'

'*Ms* Docherty,' she said brushing her hair with the palm of her hand, 'Pam Docherty. Do you want to come in, it's awfully cold standing out here?'

For a second, as the rain beat down on his wonky umbrella, Andy Fletcher was tempted. 'Thank you for the offer, Ms Docherty, but I still have a lot of houses to visit.'

He glanced down the street, seeing it stretch into the distance through the pouring rain. The blue-and-white police tape outside number 26 standing out against the grey of the sky, the trees and the houses. Manchester Grey: a particularly stubborn colour.

'If you think of anything else, Ms Docherty, please don't hesitate to contact me.' He passed over his card.

She seemed almost disappointed when she took it. 'I'll call you if I think of anything. I'll even call you if I don't.'

'Thank you, Ms Docherty.'

He proceeded to escape down the garden path, closing the gate firmly behind him.

Once again, he looked up and down the road; still another twenty-four houses to interview before he was finished. The rain was getting heavier now, sleeting across the street blown by a strong wind from somewhere in the region of Iceland.

He should have told Ridpath where to get off when he was ordered to do this job. Or he should have got a plod to do it. He hadn't served seven years and then spent six months on a detectives' course to end up knocking on doors in some poxy street in Sale.

He pulled up his coat collar and angled the umbrella to keep out the rain but it didn't help much. Already, he couldn't feel his fingers because of the cold. It was time to give this up and go and check in at the register office at Sale Town Hall. He could finish later this afternoon when more people were likely to be at home. Ridpath would never find out he hadn't visited every house at the same time.

And Andy Fletcher didn't care if he did. His boss would protect him whatever happened. Ridpath could go hang himself.

Chapter THIRTY

'Are we ready?'

'All present and correct, Sarge.'

'Right, let's get going.'

The officers, all wearing their protective gear – matt-black Kevlar helmets, NIJ level IIIA bulletproof vests, black ski masks to cover the Home Office Scientific Development Branch – also known as HOSDB – approved jumpsuits and Nomex undergarments – nodded agreement and moved away to perform last-minute checks on their Heckler & Koch rifles.

Two minutes later they were pulling out of Police HQ in their armed response vehicles, a palpable, almost physical, air of tension in the group.

Nobody was talking, nobody looking at each other. All were concentrating on their role in the upcoming job, focused on what they were about to do.

They pulled into the car park of the Morrison's supermarket at exactly 11.45 a.m.

'Last checks everybody,' Sergeant Rivers spoke quietly into the Airwave.

Inside the vehicles the PTU officers adjusted their equipment, checking each other carefully, making sure each piece of kit was operational.

'Team A, ready.'

'Team B, ready.'

'Team C and D, ready to move.'

'Wait for the go signal,' ordered Rivers. 'Gold Commander, do we have permission to begin the operation?'

Inside his own car, Steve Carruthers wiped his sweaty palms on his trousers, next to him, Helen Shipton was staring intently at the PTU vehicle in front of her.

Carruthers spoke into the Airwave he was holding, his Glaswegian accent even more pronounced. 'You have ma permission to begin, Sergeant Rivers.'

Sergeant Rivers checked his watch 11.55. Now was as good a time as any. 'All teams we have a go. Team B, go now.'

The first PTU vehicle accelerated out of the car park with Team B in the lead to enter the house at the rear of their target and effect entry over the back wall. This would take at least two minutes so Sergeant Rivers held the other teams in the car park until he received the signal that Team B were in position.

It came exactly one minute and twenty-four seconds later.

'Moving into position now, Sarge. ETA, thirty seconds. Over.'

'Right. On arrival hold position until further orders. Over.'

'Team B in position.'

'Teams A, C and D, go now. Team B hold where you are.'

'Roger that.'

The three PTU vehicles accelerated out of the supermarket car park. Team D was in the lead to block entry at the junction of Warwick Road. Team A was second in line to enter the front of the house with Team C bringing up the rear to block the corner of Keppel and Brantingham Roads after Team A had stopped at the target house.

Carruthers was biting his fingernails. The thumb was already bitten down to the quick so he started on his index finger. It was a disgusting habit but one he couldn't quit. He watched as the PTU vehicles left the car park. He could feel the vibrations of the engine of his own car, almost like it was on an FI grid desperate for the start lights. Dennis Leahey in the driver's seat was looking back at him awaiting his order.

Inside the vehicles, Team A led by Sergeant Rivers gripped their Heckler & Koch rifles, ready to go into action as soon as they heard the orders in their earpieces.

The PTU vans turned right and then at the bottom of the road, turned right and then right again onto Keppel Road. A young couple walking their dog stopped to watch the brightly coloured police vans as they raced down the road, the dog barking at them ineffectually.

As they approached the house, the driver slammed on the brakes and they slid to a halt.

Sergeant Rivers shouted in the Airwave: 'Team A, go. Team B, go.'

The back doors of the van shot open and the men jumped out of the vehicle, assembling quickly into a six-person line with Sergeant Rivers in the lead. Behind him a burly officer carrying a bright orange sledgehammer followed closely.

They advanced up the short driveway to the front door past a white van.

All clear so far.

Sergeant Rivers covered one side while the man with the orange sledgehammer swung it against the lock of the door.

There was a resounding crash of metal smashing into wood, but the lock held. He lifted up the heavy orange sledgehammer and slammed it into the lock again.

This time the door shot open, almost coming off its hinges.

Sergeant Rivers shouted 'Police, police.' He entered the dark hallway, swinging his Heckler & Koch from left to right, covering every possible danger. The two other men in his team moved past him smoothly in the coordinated actions of a well-oiled military machine, the sound of the heavy boots echoing on the bare wooden floor.

'Living room, clear,' a voice shouted in his earpiece.

'Kitchen clear,' from Team B.

The sounds of heavy boots pounded upstairs as more members of the team rushed past him. 'Bathroom, clear.'

'Bedroom, clear.'

A long silence.

Another door crashed open followed by a high-pitched male voice. 'Jesus, what the fuck is that?'

Chapter THIRTY-ONE

'Did he do this?'

Ridpath scanned the wrecked room. The drawers of a cupboard were scattered across the floor. The TV was pushed over on its side. A bookshelf lay sprawled over, its books spread across the floor. The cushions of the couch had been slit open with a Stanley knife.

Ridpath walked out of the living room and into the small kitchen. The same mess was there, too. Cornflake packets emptied onto the floor, shelves cleared, frozen food slowly melting quietly to form small puddles on the floor.

He bent down to touch a packet of frozen peas. 'Megan, can you check the bedroom?'

'Will do,' came the answer.

Ridpath heard the sound of her footsteps behind him as he brushed a tin of baked beans aside with his hand to reveal a copy of a newspaper from two days ago.

'It's the same in here, Ridpath, somebody has wrecked the place.'

Why would Tony Abbott destroy his flat before he killed himself?

Then another possibility occurred to him.

Why would someone destroy a dead man's flat?

He walked back to the living room and spoke to Albert Biggs. 'You said you mopped the corridor this morning, what time?'

'Eight thirty a.m. I always do each block once a week. Five blocks, five days, I don't work weekends.'

'The door was definitely closed this morning when you mopped?'

'Definitely. I knock on the doors when I'm mopping to see if anybody wants something disposing. I make a bit on the side selling the gear to the local rag-and-bone men. You'd be surprised how much money is to be made in rubbish. I suppose one person's piece of junk is another's antique.'

'So you knocked on Mr Abbott's door this morning?'

'Yeah, I didn't see him leave for work, so I thought it was his day off.'

'Wouldn't he be annoyed with you knocking so early?'

'Nah, he was always up early, was Mr Abbott, used to go running some mornings at seven o'clock.'

'Right, just to confirm: the door was closed when you knocked?'

'Definitely, I'd swear on my life it was.'

'You may have to. Did you see anybody unusual hanging around the area?'

Albert Biggs' index finger played with his lips. 'I might have done... I thought I saw some bloke hanging around the fence, a tall bloke he was. But you can't approach everybody you see in the area, can you?'

'You approached us.'

'Ah, that's because you looked like coppers. I always speak to the police, you never know what they're up to.'

'What time did you see this bloke?'

'About nine-ish, maybe a few minutes earlier.'

'And what did you do then?'

'I did what I always do.'

Ridpath sighed. It was like getting blood from a stone. 'What do you always do?'

'I goes round to 6C for a sup of tea and a spot of toast. She does a lovely cuppa, does Mrs Dawson.'

'So you weren't around the estate?'

'I'm always here, never leaves, it's more'n my job's worth.'

'But you were drinking tea, so anybody could have entered the flats.'

'They won't know the code.'

'1111 is hardly likely to keep anybody out for long.'

'I was only gone half an hour. It's my nineses.'

'Nineses?' asked Ridpath, instantly regretting the question.

'Other people have elevenses, I have nineses... and elevenses.'

Megan rejoined them. 'Drawers emptied, and pillows and mattresses slashed in the bedroom. Why would Tony Abbott do this before he killed himself?'

'Mr Abbott has killed himself?' asked the caretaker.

Ridpath stared at Megan Muldowney before turning to Albert Biggs. 'He took his own life on Monday night. We're checking up on the circumstances that may have led him to do it.'

Albert shook his head. 'I wouldn't have thought it of him, not *him*.' The caretaker scanned the room. 'And this is not like him either. He was always so neat and tidy, not like some of the others.'

'Did you see a note anywhere, Megan?'

She shook her head. 'None that I could see.'

'A laptop or a computer? His boss said sometimes Tony Abbott worked from home.'

She shook her head again. 'You want me to go back and check?'

'No, I think we need to get forensics in here.'

'Really? Why? He must have done this before going to the petrol station.'

'Impossible, this was done this morning.'

'How do you know?'

'Mr Biggs here says the door was closed when he did his rounds this morning before nine.'

'He could have been mistaken.'

'I know my doors,' said Biggs stubbornly.

'But the real clue is in the kitchen. The food on the floor is still frozen. Even in this weather, it would have melted if the fridge had been emptied two nights ago. Call the forensic team in, Megan, somebody has turned over this place looking for something. I want to know who did it and what they were looking for.'

Chapter THIRTY-TWO

The register office was right opposite Sale Police Station in a red brick building that proudly called itself Sale Town Hall. Andy Fletcher had walked past this place countless times on his way to the restaurants and pubs of the town but he had never been inside.

At the moment, it was covered in scaffolding for a renovation. It looked like something you would find in a kid's Meccano set, if they even made Meccano any more.

He walked round, looking for a possible entrance, before finding one up some steps on the opposite side of the building. The register office was on the second floor.

He stood inside the hallway for a second, inhaling the atmosphere of the place. The aroma of furniture polish and civic dignity was heavy in the air. Years and countless elbows had been worn to the bone shining this wood until it sweated polish like a Turkish wrestler sweats a kebab.

He slowly climbed the stairs looking all around him as he did.

On the landing, he approached the office, knocking once before entering. A young, rather pretty woman with a ring through her nose, sitting behind an old-fashioned desk, looked up briefly from what she was doing.

'How can I help you? If you need to register a birth, I'm afraid you'll have to make an appointment. You can do it online these days.'

'I'm not here to register a birth. I'm actually looking for somebody.'

'Which member of staff would you like to see?'

'It's not a member of staff. I want to find out some information.'

'The registrar is performing a service at the moment, I'm afraid.'

'A service?'

'A wedding, a couple getting married.'

He advanced and sat on the side of the desk as she checked a diary. 'Mr and Mrs Greenfield. They are both sixty-eight and first marriages for both of them.'

'Poor things, I can't imagine what their wedding night will be like.'

'Can't you? I can,' said the woman curtly. 'Full of joy and happiness.'

He pulled out his warrant card, enjoying the feeling of power as he showed it to the young woman. 'My name is DC Fletcher, and I'm here to check a birth registry.'

The woman glanced at it without being impressed. 'You'll have to wait for the registrar, she'll be here shortly.'

'Can't you help me? I'm sure it won't take you long, a smart girl like you.' He leant in closer, letting her catch a whiff of his aftershave. 'I'm looking for somebody who was born in Sale around fourteen years ago.'

'Sorry, you'll have to talk to the registrar.'

As she spoke the door opened.

'Speak of the devil,' said Andy Fletcher.

'Mrs Turner, this policeman would like to check the birth registry.'

'Would he? I presume you have some identification?'

The registrar was dressed formally in a black jacket and skirt, her hair coiffured in a style once favoured by Margaret Thatcher.

Andy Fletcher flashed his warrant card, once again producing a distinctly unimpressed response. 'How can I help you, officer?'

'I'd like to see the registration certificate of a birth in Sale.'

'Would you?'

Andy Fletcher frowned. 'I would, is that a problem?'

'Strictly speaking, yes. You see as a registrar, the 1968 Registration of Births, Deaths and Marriages Regulations clearly defines my role. Part 2, section 10, item 2 is explicit and I quote: "An officer shall not, without the express authority of the registrar general, publish or communicate to any person, otherwise than in the ordinary course of the performance of his official duties, any information acquired by him while performing those duties."'

'You can't be serious?'

'I assure you, Detective Fletcher, I take my duties exceptionally seriously. If you require that information, the registrar general has to instruct me to release it to you.'

'But I need it now, not in three months.'

'I'm sorry, the 1968 regulations are quite clear. As an officer of the law you wouldn't be encouraging me to break it would you?'

'No, of course not but—'

'If you have the mother or father's name, you could find the information you want from the General Register Office by paying the usual fee. Of course, you'll need the index reference numbers first.'

'Where do I find them when they're at home?'

'You could visit Manchester Central Library or go online at FreeBMD.'

'Right, but afterwards I'd still need to order the cert from the General Register Office.'

'Correct.'

'And how long would that take?'

'Fifteen days if you don't have the reference numbers, four days if you do. Of course, you could get it sent out by tomorrow at the latest if you pay £38.50 and apply before four p.m.'

'£38.50?'

'That does include VAT.'

'I should bloody hope so.' He changed the tone in his voice, almost wheedling like a young child. 'But we're investigating a murder and I need that information now.'

'A murder? Not the woman in Handley Street?'

Fletcher nodded his head. 'I need to know who the father of her child was. She's in a children's home at the moment and we need to discover if there are any relatives.' He was laying it on thicker than a bricky with his trowel.

The registrar appeared to make a decision. 'In that case, we can make an exception as long as you promise to follow up with a note to the registrar general for me.'

'Of course,' said Fletcher, 'as soon as I get back to the office.' He'd crossed his fingers and, when you do that, a promise is not a promise.

She walked over to a filing cabinet. 'Fourteen years ago, you said the birth was?'

'Roughly around then.'

'You don't know the birth date of the child?'

Andy Fletcher realised he should have checked with the school first. They would have all Anita Forsyth's details. 'We're not certain,' was all he finally answered.

'So we need to check all the quarters of 2010. What was the name of the mother?'

Fletcher checked his notes. 'Jane Forsyth.'

The woman ran her fingers over the files. 'Nobody of that name registered a birth during the first quarter. Are you sure it was done here?'

Fletcher shook his head. 'I heard she lived in Sale and the birth was at Trafford General.'

The woman frowned. 'Usually, they would register with us. By law, the mother and father have to register the birth within forty-two days. It's extremely rare for people not to come to the office. Let me check the next quarter of 2010 for you.'

She opened a different drawer and scanned a block of files. 'Here it is. Ms Forsyth registered the birth on June 29, 2010, the child, Anita, was born on the 20 June, 2010 in Trafford General Hospital.'

'Could I see that?'

The registrar handed over the single sheet of paper. Andy Fletcher quickly scanned it. 'There's no name, address or occupation for the father, that area is blank.'

'It usually means the mother chose to register the birth without including the name of the child's father.'

'Why?'

'They weren't married or in a civil partnership, the father didn't attend the register office with the mother, or the mother simply did not want to recognise this particular man as the father of her child. You take your pick.'

'Right.' He held up the birth certificate. 'Can I take this with me?'

The registrar gently took it from him. 'Of course not, this is the original of the long-form certificate. You can apply for a short-form copy if you like, or take notes now. But this stays here.'

Fletcher shrugged his shoulders. 'Suit yourself,' he mumbled and began to take down the details in his note-book.

'If we're finished here, I have another wedding to perform in five minutes' time, so if you will excuse me.'

'How was the Greenfield wedding, Mrs Turner?' the receptionist asked.

'Wonderful, it was so lovely seeing people discover love in the twilight of their years. I must rush off now, Jenny, I'll be back at two after the ceremony. Make sure you file Ms Forsyth's long-form certificate back in its correct place.'

'Will do, Mrs Turner.'

'Good day to you, DC Fletcher. Do not forget to send an official request through to the registrar general and copy me. Jenny will give you my email address.'

And with those words, she was gone.

Andy Fletcher scurried over to the receptionist's desk. 'Are you sure I can't get that certificate?'

'Positive.'

'But it would help me immensely – my bosses will kill me if I don't come back with it.'

'Sorry, I can't release this. But I promise to look out for your obituary in the newspaper.' She stood up and walked over to the filing cabinet.

'How about a quick copy? Surely you could just use your photocopier? It won't take you a second.'

'You heard the registrar, Detective Fletcher.'

'Andy, please.'

'I suggest you apply for your information through the official channels, Detective.'

'Come on, just photocopy this one piece of paper for me and I'll take you for dinner tonight, my treat.'

'You'd take me to dinner and you'd pay?'

'Of course.'

'Detective Fletcher, while the thought of having dinner with you is terribly attractive, unfortunately I have to clean a septic tank this evening.'

'So the answer is no.'

'You know, Detective Fletcher, with an intuition like that, you're destined for a stellar career in the police force. And yes, the answer is a definite no.'

She placed the certificate back in its correct file and closed the cabinet with a clang.

Chapter THIRTY-THREE

Steve Carruthers walked past the shattered door, still hanging off one hinge, followed by Dennis Leahey, with Helen Shipton bringing up the rear.

They were met in the hallway by the sergeant and led upstairs to the first floor.

'Is this where you found it?'

'Yes, sir. The rest of the house is clear. It looks like it hasn't been lived in for a long time. The beds are covered in dust and the kitchen looks like something out of the 1960s.'

They strode into the first-floor bedroom. On the wall directly facing them somebody had sprayed in thick black paint: 'I am guilty but you'll never save me.'

'What the fuck does that mean? What's he guilty of?' Dennis Leahey said.

'I haven't a clue but I do know it doesn't sound good. Dennis, get a team of officers from MIT and canvas the local area. Find out if any of the neighbours saw the person who lives here and the last time they were here. Discover anything and everything you can on Mr Ronnie Rellik. I noticed there are no flyers or junk mail in the hallway so somebody must have been here recently to take it away or dump it somewhere.'

'On it, boss.'

Leahey ran out of the room, his feet making a heavy noise on the bare wooden boards as he went down the stairs.

'Nothing anywhere else in the house, Sergeant?'

'Nothing my men have found sir, but we've just been concentrating on making sure the place was empty.'

'Right, your men in the house can stand down but leave the vans blocking the end of the street. I don't want anybody coming near here until we've searched this place from top to bottom.'

'I'll organise the road block, sir.'

'Helen, can you get on to the CSIs? I want a full team down here and this place gone over with a fine-tooth comb. I want DNA or at least fingerprints from Mr Rellik. And don't forget the white van in the driveway. I'll lay ten to one it's the same van your ANPR picked up last Wednesday morning, driving from Saddleworth to Manchester.'

But Helen Shipton wasn't listening. Instead she was staring up at the light fixture hanging down from the ceiling. Slowly she lifted her arm to point at it.

'Do you see above the light socket?'

Carruthers followed her pointing finger upwards. An old cord was hanging from a plaster rosette decoration in the middle of the ceiling but the light socket was missing the bulb.

'What is it?'

'Just above the light, there's something there.'

'Get me a chair or a ladder, Sergeant.'

The PTU officer ran out of the room, returning a minute later with an old bentwood Windsor chair.

Carruthers climbed up and reached above the socket, pulling off a small cube with a glass lens. A thin wire ran from the cube along the flex into a hole in the ceiling. He yanked the cube and the wire broke.

'What is it?' asked Helen.

Carruthers held it close to his face. 'If I'm not mistaken, this is a camera. The bastard has been watching us as we raided his house. Check the other light fixtures, Sergeant, but don't touch anything you find: we'll need forensics to look at them for prints.'

The sergeant left the room, shouting orders to his men.

'Helen, get onto the CSIs now. Tell them I need a team here yesterday to turn over this house. I want it and the white van dusted like an Arbroath smokie.'

'On it, boss.'

Carruthers turned the camera around in his fingers, examining it from every angle. The bastard knew they would come here and had been watching them all this time.

What the hell were they dealing with?

Chapter THIRTY-FOUR

'Come on, Megan, let's leave them to it. There's not much more we can do here.'

Ridpath was standing outside Tony Abbott's flat, watching the CSIs in their white suits go in and out while others were dusting window ledges and door architraves looking for fingerprints.

Next to him a large forensic specialist was eating an even larger bacon, lettuce and tomato bap noisily, reminding him he hadn't eaten so far that day.

Megan joined him. 'Where are we going, Ridpath?'

'I think we need to visit Tony Abbott's wife first – what was her name?'

'Charlotte Abbott.'

'We need to tell her what happened to her husband before she reads it in the papers. Afterwards, I want a quick look at the petrol station again and then we have to see Superintendent Durrow. Afterwards, we'll go back to Sale nick and find out what Andy Fletcher has discovered, if anything.'

'I'm not looking forward to seeing Charlotte Abbott.'

'Neither am I.'

A small man in a Tyvek suit, still wearing his mask, joined them. 'We're not finding much, Ridpath, but we'll bag what we see and take a look at it in the lab. No fingerprints so far. Whoever turned over this flat must have been wearing gloves.'

'Have you found a laptop or a computer yet, George?'

The crime scene manager shook his head. 'Nor any mobile phone.'

'He must have had both for his job. I'll get the mobile number from his boss.'

'Right.' He held up an evidence bag containing a certificate. 'We did find this in one of the drawers.'

'What is it?'

'A decree nisi. His divorce came through a year ago.'

'Nothing else?'

'That's it.'

'No pictures or photo albums?'

'We didn't find any.'

'Strange. Who doesn't have pictures at home?'

'A man who keeps them on his phone? Lots of people don't print out their pictures any more, Ridpath.'

'Thank you, Megan, is that Gen Y or Gen Z speaking?'

'Both. I don't have any photos at home either,' added George.

'But Tony Abbott was more my age...'

'Perhaps, he was a bit more... modern.'

'I'll ignore that remark, DC Muldowney. Meanwhile, make yourself useful and take a picture of the decree nisi and follow up with the courts. We'll have to inform his ex-wife when we see her.'

'Right, Ridpath.'

'Okay, George, we're off. Call me if you find anything useful, particularly that laptop.'

'Will do.'

Megan was just finishing snapping a photo of the document in its bag with her phone.

'Come on, I'm starving, let's grab a Greggs on our way to the petrol station.'

'Why are you obsessed with his laptop, Ridpath?'

'It strikes me as strange that it's missing. He definitely wasn't carrying it when he went to the petrol station and, reading the reports of the Forsyth murder, no laptop or mobile phones were found there either.'

'You can't think there's a link between the two cases?'

'Can't I? Why did they both use exactly the same words: "I'm doing it to save her"?'

'Just a coincidence.'

'I don't believe in coincidences, Megan, and as a detective, neither should you.'

They walked down the steps to where their car was parked. Outside the flat, a small crowd had gathered, held back from the entrance by a thin blue-and-white line of police tape and one very burly sergeant.

Ridpath ducked under it and was immediately accosted by a reporter who stuck a microphone connected to a recorder in his face.

'Steve Rockford from the *Evening News*. We understand the man who lived here took his own life on Monday evening. Was he the man at the petrol station? What are the CSIs looking for? Are you investigating Tony Abbott?'

'I thought your lot would be keener on reporting on the home invasion in Saddleworth rather than wasting your time round here.'

'That's last week's news, mate.'

Ridpath scowled. Out of the corner of his eye, he could see Albert Biggs standing to one side holding a twenty-quid note in his hand. The reporter had obviously just finished interviewing him.

Ridpath tried to push past the man, but he adjusted his position and blocked his way. Ridpath realised he wasn't getting away so easily.

'Obviously, I cannot comment on an ongoing investigation. My thoughts, and the thoughts of the entire investigation team, remain with the family of Tony Abbott. A cordon will remain in place whilst officers work in the area. We know there will be some disruption to the local community as a result of our work, but it is important that we do this so we can provide their loved ones with the information they need to process this news. Thank you for your time.'

He pushed past the reporter again and this time he let him go. He had his story now and would be happy to phone it in to his sub at the paper.

Ridpath reached his car and slipped into the driver's seat. 'I hate reporters. Leeches all of them, who would sell their mothers for a few column inches and a byline.'

'You sounded convincing.'

'It's a speech my old boss, Charlie Whitworth, taught us. I use variations of it every time. It means nothing but it keeps them happy.'

'I sometimes feel sorry for them, standing out in the cold in all weathers waiting for titbits from investigating officers.'

'Don't ever feel sorry for people like them. Our reporter there will interview the neighbours, perhaps find an old photo and splash the results on Page Six, next to the opening of a new restaurant. He'll forget there is a man's family somewhere, perhaps with kids too, who will be torn apart by the story. Meanwhile, he will have moved onto his next article, leaving behind a troubled, grieving family and we have to pick up the pieces.'

'You don't like them, do you?'

'Like I said, most reporters would sell their own mothers for a few column inches.'

'They can't all be like that.'

'They can and they are. They wouldn't be reporters unless they were leeches. Woodward and Bernstein died long ago. And that whole "speak truth to power" is the biggest lie ever told. Anyway, enough of my hobby horse, a Greggs sausage roll is calling my name. I'll buy you a pasty and coffee, if you want?'

'Last of the big spenders, huh, Ridpath? You really do know how to treat a girl.'

'Years of practice, Megan, years of practice.'

He started the car and revved the engine, then stopped. 'But in all seriousness, there's something about this case that worries me. Why would anybody want to search the flat of a man who had just killed himself?'

'I don't know, Ridpath.'

'Neither do I, but we're going to find out.'

Chapter THIRTY-FIVE

He unlocked the door and walked into the house. The timing was perfect.

He'd watched the whole performance of the police raiding the Keppel Road house from the comfort of his car parked less than two hundred yards away. It was amusing that his little plan warranted so many coppers invading his space, all armed to the teeth.

He'd expected them to find him using ANPR, but not that quickly. He thought he would have time to execute his plans for Robert Wallace before they were all over him like measles.

But it wasn't a problem. He'd foreseen this possibility and planned accordingly.

For a second, he stopped in the hallway, going over in his mind his last visit to the house on Keppel Road. Had he left anything behind?

The van was wiped clean of fingerprints. They'd check the registration and find that it had been bought by a Ronnie Rellik from a second-hand dealer in Ashton-on-Mersey for 4,000 quid in cash. The dealer might remember his face, but he doubted it and, after six months, the CCTV would have been taped over long ago.

He'd realised when he was walking around Manchester planning this work he would need another identity if his plan was to be executed properly. And so, Ronnie Rellik was born. It had been relatively easy to rent the house in that name once he'd kicked out the sitting tenant, put himself on the electoral register and changed the gas and electric bills, even opened a bank account.

The house itself was clean: he always wore gloves when he was inside. It had been bought by his parents over thirty years ago as a nest-egg for himself and his brother. It had been rented out since then to a variety of students and ne'er-do-wells. He'd even moved in there himself fifteen years ago for a short time. It was part of his parents' plan to make him more independent. But he hadn't lasted long, he missed his mother, father and brother too much, and they missed him. He'd moved back home within four months.

It was good that they'd spent their last years together but they should have had longer.

They had all died well before their time.

Ronnie Rellik was brought to life from out of the whispers of that dark place. He would return there just as soon as he had finished with Robert Wallace.

Death and life, both come from darkness.

He strode up the stairs to the attic and unlocked the door. Just one picture was still not on the wall. Just one death to go.

As soon as he logged into the chat room, he saw his target had left a message for him twenty minutes ago.

PropMan76: Are you there?

Ten minutes later there was another message.

PropMan76: Are you there? I'm going spare here.

He sounded wired, at the end of his tether.

Perfect.

He tapped in a short message.

> **Rellik:** Hello, did you read the instructions?

The response came back immediately, he must have been poised over the laptop like a vulture waiting for a wanderer in the desert to die.

> **PropMan76:** I read them but the last instruction is to kill myself, I don't understand. Are you serious?
> **Rellik:** Very.
> **PropMan76:** I don't get it. How am I supposed to kill myself?
> **Rellik:** You will be told at the appropriate time.
> **PropMan76:** When?
> **Rellik:** When I'm ready to tell you.
> **PropMan76:** I can't do it. I can't go on like this any more. My wife wants to go to the police.
> **Rellik:** If she does, they won't be able to save you or your family. I will take great pleasure in killing your children. The Ashtons watched me kill theirs, helpless as I slashed the throats of their kids…
> **PropMan76:** The police are looking for you.
> **Rellik:** Let them, they'll never find me. Do what I want or else your family will pay.
> **PropMan76:** Not if I go to the police.
> **Rellik:** The police can't protect you. They couldn't save the Ashtons. They couldn't save Jane Forsyth. They couldn't save Tony Abbott and they can't save you. If you want to save your family's life, you know what to do.

> **PropMan76:** But if I do what you want, I'll never see
> them again.
> **Rellik:** But they will be alive and you will have saved
> them. Your choice: yourself or your family?
> **PropMan76:** Why are you doing this to me? To us?
> **Rellik:** You know why.
> **PropMan76:** I didn't mean for anyone to get hurt. I'm
> sorry.

A long pause.

> **PropMan76:** I have money, I can sell the house and
> give you money. We have some savings, I can give
> you everything we have. You could be rich, you don't
> have to do this.
> **Rellik:** Just do what I told you to do. If you want your
> family to live…

He logged out of the chat room. The camera was still on
of course. He watched the man with his head in his hands,
all alone with his fears and his decision.

He hoped Robert Wallace made the right choice. He
didn't want to kill the children. They bled far too much.

Chapter THIRTY-SIX

Ridpath and Megan Muldowney walked up the short garden path and knocked on the front door. The house was one of those classic red-brick, detached places that had been built by the thousand as Manchester expanded into the suburbs during the 1930s. Back then, it had cost just 350 pounds, nowadays it was worth a fortune.

A young girl answered the door.

'Hello, is your mother in?' asked Ridpath.

'Mum, someone to see you,' she shouted over her shoulder before turning back to Ridpath. 'If you would like to wait, she'll be down in a minute.'

The girl then vanished inside, leaving the door open. Ridpath could hear the sound of feet running down carpeted stairs. An elegantly dressed woman came to the door a few moments later. 'Can I help you?'

Ridpath took a deep breath. 'Are you Mrs Abbott, Mrs Charlotte Abbott?'

'I used to be Mrs Abbott but now I use my maiden name, Rowlandson.'

'I'm DI Ridpath and this is DC Muldowney, could we come in? I'm afraid we have some bad news for you.'

'Bad news? Is it about my father?'

'It's about your husband – your ex-husband,' Ridpath corrected himself, 'Tony Abbott. Could we come in?'

The woman opened the door wider and stepped aside. 'If you'd like to go through to the front room.'

The front room was neat and tidy, everything in its place and a place for everything. Along one wall, on either side of what used to be a chimney, two bookshelves were heavily laden with books.

The woman saw Ridpath staring at them. 'I'm a teacher, an English teacher.'

Ridpath nodded, looking for somewhere to sit. He felt like his mere presence dirtied the place somehow.

Eventually Mrs Abbott sat down on the settee and Ridpath sat facing her, his notebook in his hand. Megan remained standing at the door.

For a moment, a shroud of silence covered the room with the only sound that of a clock ticking away loudly on the mantlepiece.

It was Mrs Abbott who spoke first. 'You said you had some news about Tony?'

'Bad news I'm afraid.' Ridpath took another deep breath. He had told people about the deaths of family members before but it was never easy, and the more he did it, the harder it became. 'Tony Abbott passed away. He took his own life on Monday evening.'

The woman's face displayed no emotion. 'He took his own life?'

'That's correct. I'm terribly sorry to bring you this bad news but we felt you needed to know just as soon as we identified him.'

'Identified him?'

Ridpath realised this was the question he was dreading the most but this woman deserved to know the truth, or as much as he could tell her.

'Tony killed himself by pouring petrol over his body and setting it alight.'

The woman's hand flew to cover her mouth and her head bowed.

'I'm sorry, the details are shocking,' Ridpath continued, 'but we felt you had to know the whole truth for your daughter's sake and in case you are visited by the press.'

She nodded once without saying a word.

'You understand what I've just told you?'

She nodded again. 'Tony took his own life.' Then she looked up and stared into Ridpath's eyes. 'He did it to save us.'

Ridpath frowned. 'What did you say?'

'Tony, he took his own life to save us.' Her eyes narrowed as if she realised she had said too much. 'Thank you for coming to see me. But if you don't mind, I need to cook Dorothy's dinner now.' She stood up.

Ridpath remained seated. 'Why did you use those words. "He did it to save us"?'

'I don't know,' she mumbled, 'they just came out. Now, if you have nothing else to tell me, I'd like you to leave so I can cook my daughter's dinner.'

'There is one thing I must ask, and please forgive me if this sounds a little strange. But did your ex-husband have any sadomasochistic tendencies?'

The woman looked surprised. 'What?'

Ridpath took a deep breath and asked again. 'Did Tony Abbott have any sadomasochistic tendencies. Did he like to hurt you or hurt himself?'

Charlotte Abbott visibly winced, pursing her lips together. 'I don't know what you are talking about, Inspector...?'

'Ridpath.'

'Tony had no sadomasochistic "tendencies" as you call them. He was a loving father to his daughter, and my ex-husband. Now, I have asked you once and I will say again, I would like you to leave.'

Ridpath stood up and glanced across at Megan, who took two steps towards them.

'You seem distraught, Mrs Abbott. Is there anything I can do to help? Would you like a Family Liaison Officer to stay with you?'

'I've told you once already, DI Ridpath, my name is Rowlandson, Charlotte Rowlandson. I don't have to remind you that Tony and I are divorced, but thank you for telling me about his… demise.' She used her hands to smooth down her skirt. 'Now, if you could both leave.'

'Are you sure, Ms Rowlandson? I could ask a family officer to stay with you.'

'For the last time, DI Ridpath,' she raised her voice, 'I don't want anybody to stay with me and I want you to leave.' She pointed towards the door.

Ridpath held his hands up. 'I'm sorry if I have offended you inadvertently, Ms Rowlandson.' He reached into his inside pocket and pulled out a card, offering it to her. 'If you need anything, anything at all, just call me at any time.'

The woman didn't take the card.

He reached over and placed it on the mantlepiece. 'I'll leave it here.'

'Please go. Both of you, please just go.'

Chapter THIRTY-SEVEN

Megan Muldowney fastened her seatbelt across her chest. 'That was weird.'

'Wasn't it? I've told a few wives their husbands had just died or killed themselves, but I've never had a reaction like that.'

Ridpath switched the engine on, more to get the heater in the car going than to actually drive anywhere. He wiped the windscreen with a tissue he found in his glovebox and switched the blowers to full to clear the last bits of condensation.

'It was almost like she knew he was going to do it and we merely confirmed the news for her.'

Ridpath glanced across at Megan. That had been quite an astute statement from a young detective fresh out of Edgehill.

'What did you make of her?'

'High maintenance. I don't think I could live in that house. So clean you could eat your dinner off the floor. Almost clinically clean. Why did she order you out of the house; you were only offering her help and the company of a FLO.'

'I don't know. It was like she didn't want me there.'

'The kid seemed well looked after though and polite enough.'

'Perhaps too polite. Megan, I want you to check out Mrs Abbott—'

'Ms Rowlandson.'

'Right. Check out the background, where she works, her employment record, all that sort of stuff.'

'What am I looking for?'

'I won't know until you find it.'

'That's helpful.'

'I'll ask about her when we meet Tony Abbott's colleagues.' Ridpath paused for a second, turning down the car's blower, the noise was distracting him. 'One other thing worries me.'

'What's that?'

'Something she said. "He did it to save us." It was almost like she let slip those words accidentally.'

'You can't still think there's something going on, Ridpath. It's the sort of thing somebody would say if they'd just heard that sort of news.'

'Would they? Didn't you notice it was after she said those words that she became flustered and ordered us to leave?'

'That was a bit weird. I'd want any help that was offered if I were in her place. Even if it was a police FLO. She definitely didn't like the questions about sadomasochism, did she? But I don't suppose anyone wants to suddenly find out their ex-husband was involved in S&M.'

'I shouldn't have asked that question, not at that time. Stupid of me. But her reaction to his death didn't feel kosher. Something is not quite right there. Why do we now have three people using nearly identical words in two separate incidents; one an apparent murder, the other an apparent suicide.'

'Apparent? You saw the video. Tony Abbott walked into a petrol station, paid for the petrol using a credit card and then set himself alight. If that's not suicide, I don't know what is.'

Ridpath put the car in gear. 'Let's take another look at the petrol station, a couple of things are bothering me.'

'Like?'

'I'll show you when we get there.'

Chapter THIRTY-EIGHT

'We can't go on. How do we stop this?' his wife asked.

Robert Wallace was sitting on the couch, an open laptop by his side, his head resting on his chest as if sleeping. Opposite him, his wife was pacing up and down the living room, smoking endless cigarettes. In front of the patio doors, a dog sat staring out over the garden.

'I don't know, I just don't know.'

The man lifted his head for a few seconds. His eyes were rimmed red, his face grey, tiredness seeping from every pore.

'He's going to kill us all if you don't do as you're told.'

The man slowly shook his head. 'I can't, I can't do it.'

The dog left the doors and walked over to the man, nudging his knee with his head.

'Benjy wants to go out,' she said.

'We can't take him for a walk, we can't go out. He told us we mustn't leave the house until I'm ready to do it. He might be watching.'

The dog began to whine.

She grabbed hold of its collar roughly and dragged the dog across the floor, opening the patio doors and slinging him out into the cold. The dog looked back at the woman for a second before scampering away to the bottom of the garden.

'There's no need to treat Benjy like that.'

'He was annoying me with his whining.'

Robert Wallace fell silent for a few seconds before asking, 'Where are the kids?'

'Upstairs on their iPads.'

'Have you checked on them?'

'I went up five minutes ago, you saw me. They're fine.'

Martha Wallace stubbed her cigarette out in the ashtray and immediately lit another, continuing her pacing up and down the room. 'What are we going to do?'

The man stared down at the ground. 'I don't know.'

She paused for a moment, standing in front of him, staring down with disdain. 'You're the big-shot property developer, you *should* know what to do.'

He launched himself from the couch and pushed her away. 'I don't know what to do, understand?'

'Don't you have any contacts in the police we can talk to?'

'You heard what he said: if we go to the police he will kill us like he killed the Ashtons.'

'The police can protect us.'

'The Ashtons went to the police and he killed them all. Do you want that to happen to us?'

She continued pacing up and down, up and down, a cloud of cigarette smoke over her head. 'Why did you do it?'

'I don't know. I'd been drinking over lunch and then had a few more at the club. I should have gone straight home but I didn't. When it happened I panicked.' He pointed to the new conservatory. 'You enjoy the fruits of my work every day, don't forget that. What's it going to be this year, the Caribbean or Thailand?'

His wife's face softened and she laid her head on his shoulder. 'It's going to be nowhere. Without you we have nothing. What are we going to do?'

He turned away from her. 'I don't know; I don't know anything any more.'

'Why don't we run away, go to Spain... or... or... Thailand, he'd never find us there.'

'What would we do with the kids? Leave them here?'

'Take them with us obviously, make it an adventure.'

The man shook his head. 'He'd find us, I *know* he'd find us.'

Her mobile phone rang. They both jumped at the noise.

'You'd better answer it, it might be him?'

'Why would he call me?'

'I don't know, just answer it.'

'Hello.' She listened as somebody spoke at the other end.

'This is her speaking.' She covered the mouthpieces of her phone and said, 'It's Robyn's school.'

She nodded her head a few times and mumbled a few uh-huhs and yesses before answering. 'She's still not feeling well, but hopefully she'll be better in a few days. Have we taken her to a doctor yet? Not yet, you know how difficult it is to get an appointment. But we'll take her tomorrow if she's still not well. No problem, thank you for your concern.'

She ended the call. 'Her school was asking after her, what are we going to tell them?'

'I don't know.'

'You don't seem to know anything any more.' She clenched her jaw. 'We have to go to the police: we can't go on like this.'

'Don't do that, let me talk to him one more time. Get him to change his mind, offer him money again. We could sell the house, give him everything we have.'

'You heard him, he's not interested in money. He won't stop until you do as he says.'

'I can't kill myself, just can't.'

She stared at him without pity. 'Tony did.'

Chapter THIRTY-NINE

They parked the car on the road next to the petrol station. The place was still surrounded by a cordon of police tape but there were no coppers present. Instead, a large handwritten sign stood guard at the entrance.

This Petrol Station is closed until further notice.

The sign was sodden from the rain and the letters were beginning to bleed. For a moment, Ridpath thought the sign was crying. Then, for the second time that day, he ducked under police tape.

The shop was closed and all the neon lights that usually illuminated petrol stations were switched off. Without the exuberance of electric blue, sparkling yellow and fluorescent green the place looked sad and isolated. The sort of place Edward Hopper would have depicted in his paintings.

Ridpath walked over to Pump 8. All that remained of Tony Abbott was a dark stain on the ground next to an even darker oil slick.

'What are we doing here, Ridpath?'

Megan Muldowney rushed to get under the canopy of the station, out of the rain. She shivered and turned up the collar of her coat.

'I just wanted to see the place in the full light of day.'
He examined the pump closely.

'And?'

'And I remember the witness saying Tony Abbott wrote something on the pump before he killed himself.'

His eyes scanned the top and sides, but the whole panel had been removed and all that remained was the inner workings of the pump itself.

'I remembered that too, so I asked the CSIs to look at it. They must have removed it to the lab.'

Ridpath eyed the female detective. 'That was a good move.'

'Thanks, but it seemed the obvious thing to do.'

'Who was the crime scene manager?'

'Terri.'

'Can you call her? Check out if they've had time to examine the panel yet. I'd love to know what he wrote.'

'Could be a suicide note.'

'Could be.'

Megan wrote a message to herself in her notebook. 'You said there were a couple of things that concerned you.'

Ridpath was now looking all around the station. 'I also wondered how Tony Abbott managed to get here.'

'The CCTV shows him coming from that direction.' Megan swivelled to point back down the road.

'The caretaker said he didn't have a car.'

'So?'

'Did he come here by bus?'

'I don't know.'

'Who takes a bus to a petrol station and then kills himself?'

'Somebody who was extremely unhappy?'

'But we passed four petrol stations on the way here. The A56 is one of the main routes out of Manchester, why not use one of those petrol stations?'

Megan shrugged her shoulders.

'Get on to the bus companies and check all the buses that travelled the route in the hour before eight p.m. on Monday. They all have CCTV of the passengers who board the bus and there may even be CCTV from the stop he used.'

'What if he didn't come by bus?'

'We're going to check that now.'

Taking one last look around the station, Ridpath marched off down the road, followed by Megan, hurrying to catch up.

'Where are we going, Ridpath?'

'To see if we can find his car.'

Megan stopped, seeing cars everywhere. On the A56, in the side roads, even parked in a car showroom.

'But how will we know which one is his, even if he did use one?'

Ridpath stopped too and walked back to her. 'We don't, but put yourself in his shoes. We know which direction he came from, right?'

'That way.' She pointed down the road.

'So, parking along the street here is impossible, therefore he must have put the car somewhere. Perhaps a supermarket, there's a Tesco and a Sainsbury's over there. Or he put it in…'

'The Stanley Square multi-storey. But we still don't know which car we are looking for.'

'That's why I'm just going to make a phone call to an ex-colleague.' He dialled a number. 'Hiya, Danny, Ridpath here, how's traffic treating you?'

Megan could only here one side of the conversation.

'That bad, huh. Your boss is an arsehole. What's his name?' A few nods of the head. 'Durrow? I'm meeting him in –' Ridpath checked his watch '– forty-five minutes. Anything I should know?'

Ridpath kept nodding his head. 'Really? Sounds like one of those bastards we keep promoting. Listen, Danny, I need a favour – what cars are the traffic investigators driving these days? Uh-huh, grey Peugeot 3008s, okay. Double aerials and lights? Great. One last thing, did you know an inspector called Tony Abbott? Uh-huh, uh-huh, good to know. Sorry, can't tell you now, but I promise I'll give you a heads-up after meeting your boss. See you Danny. What's that? Not if you see me first. Very funny. Ta, mate, you've been a great help.'

He turned back to Megan, but she spoke first. 'If he used a car, we're looking for a grey Peugeot 3008, with two aerials and police lights on the windscreens and behind the grill.'

'You've got good ears.'

'What did he say about Tony Abbott?'

'A good man and a great traffic investigator apparently, one of the best. A couple of months ago, he seemed to lose the plot, became a bit of a loner.'

'Same time he moved into the flat.'

'Yeah, another coincidence…'

'And you don't believe in coincidences.'

'Right first time, Tonto.'

'Come on, let's check out the car parks.'

After twenty minutes of searching, they found the car they were looking for on the top floor of the Stanley Square multi-storey, parked in a corner all on its own. It matched the description given by Ridpath's colleague to a tee: two aerials, eight lights attached to the front and rear windows, more lights behind the grill. The only addition not mentioned was a white parking notice stuck under the front driver's-side windscreen wiper.

Ridpath wrote down the registration number.

'How can we be sure this is the car Tony Abbott used?'

'We can't. Yet. But it's definitely an unmarked police car and looking at the parking notice, it's been here for a couple of days at least. My bet's that Superintendent Durrow is missing one of his motors. Now we have the registration, easy to check with the motor pool at Eccles nick.'

Megan glanced at her watch. 'Speaking of Durrow, I reckon we need to drive over to Eccles right now.'

'Right, His Highness said we shouldn't be late. Let's get a move on.'

'What are we going to do about the car?'

'Nothing right now. We'll ask the motor pool if Tony Abbott took it out over the weekend. If it is his, we need a forensic team down here to check it out. Plus, you need to go through all the car park CCTV footage from the day of the incident.'

'Why are we doing so much work on an open-and-shut case of suicide, Ridpath?'

Ridpath sighed. 'Because I don't think it's so open nor is it shut. Come on, we have a superintendent with delusions of grandeur to visit.'

Chapter FORTY

Back at Police HQ, most of the MIT detectives were sitting in the Operation Chancellor incident room, waiting for the meeting to start. There was a sense of expectation as Steve Carruthers stood up.

'Right, as you may or may not know, we discovered the house which our perp probably used before and after he committed the crimes last Wednesday. The CSIs are in the building as we speak but their initial word is that it's as clean as a whistle, forensically speaking. Even the white van parked at the front has no fingerprints or DNA so far, but we'll keep looking on the off-chance some will be found. It looks like our perp is forensically aware.'

'That was clear from the lack of trace elements in the Ashton house, boss.'

'Aye Dennis, but we can always hope. The bastard must make a mistake sometime. What about you, Chrissy? Discovered anything?'

'Like I said before, Ronnie Rellik has been on the electoral register for the last six months but not before that. I've gone back through it until 2010 and nobody with that name was registered to vote before. I've been on to the Land Registry to find out who actually owns the house, but they are yet to get back to me. A bit slow, that mob...'

'Do you want me to give them a kick up the arse, Chrissy?'

'Maybe you'll have to if they don't get back to me soon.'

'Any time you want, I'll be happy to do it. Anything else?'

'I put the man's name through HOLMES and all the police databases. Nothing has come back yet. I could try the Passport Office next to see if he's ever travelled abroad, as the name isn't common, but they're even slower than the Land Registry.'

'What about Interpol and their databases?' said Dennis Leahey. 'The name could be Polish or East European.'

'Since we left the EU, we don't have automatic access to either ECRIS or SIS II…'

'What the hell are they?' asked Alan Butcher.

Chrissy closed her eyes and sighed. 'ECRIS is the European Criminal Records Information System and SIS II is the Schengen Information System. The former provides data on criminals in the EU while the latter shares data on criminals moving across its borders. Both operate in real-time but are restricted to EU member states. When the UK left the EU on January 31, 2020, access to that data was lost. The plan currently under development is to build a new data-sharing architecture encompassing the UK, the EU and other "international partners", but it seems like it's a long way off.'

'Why?'

'The crackdowns on the right to protest and the right to seek asylum by the last government offended some of the EU member states, so they're dragging their heels.'

'And we can't get information?'

'We can, it just takes longer. We have to go through the liaison committee at Europol.'

'How long will that take?' asked Steve Carruthers.

Chrissy shrugged her shoulders. 'How long is a piece of string? It could take three months or more.'

'Keep going, anyway, Chrissy.'

'Will do, boss.'

'How about you, Jasper? How did you go tracking the van through ANPR on Wednesday?'

'Without Helen, it wasn't easy. I tracked it to Hyde but then lost it in a dead area for ANPR. They haven't fixed the cameras since we had the power surge last week. Sorry boss...'

'Could you do it the other way?' suggested Helen Shipton. 'Track it from the area around Keppel Road where we know it was parked and see what route it followed?'

'Could do, wish I'd have thought of that.'

'You'd better assist Jasper with the ANPR search,' said Carruthers.

Helen Shipton's face looked like it had just been dragged through a hedge of poison ivy backwards.

'Will do,' she said without any enthusiasm. Jasper Early on the other hand, had a smile as big as the *Titanic* plastered across his face.

'Finally,' said Carruthers, 'how was the house-to-house in Keppel Road?'

Dennis Leahey opened his file. 'We didn't find out a lot. Ronnie Rellik wasn't even known by most of the neighbours and even fewer remembered seeing him or talking to him. Most said he was a quiet man, tall though, above average height apparently. They hardly ever saw him. One neighbour reported him putting out his bin for the council a week ago but that was the last sighting.'

'Any description?'

'A tall man wearing a black hoodie, is all I got from the woman. She couldn't give me anything else.'

'At least it tallies with the description from the ex-copper in Saddleworth,' said Alan.

'Aye, and roughly 250,000 people in Manchester would fit that description.'

'How about the van?'

'She said she only noticed it about six months ago. It hardly ever moved from the driveway and was always parked there. She thought somebody may have dumped it.'

'Anything on the reg?'

Dennis checked his notes. 'It was bought from a dealer in Ashton-on-Mersey six months ago. The buyer, a Ronnie Rellik, paid 4,000 pounds in cash. And before you ask, boss, there was no CCTV of the transaction.'

'Shit. Anybody got anything?'

The room remained silent.

'So, let me get this right. We have a possible suspect but we don't know anything about him other than he seems to have no past. We have a house where he lived where nobody even knows what he looks like. We have a van which he purchased but nobody remembers seeing it on the road. And most importantly, we have four members of a family who were murdered in cold blood but we have no idea by who or why.' His eyes scanned the room. 'Have I described the present situation correctly?'

Again, silence in the room, which was broken by Carruthers slamming his fist onto the table.

'Right, I have to make a report now to Claire Trent and she, quite rightly, is going to hand me a pair of bollocks on a silver platter. Unfortunately, both those bollocks will be mine. So when I come back here in an hour's time. I want ideas and a plan for moving this investigation forward.'

He put his index finger up in the air and paused, scanning the room once more.

'A word of warning. Waiting for our perp to kill again or make an error is not an option, understand?'

Chapter FORTY-ONE

Superintendent Matt Durrow's office in Eccles Police Station was bigger than most football pitches.

At one end, a couch and three comfortable armchairs surrounded a wooden coffee table laden with books, most of which featured images of cars. To one side, a bank of windows looked out over a vast car park filled with unmarked, undercover and marked police cars, vans and tactical vehicles. At the other end, Matt Durrow sat in his shirtsleeves behind an enormous desk, piled high with papers, documents and files.

When Ridpath and Megan Muldowney entered the room, the superintendent didn't get up to greet them. Instead, he remained behind his desk, staring into a large file filled with numbers.

The station itself was one of those places that looked more like a warehouse or an aircraft hangar than a police station. There was no public reception area or friendly sergeant ready to answer inquiries. Instead, Ridpath had picked up a phone outside the main door and it had been answered after ten rings by a disembodied voice at the other end of the line.

'DI Ridpath and DC Muldowney to see Superintendent Durrow.'

The only response was a loud click from the door. Megan pulled it open and they went in. A set of stairs led upstairs to another door where a female civilian officer was waiting.

'DI Ridpath? The super will see you now but he asked me to tell you he has only fifteen minutes before he needs to jump on a call with the chief.'

She led them down a long corridor to a large pair of double doors with a single boilerplate on the outside.

She knocked gently, waited for an answer from inside and went in.

'DI Ridpath and DC Muldowney, sir.'

Durrow didn't look up.

'You can sit at the desk,' said the civilian, 'but remember you only have fifteen minutes.'

Ridpath thought there would be less ceremony meeting royalty. He crossed the acres of carpet to the desk and pulled out a chair. Seconds later he was joined by Megan.

Durrow deigned to look up from his file, staring across the table at the two detectives as he closed it, pulling another one from a pile in front of him.

'Good afternoon, sir, we're here to—'

Durrow held up his hand to stop Ridpath speaking. 'I rang your unit, DI Ridpath, and spoke to your direct supervisor, a DCI Carruthers, a man with a strong Glaswegian accent.'

Durrow sniffed twice. His own accent wasn't Scottish nor was it from Manchester. Ridpath guessed he was from one of the Home Counties.

'He tells me you work for both the coroner and MIT but at the moment you're seconded to Sale Police Station. How is Ron?'

'Inspector Pleasance? He's fine, sir. I'm here today—'

'I was on an anti-terrorism course with him last year down in Camberley. A good man; bright, well spoken, he'll go far.'

Ridpath could hear the implied criticism of Steve Carruthers.

'Now, I haven't much time – I have a call with the chief at two forty-five. This is about Tony Abbott isn't it?' If the man had stopped talking for a second, Ridpath would have explained everything. 'I'm afraid I didn't know Inspector Abbott that well, I've only been in this post for six months. Before that I was with traffic in Surrey.'

Another import, thought Ridpath. GMP was filling up with them quicker than they could retire the existing officers.

'I'm afraid to say that Inspector Abbott killed himself on Monday night. He walked into a petrol station, poured petrol over his body and set himself alight.'

The superintendent's face changed, turning almost green. 'What an awful way to die.'

'You said he was on administrative leave when I spoke to you earlier. Was there any reason why he was given that leave?'

'I don't know. You'll have to check with his direct supervisor, Chief Inspector Howarth.'

'You don't know, sir?'

'I can't be expected to know the ins and outs of every officer under my command.'

'Of course not, sir. But I presume an application for administrative leave may have been brought to your attention.'

'It wasn't.' Durrow's eyes narrowed. 'Why is MIT investigating this case?'

'My boss asked me to look into it and one other at Sale Police Station. They are a little short-staffed at the moment.' A long pause. 'And of course, GMP needs to know if there were any exigent circumstances that may impact the force's reputation behind Inspector Abbott's decision to take his own life.'

'Exigent circumstances?' The man seemed almost as surprised as Ridpath was when he used the words. Eve had taught him the meaning last weekend.

'Yes, sir. Bullying, racism, unfair treatment at work. That sort of thing.'

'I can assure you there is nothing like that in my unit.'

'That's good to know, sir.' With that, Ridpath stood up. 'I know you are a busy man, so I won't bother you any longer. I presume I have your permission to talk to Inspector Abbott's direct supervisor and his colleagues? To ask them about Tony Abbott and his time in the unit?'

Durrow stood up too. 'Of course, I'll instruct HR to let you see his files. I'm sure you'll let me see your report when you are finished.'

'Above my pay grade, sir. That will be Detective Chief Superintendent Trent's and DCI Carruthers' decision.'

Ridpath turned to go and then turned back, taking out his notebook. 'By the way, are you missing a car, sir? YR22 XFG?'

Durrow looked down at his desk and touched a paper lying there. 'I received a report from the head of operations an hour ago. Apparently, it hasn't been seen since Saturday and the tracker on it was disabled.'

'I'm happy to tell you we've found it, sir. Just as soon as forensics have finished, we'll return it to you. I presume it was checked out by Inspector Abbott?'

Durrow looked at the paper. 'Last Saturday at eleven a.m.'

'I'll let your head of operations know where it is. Thank you for your time. Come on Megan, we have work to do.'

They left Superintendent Durrow sitting behind his desk, staring into mid-air.

He looked lost.

Chapter FORTY-TWO

Detective Constable Andy Fletcher arrived back at Sale nick just before four o'clock. After visiting the register office, he had enjoyed a long, leisurely lunch, visited Anita Forsyth's school and then decided to go back to Handley Road to finish the house to house.

The prospect of an angry Ridpath had finally convinced him that he was better off doing the work than pretending he had done it.

He would now be able to report that it was a waste of time. None of the people who answered the door knew Jane Forsyth. The only thing they were vaguely aware of was the police tape and the fact that somebody had been murdered on their street. It made them vicarious celebrities. Quite a few had already been interviewed by the papers and the local evening news programme. Nobody had anything of substance to say but that didn't stop them. Five minutes in front of the cameras was all they were looking for.

Fletcher grabbed a cup of lukewarm water that was laughingly referred to as tea in Sale station and settled down in front of the computer. His last remaining task before the meeting at six p.m. was to see if there was any information about Jane Forsyth online. This was the sort of work he enjoyed, in a warm office in front of a computer, searching for information. Not tramping the streets, asking stupid questions and receiving even more stupid answers.

He went on to Facebook and checked all the accounts with her name. Over one hundred and fifty, but none resembled her. With a name like Forsyth, most of the women seemed to be based in Scotland. Instagram and X provided no help either – too many similar names. Who'd have thought there were so many Jane Forsyths in the world?

Next, he tried the local electoral register. This time he had better luck. Her name came up on it for the last three years, which indicated she had lived at number 26 for at least that long. No other name was listed for the address though. It seemed that Jane Forsyth was as single as her neighbour had said.

So then who was the father of her child?

Fletcher checked his notes from the register office. That had been a dead end with nobody listed in the box marked father. Perhaps the father was named in the medical records of the hospital? It was a long shot, but he could try to get a court order under the Police and Criminal Evidence Act of 1984. That was the procedure he had been taught at Edgehill.

He made a note to ask Ridpath about it.

Finally, he decided to find out more about where Jane Forsyth was born. He typed in her name and birth year into the FreeBMD website and waited for a response.

Nothing. Zero matches.

Either she had given the wrong birth year or she was born in Scotland or Northern Ireland. Of course, their records were held in different databases. Then it occurred to him, she might not have been born in the UK at all.

Shit.

A shadow loomed over him.

He turned his head. Inspector Ron Pleasance was staring at his computer.

'What are you doing, Andy?'

'Ridpath asked me to find out more about Jane Forsyth. He has questions about her background and wants to know more.'

'Does he? And why is that?'

'I dunno, sir. It's like I told you, he thinks there are "anomalies" in our case.'

'He's got you spinning wheels, hasn't he, Andy? Ridpath hasn't changed in all the years I've known him.'

'What do you want me to do, sir?'

'Just carry on for the moment. Let me sort him out, you just do what you're told.' A long pause. 'But keep me informed, understand? I don't want Ridpath screwing this up.'

'Right, sir. Of course, sir.'

'Good man.' Inspector Pleasance patted him on the shoulder.

'I won't be able to make squash this evening, sir. Ridpath has called a briefing at six.'

'Has he? Well, never mind, there will be other games of squash once Ridpath has been put back in his box at MIT. It won't be long, don't worry.'

After Pleasance had returned to his office, Andy Fletcher proceeded to arrange his notes and write up the one useful interview with Pam Docherty. Before the meeting, he would print out the pictures of Tony Abbott and the post-mortem shot of Jane Forsyth and place them on separate boards on the wall of the room.

This was the work he enjoyed doing…

Chapter FORTY-THREE

Eve arrived home to an empty to house. She was used to it now, but it still made her heart jump every time she opened the door. She half-expected her mother to come out from the living room and give her a big hug.

But she never did.

Instead, Eve dropped her school bag next to the coat stand in the hall. She walked through to the kitchen and went to the fridge to get herself a glass of milk. She fancied the comfort of some Nutella on toast so she popped the bread into the toaster and searched for the spread in the cupboard.

Strange, she was sure there had been some there. She must have eaten it all.

For a second she had the weird feeling that somebody was watching her. She went to the window and stared out at the houses opposite and down the street.

Nobody was there.

'Just because you're paranoid, doesn't mean they're not out to get you,' she said out loud.

She checked the back and front doors were locked and glanced up the stairs. Had she just heard a noise?

She stood still listening for any movement or sound of breathing.

Nothing.

Then a loud pop from the kitchen. She jumped and her heart skipped a beat. Picking up an umbrella to hold as a club she tiptoed towards the kitchen, listening for any sound.

Slowly, she pushed open the door, raising the umbrella over her head ready to strike down.

The kitchen was empty. The toast standing tall from the toaster, waves of heat rising from the brown bread.

She relaxed, lowering the umbrella to her side. She really would have to get her act together. She was so jumpy and nervous all the time.

'I didn't mean to startle you.'

A voice from behind her.

Not her dad's voice.

Not her mum's voice.

Billy Diamond's voice.

She turned around, raising the umbrella ready to strike. He was standing there, a smile on his face, his hands raised in surrender.

'What are you doing here? Get out! Get out now!'

'I just came to say sorry.'

'Sorry? You broke into my house, scared the living shit out of me, just to say sorry? Get out. My dad will be home soon.'

He kept his hands held up. 'I said I just want to say I'm sorry. I was hoping you could find it in your heart to forgive me.'

'Forgive you? You tried to kill me. Get out, get out now.'

'I'll leave, but please don't tell your dad. If you do they'll put me straight back inside. It's not good in there, not safe.'

'Just get out.'

He put his head down. 'I'm sorry for what happened. I was groomed by Harold Lardner. He made me do it. Please forgive me.'

'He made you attack me?' she shouted. 'You did that, you made my life hell.'

'I'm sorry, I'll go now. Just wanted to say sorry to you myself.'

'Get out.'

He turned to go back into the living room.

'Not that way. Out through the front door so I can see you.'

He nodded. 'I'm sorry.' He repeated, opening the front door. 'You should get your dad to fix the rear window, it's too easy for somebody to break in.'

'Just GO!'

'Please don't tell your father I've been here. If you do, I might just have to return, they'll put me back inside.'

He smiled and was gone.

She rushed to slam the door behind him, attaching the security chain with fumbling hands. Why wouldn't the bloody thing work?

Finally. She hooked it over and breathed out.

Leaning back on the door, she slid to the ground and her body began to tremble uncontrollably.

Why did it always have to happen to her?

Chapter FORTY-FOUR

Ridpath was rushing back through the busy traffic along the M60 to attend the briefing at six. He'd sent Megan off to check on Tony Abbott's car and the forensic teams at the man's house while he had interviewed the colleagues at the Road Policing Unit.

Their opinions all seemed to agree.

'Tony was a great guy, quiet, sober, just did his job well.'

'He didn't say much but he was a nice guy, always willing to help.'

'One of the good guys. He took over one of my shifts when my mum died and never asked for anything in return.'

They had all been shocked when told he had killed himself. The consensus being that it was totally out of character. The reaction was best summed up by another accident investigator, David Doyle. 'I couldn't imagine somebody less likely to kill themselves. He just seemed to be happy most of the time and he loved his job, why would he kill himself?'

The information from his colleagues was confirmed by Tony Abbott's direct supervisor, Chief Inspector Howarth. 'A lovely man, brilliant at his job, worked for me for seven years. Detailed, forensic and good with witnesses. He never missed a trick did Tony. I'll miss him.'

'Did you know his wife, Charlotte?'

'I met her a couple of times, a teacher I think. They were never the most sociable people. Her family were quite well off. Tony came from the area around Old Trafford. A bit of a marriage across the tracks. They bought their house with money from an inheritance on her side.'

'When was that?'

'Five years ago, I think. They were renting before that. Tony was happy they finally owned their own place.'

'Do you know why they divorced?'

'Not really, I don't think she was the easiest person to live with. He seemed happier after the divorce, told me he was glad it was all over.'

'No women after that?'

'A few dates I think, but he was in no hurry. Once bitten, twice shy if you know what I mean.'

'So the divorce wasn't the trigger for his suicide.'

The man shook his head. 'I don't think so. Tony seemed happier after the divorce than when he was married. They both seemed to get on better when they weren't living together and he had his daughter every weekend, which made him happy.'

'Why did he ask for administrative leave?'

'The official reason was that he was moving house...'

'But...?'

'Unofficially, he told me he had a few things to sort out. A month ago his mood changed. He seemed preoccupied, worried about something. When I asked him, he said something from his past had come up, told me he needed to handle it.'

'He didn't give you any details.'

'If I'm honest, I didn't ask. Tony was one of my best investigators, if he told me he needed a week off, I'd give it to him, no questions asked.' The inspector shook his head. 'But to kill himself like that… I can't imagine Tony doing it. Why kill himself at a petrol station of all places?'

The last was the question that Ridpath was finding most difficult to answer.

After parking at the back of the nick, he found Megan Muldowney and Andy Fletcher sitting in the briefing room when he arrived back at 5.50 p.m. Both were drinking from large mugs of warm tea.

The walls of the room had been plastered with enlarged photos of Tony Abbott and Jane Forsyth alongside the information that Andy Fletcher had collected on the latter.

'Right, let's get started.'

Fletcher had put two clean white boards at the front of the room, ready for questions or observations from the team on either case. One was marked Anita Forsyth and the other Tony Abbott.

'Let's start with you, Andy: take us through what you found.'

'Not a lot. The mother, Jane Forsyth, doesn't seem to have any online presence at all, as far as I can see. No Facebook, Instagram or X accounts. I can't even find out where she was born as she doesn't come up in any search in England. I'll widen it later to Scotland and Northern Ireland but as of now, I don't know. As for the school, they said Anita was a bright girl, especially good at maths. According to them, she had a chance to get good marks at her GCSEs, got on well with her school friends and the teachers. They're all in shock at the news.'

'You didn't tell them why we were investigating?'

'No, but they knew anyway. I guess everybody knows. The *Evening News* was sniffing around the area and Handley Street.'

'Did the neighbours tell you anything?'

He shook his head. 'She seems to have been a bit of a loner. The only neighbour who knew her at all was a Ms Docherty from number 18. She went to yoga classes with her and their kids were the same age. She says she noticed a change of mood from her about a month ago. Hasn't talked with her since then.'

'Strange, that's what one of his colleagues said about Tony Abbott,' said Ridpath, 'a change of mood a month ago.'

'You're still not trying to link a suicide with our murder, are you?'

'Until somebody explains to me why two people used exactly the same phrase, then I'm going to be looking at both incidents and trying to understand them.'

'There doesn't seem to be much of a link. It's not like they knew each other.'

'You mean, "I'm doing it to save her" is just a coincidence?' Ridpath glanced across at Megan Muldowney who was writing in her notebook. 'For a copper, there is no such thing as a coincidence.'

He wrote four big question marks beside Anita Forsyth's name. 'Did you find out who her father was?'

'No. According to the register office, no name was listed.'

Ridpath sniffed twice. 'So you haven't found out much at all.'

'We could apply for a court order for her medical records.'

'I've a better idea, let's talk to the girl herself. Where is she being held?'

'She's in Ford Avenue Children's Home. But the social workers won't let me anywhere near her.'

'Are you surprised after interviewing her in a police station?'

'For god's sake, Ridpath, she strangled her mother, I had to interview her.'

'So you say…'

'It's what the pathologist and the forensics say.'

'Megan, set up a meeting tomorrow and make sure her social worker is present. We don't want any more allegations of police forcing confessions. Ask them to call me if there is a problem.'

Fletcher didn't answer, his mouth opening and closing like a beached fish. Again.

A knock came on the door. The same PC as before popped her head around the door.

'Hiya, Inspector Ridpath, we've had a call from a Mrs Challinor. She'd like you to call her back…' She stopped speaking and stared at one of the photos on the wall. 'Why have you got a picture of Tony Abbott up there,' her gaze shifted to the other photo, 'and Jane Forsyth, what's she doing there?'

'You know them?' asked Ridpath.

'Worked with them in road policing years ago.'

Chapter FORTY-FIVE

'How long do you have left?'

'Until tomorrow afternoon.'

'What are we going to do?'

'You keep asking me. I don't know.' The man buried his head in his hands. 'I wish I never got involved in it.'

'But you did.'

'Only because you told me to. You wanted this house, you wanted the money, you wanted the holidays, you wanted the golf club. We were happy where we were.'

She came over to sit beside him. 'Like I keep saying, we have to go to the police, it's our only option. They can protect us.'

He moved away from her. 'No. Never. The Ashtons went to the police and look what happened to them. He would kill Robyn and James. The police can't protect us forever.'

'Then offer him money, everything we have.'

'I told you, I even offered him the house. He's not interested.'

The woman's eyes narrowed. 'What if we tricked him? He said he'll give you the final instructions just before you do it. What if you tell the police and they catch him while he's with you? He can't kill us if he's in jail, can he?'

The man's head came up and his eyes brightened. 'It might work. I could ring the police and they could watch while we met. All they'd have to do is follow me to the location and then they could grab him.'

'What happens if they ask you why he's threatening you?'

'I'll just tell them he's an ex-client and we're having a business dispute.'

'You'll need proof. I thought Signal's messages disappear?'

'They do, but not if I screenshot them.'

Their daughter appeared at the door. 'What were you talking about? And why are you crying, Daddy?'

The woman got up and picked up her daughter. 'Nothing, sweetie, Mummy and Daddy are just chatting.'

'When can we go back to school? We're not sick or anything and I want to play with my friends. James is missing his football.'

'Soon, you can go back soon, Robyn. But there's a Covid outbreak at your school, so you can't go for a couple of days,' Martha lied shamelessly.

'Do we have to do homeschooling again, Mummy?'

'I don't think so, sweetie, not this time.'

'I hated home schooling. Daddy is the worst teacher.'

'Now go back upstairs and play with your Xbox, Mummy and Daddy have to talk.'

'But I don't want to play with my Xbox, it's boring. I want to go to school.'

'Come on, I'll go and play with you. See if you can beat me on Roblox.' She turned back to her husband. 'Perhaps you could chat with him now and save the messages. It can't hurt.'

He nodded once and picked up his laptop, logging on to the special account he had given them on Signal.

PropMan76: Are you there?

The answer was immediate.

> **Rellik:** Did you understand the instructions? You have less than twenty-four hours left.
> **PropMan76:** I need to talk to you in person. It's the least you can let me do.
> **Rellik:** Why? You have your instructions. Just follow them.
> **PropMan76:** But I need to talk to you.
> **Rellik:** It's too late. Just follow the orders.

This wasn't working. He paused for a moment his fingers hovering over the keyboard, he had to try another angle.

> **PropMan76:** I don't understand the instructions.
> **Rellik:** What don't you understand? They are very simple. Just follow them exactly.
> **PropMan76:** If I don't kill myself, you are threatening to kill all my family including my children, correct?
> **Rellik:** I have told you many times, there will be consequences for not obeying my orders. The death of your family is one of those consequences.
> **PropMan76:** So you will murder them in cold blood, just like you murdered the Ashtons in Saddleworth?

He waited, unable to breathe. This was the key line. If he said yes, he would be admitting to the murder of four people. The police couldn't ignore such evidence: they'd have to protect him and his family.

> **Rellik:** As I said, there will be consequences if you do not follow my instructions.
> **PropMan76:** The consequences are if I don't kill myself, my family will die?

A long pause.

> **Rellik:** Correct.

There he had him. He quickly screenshotted their conversation before it was deleted from Signal.

> **Rellik:** Go out to your garden and look behind the shed.
> **PropMan76:** Why?
> **Rellik:** I know you are considering going to the police. Do not even think about it.
> **Rellik:** It's time to show you how serious I am.
> **Rellik:** Go to your garden and look behind the shed.

How did he know what he was planning?

Robert Wallace looked over his shoulder to see if anybody was watching. But that was illogical, how could anybody see what was happening inside their house?

> **Rellik:** Look behind your shed. NOW.

Robert Wallace stood up, went out the back door and ran across the lawn, a large square of grass that took a fortune to upkeep but worth every penny according to his wife. He reached the orange shed where the gardener kept his tools, and slowly edged around the side to the back.

He turned the corner and let out a scream, which he quickly stifled with his fist.

He closed his eyes. How could this be happening to him? He'd worked all his life, cut a few corners it was true, but created homes for people. HMOs were useful for those who couldn't afford anything better. So what if they had mould in them? They lived in Manchester, for

God's sake, one of the wettest places on earth. Of course, there was going to be mould.

He opened his eyes again.

Their dog, Benjy, was hanging from the apex of the shed, a rope wrapped around his neck and his tongue hanging to one side.

He walked slowly back into the house and straight into the living room. There were three messages on the laptop.

> **Rellik:** Do not go to the police.
> **Rellik:** Obey my instructions.
> **Rellik:** You have just sixteen hours left to comply.

Chapter FORTY-SIX

'Say that again, Melissa.'

'I worked with them in road policing years ago.'

Megan pointed at the two pictures. 'What? They knew each other?'

'More than that, actually. Jane was Tony Abbott's civilian researcher then. They worked cases together closely. When there was a serious accident, she used to do all the documentation checks: insurance, registration, driving licence, warrants, that sort of stuff, while Tony was out in the field. They would write up the case together; thick as two thieves, if you'll pardon the expression.'

'You said "used to do". When did they stop working together?'

'About five years ago, just as I was transferring out of roads and back into division. One day she just decided she didn't want to work any more and packed it in. Just a couple of weeks' notice, I think. I heard she sold up where she was living in Old Trafford and bought a new house in Sale. Don't know what she did after the police, though.'

Andy Fletcher interrupted. 'I couldn't find out what she was doing. One of the neighbours said she spent a lot of time on the computer, but nobody else knew anything.'

Ridpath ignored him. 'Was there any bad feeling between Tony Abbott and Jane Forsyth?'

'Not that I remember. He was very happy for her, came to her leaving do and everything.'

'Were they having an affair or anything like that?' asked Megan.

'I don't think so. Jane said she was gay, wasn't interested in men.'

Andy Fletcher interrupted again. 'But she had a child, a daughter.'

Melissa Danvers shrugged her shoulders. 'Mistakes happen, perhaps she was in a relationship with the father back then, but when I knew her, she definitely had girl-friends.'

'Do you know who the father was?'

'She never mentioned him to me. I don't think it was important to her. All she cared about was her daughter.'

Ridpath nibbled the skin at the top of his thumb. 'You said she was living in Old Trafford and then moved to Sale five years ago: how could she afford that?'

'I don't know. She wasn't much of a spender, was Jane Forsyth. Even brought her own sandwiches to work.' She jerked her head towards the door. 'I'll have to go back out front otherwise His Lordship is going to have kittens.'

'Anything else you can tell us, Melissa?'

'Not a lot. Like I said, I never really knew Jane. She was very much a loner, kept herself to herself. The person she was closest to was Tony.' She glanced at the photos on the wall again. 'What's all this about? Why are you investigating Tony and Jane?'

'Sorry Melissa, we can't tell you at the moment,' said Ridpath, 'but as soon as we have more information, you'll be the first to know. Thanks, Melissa.'

She looked at the pictures again, nodded once and left the room, leaving behind her a stunned silence. It was Ridpath who broke it.

'Now we have more than just words, we have a concrete connection between these two people.'

'It could be a coincidence, Ridpath,' said Andy Fletcher.

'A coincidence that two people die within three days, and they say exactly the same things as they do it? The two deaths have to be connected.'

'You think it was a suicide pact?' asked Megan. 'They decided to end it all together.'

'But they didn't end it together, did they? One was apparently killed by her daughter and the other set himself alight in a petrol station. If it was a suicide pact, they would surely have done it at the same time in the same place.' He shook his head. 'And why was Tony's flat wrecked as if somebody had been searching for something? And why, if Jane Forsyth was working with computers, did we find no laptops or mobile phones in her home? It doesn't make sense, none of it makes sense.'

Ridpath glanced across at the clock on the wall.

'Shit, is that the time? I need to make a phone call. Megan, can you check with HR and get Jane Forsyth's work details? I want to know when she started working and why she left five years ago. They will have performed an exit interview with her.'

'On it, Ridpath.'

'Andy, I want you to ring Chief Inspector Howarth, Tony Abbott's boss. Ask him about Jane Forsyth and find out exactly which cases they worked on together. Get the files for all the cases if you can.'

'Okay, will do.'

'One more thing, can you see if Sale has a local BDSM community?'

'A what?'

'BDSM. Bondage and discipline, dominance and submission, and sadomasochism,' answered Megan without looking up.

'Why do you want to know about those sorts of pervs?'

Ridpath sighed. 'Because Tony Abbott was wearing a row of fish hooks around his thigh. When you find the BDSM group, show them a picture of Tony Abbott and see if they know him.'

'Can't Megan do it, she seems to know all about it.'

'No, I want you to follow up.'

'What are you going to do?'

'I need to make a couple of phone calls.'

Andy Fletcher sat in his chair not moving.

'What are you waiting for? Get a bloody move on.'

Chapter FORTY-SEVEN

Ridpath stepped out into the corridor, slamming the door behind him and pulling out his mobile phone. It rang ten times before it was answered. 'Hi Eve, just thought I'd check in with you. How's things?'

'Okay…'

'Listen, I'm going to be working late tonight, for at least another couple of hours. Are you going to be okay on your own?'

'When are you coming home, Dad?'

'Soon, a couple of hours at the most. You sure you're going to be okay?'

'I suppose so.'

'Are you sure? You don't sound okay.'

'I'm fine, Dad, nothing to worry about.'

'Did you eat yet?'

'Not yet, but I'll warm up the pizza from yesterday,' Eve lied.

'You want me to bring something back for you? Fresh pizza, a McDonald's, anything you want?'

'No, just come home soon.'

'I will. You sure you're all right? Your voice sounds a little down.'

'Just tired, Dad. Come home soon.'

'Will do.'

'Have you called Mrs Challinor yet?'

Shit, Ridpath said to himself. 'Just about to call her as soon as I finish this chat. You still want to meet her on Saturday?'

'Yes, Dad. Come home soon.'

The call ended. Ridpath stared at his phone for a long time. Was something wrong? Her voice sounded subdued, almost resigned, without any life or energy. He'd finish this as quickly as he could and head off home, have a chat with her and find out what was wrong. Something must have happened at school.

He was about to return to the meeting room when he remembered he had one more phone call to make.

'Mrs Challinor.'

'Ridpath, I was hoping you'd call. How's the investigation into Jane Forsyth's death?'

'Not good, I'm afraid. Too many errors. We're interviewing the daughter, Anita, tomorrow.'

'Careful, Ridpath. Interviewing a fourteen-year-old girl after the death of her mother isn't going to be easy. If I were you, I'd postpone for at least a couple of days. Give her time to get over what happened.'

'I can't. The inspector here is pushing for an arrest with the case going to the CPS.'

'Idiot.'

'I couldn't agree more. There's something else, too…'

'What?'

'We've just found links from that case to the man who killed himself at the petrol station on Monday evening.'

'Really? Why would the death of Jane Forsyth and that man be linked?'

'They worked together five years ago, Coroner.'

'Might be nothing, just a coincidence. But you don't believe in coincidences, do you, Ridpath? Well, keep me informed of how you are proceeding and be careful with that interview.'

'Will do. There's one more thing. Eve would love to spend time with you at the weekend if that's possible. I think she needs to talk to somebody who's not her dad or her therapist.'

'No worries, I'd love to have her out to the cottage. Sarah would love to see her, too. Why don't you come as well?'

'I think Eve wants to be away from me for a while.'

A long sigh. 'Ridpath, what your daughter needs is more time with you, not less. You come along as well. Sarah and you can go for a walk while I chat with Eve. That's an order, Ridpath. I'll cook lunch. Agreed?'

'Agreed, Mrs Challinor. How can I say no?'

'You can't. See you on Saturday. In the meantime, keep me informed of developments in the Forsyth case. No surprises, understand?'

'Understood.'

Ridpath ended the call. Should he be spending more time with Eve? Perhaps Mrs Challinor was right. After this case, he'd arrange holidays for them during the Christmas break. Just the two of them, nobody else, father and daughter time.

He looked through the glass of the meeting room. Inside he could see Megan and Andy pasting something on the wall. He hoped it was good news for a change.

Chapter FORTY-EIGHT

He lay on the old couch, staring at the ceiling above his head. He was feeling tired, but exhilarated. Killing the dog had always been part of the plan. Sometimes people needed a little encouragement.

He thought about having a short nap but decided against it. Too many thoughts, too many images were running through his mind. One memory above all forcing itself into his consciousness like a twenty-stone prop forward: his parents packing for the short trip away in Scotland.

It was a week he and his brother always looked forward to. The cottage, perched next to Loch Lomond, with windy views across the choppy water. Walking across the moors, the heather scratching his legs. Treks through the forests, crunching the pinecones between his feet, his mother encouraging him not to dawdle with an impatient wave of her hand. His father late at night, reading his book with a cut-crystal glass of golden whisky at his elbow next to a small jug of water, 'A Gift from Bonnie Scotland' proudly emblazoned on the outside.

His mother preparing a picnic basket for them all on the journey. 'I don't like to stop at the motorway places, the food is always so expensive and the quality so bad. We'll come off like we always do near the Lakes and find a nice place to park and eat our lunch.'

They always split the journey, never driving all the way to the cottage in one day. Inevitably they stopped at the same B&B near Gretna Green. Their parents had married there back in the Eighties and they loved the place with a passion.

He and his brother packed the foldaway seats in the back of the car. When they were close to the Lakes, their father would start to look for a lay-by or parking spot where they could put everything out at the rear of their old Rover. Mother even packed a tartan blanket and the bright green plastic plates which came with the picnic hamper.

Home-made scones, Quiche Lorraine, Scotch eggs, dainty little finger treats filled with either boiled egg and mayonnaise, coronation chicken or cucumber, depending on the time of year. And, of course, his mother's special cheese and onion sandwiches, all washed down with a thermos flask of hot sweet tea and Robinson's barley water for himself and his brother, Mark.

In many ways, they were a family of the 1950s, not of the new millennium. His mother and father had become parents late in life and, by the time he was born, were already set in their ways. They lived a comfortable, insular middle-class life: *The Daily Telegraph* every morning, his father going off to work at the insurance office until he retired at sixty-five with a watch and a handshake, the library every Wednesday, bridge on Friday, church on Sunday, cheese and onion sandwiches all year round.

He could still taste the food in his mouth. Parking in the lay-bys of the Lakes, on those many trips back to Scotland. His father leaning forward in his checked flannel shirt, offering his wife the last scone because she could never resist it.

The memories were always there, haunting him. When would they go away?

The last time they'd left for Scotland always stayed though, the sky blue and the scent of autumn in the air. He'd always remembered the last hydrangeas at the bottom of their garden, his mother picking a few and bundling them up in old newspaper.

'They'll be perfect for the cottage.'

Mother's family had owned the cottage for years. She had been going to it since she was a young girl and still she looked forward to visiting it every spring, summer and autumn.

Perhaps it held happy memories for her, too, or she was always comfortable there, wrapped up in the past. He would never know now though.

Everything around the house in Chorlton had changed, but they had remained the same; kind, courteous, old-fashioned. His mother must have been the last person on earth not to have a mobile phone. 'Why would I have one of those horrid things, dear? I know when your father is coming home and nobody else is going to call me.'

That day had seemed like any other day. After a lot of messing around, mainly because their father had insisted the car be checked over by the garage before they left on a long drive, they had finally packed everything and everybody into the car and, at eleven thirty a.m., they were on their way.

His father, as he always did before starting the engine, said, 'Everybody aboard, so let's cast off: just two hours sailing to the Lakes, an hour for lunch and then a wee tack to Gretna, arriving just as the harbour lights start to come on.'

He didn't know why his father always used nautical terminology. It was something else he had forgotten to ask him.

He and his mother were in the back seat – they loved playing travel Scrabble on the journey – while his brother occupied the seat in front, a map on his knees. He was the designated guide even though his father had driven the route so many times he knew it off by heart.

They had driven down Edge Lane and onto the A56 in Stretford, filtering onto the right lane prior to turning right to get onto the M60 Ring Road and head north. His father was just accelerating away from the lights when his mother exclaimed, 'I've forgotten the butter.'

'What?' his father had asked.

'The butter for the scones, we don't have any.'

'We can buy it en route.'

'But it's not the same. I like *our* butter.'

'Would you like me to go back, dear?'

'If it wouldn't be too much trouble, George.'

His parents were always unfailingly polite to each other. It was a consequence of their upbringing, he supposed. They never showed any outward emotion but he knew they loved each other. And, above all, he knew they loved him, despite his quirks and foibles.

'I'll take the slipway to Carrington before we get on the M60 proper and we can loop back to home.'

Father looked in his mirror, signalled left, manoeuvred, checked the mirror again as they entered the slipway for Carrington. He was always such a meticulous driver. Not the quickest on four wheels but always aware of the road and other users.

They reached the roundabout at the bottom of the slipway and Father indicated left. The car moved out around the roundabout when he heard the horrible sound of crunching metal, felt himself thrown backwards and across the back seat, looking up at the car grill of a big Mercedes pushing its way into their Rover.

They whirled and suddenly he was upside down and falling. The door swung open and he was flying through the air, the wicker corner of the picnic hamper hitting the side of his head.

The ground came up and he hit it, lying there face up staring at the blue sky, unable to move. His mother was lying next to him, her legs and arms twisted like a Chinese contortionist.

He lifted his head as far as he could. They were in a ditch at the side of the road. Ten yards away the Rover had come to rest upside down with its bonnet facing them.

He could see his brother's face through the windscreen. There was nothing left of it but blood and bone. Next to him, his father was unconscious with his bloodied head resting against the driver's side window.

A well-dressed man was outside the car, above him, looking down.

He remembered gasping, 'Help me, help me,' and reaching his arm out towards the man who seemed so far, far away.

There was the overpowering smell of petrol followed by a loud whoosh and the blue flames began to lick the outside of their Rover.

He reached out again to the man above him. 'Help me.'

The man stared down at him and did nothing, finally vanishing from view.

He would remember the look on the man's face for the rest of his life.

Fear. Naked fear.

He turned back to see his father awake now, his face swallowed up by the flames as they engulfed the car. And heat, overpowering heat…

He must have blacked out then because he next woke up in a hospital and a doctor told him his father and brother had died at the scene but his mother had survived for three days, pumped full of drugs, before she too, succumbed to her injuries.

They had never made it to Scotland.

Over a year he had spent in that hospital bed. They said he would never walk again but he had proven all those Doubting Thomases wrong.

So wrong.

He walked and he planned and he imagined their deaths.

All of them.

He opened his eyes. The street outside the house was dark now, the trees rustling in the wind.

They buried his parents and his brother in Southern Cemetery, in graves next to each other. He had been unable to attend, still in Manchester Royal in an induced coma.

When he could finally visit his parents' grave, he planted daffodils on that day and every year from then on. They flowered just where his mother's head lay. She always loved daffodils.

Tomorrow was the anniversary of their deaths.

The Ashtons, Jane Forsyth and Tony Abbott had paid for what they did to his parents, paid for what they did to him.

Only one man remained: Robert Wallace.

Tomorrow was going to be a big day.

Chapter FORTY-NINE

It was well past ten p.m. before Ridpath arrived back home. He opened the door, shouting that he was back as he always did.

This time Eve didn't reply, nor did she come out of her room. He ran upstairs to her bedroom and knocked on the door.

No answer.

He shouted again, leaning over the banister and directing his voice downwards.

She wasn't at home. What had happened to her? He had told her so many times never to go out on her own, and particularly not now when Billy Diamond had been released from prison.

He was about to ring her mobile phone when the front door opened and she came in.

'Where have you been?' he asked from the top of the stairs. 'I've just got back and you weren't here.'

'I went to Maisie's. I didn't want to be here on my own.'

Her face was pale, her eyes red, as if she'd seen a ghost.

'Did anything happen? Did you have a bad day at school?'

She slowly took off her coat without answering him.

'What's wrong, you don't seem yourself?'

'And what's myself, Dad? You didn't come back from work so I went out to see Maisie. What's wrong with that?'

He came down the stairs towards her, deliberately softening his tone. 'Did you eat?'

'Maisie's mum cooked for us.'

'Broccoli bake again?'

She wandered through to the kitchen. 'Nah, some nut crumble or something. Terribly vegan and terribly healthy, I felt almost virtuous eating it. They were all drinking kombucha and eating the smelliest kimchi. They're into this stomach biome stuff, all about gut health and tons of bacteria.'

'Bacteria?'

'Apparently, Maisie's mum has cultivated a love of friendly bacteria, whatever that is.'

'In my day, bacteria was bad for you.'

'Yeah, well, the world has moved on from the Neanderthal era.' She reached into the fridge and poured herself a glass of milk.

Ridpath felt she was being too chatty, too blasé. 'Are you sure you're okay? You seem a little… on edge.'

'Must be the history test we have tomorrow. Anyway, I'm going upstairs to revise.'

She brushed past without looking at him, still carrying her glass of milk.

'Are you sure everything is good?'

She turned back suddenly. 'Listen, Dad, why all the questions? You weren't back here again when I got home.'

'I was working a case.'

'I know, you rang me. So I went out to Maisie's. Now I'm going up to my bedroom to relax and revise. Is that okay or do you want to sit there and ask me more stupid questions?'

Her voice had risen to just below a shout and her face was contorted in anger, not helped by the fact that her thick mascara was beginning to run.

What had happened to his daughter?

She stared at him disdainfully before launching herself upstairs.

He followed her with his eyes until she went out of sight, hearing the terrible finality of her bedroom door slamming.

He hadn't handled that encounter particularly well. But he was sure there was something wrong.

He reached into his pocket and made a phone call.

'Hi, Ridpath, long time no see.'

'Hello, Mrs Knight, I just thought I'd ring to say thank you for feeding Eve tonight.'

There was a pause. 'Sorry, I haven't seen Eve since I dropped her off from school.'

Ridpath thought quickly. 'Oh, I must have misunderstood what she said. Thanks for giving her a lift home. I just wanted to ring to say that.'

'No problem, I hope she's okay.'

'She's fine, just worried about the history test.'

'Why? They already did that this morning. I would have thought she would be happy it's all over.'

He pretended to laugh. 'There I go again, getting it all wrong. Anyway, thank you for picking her up. If you ever need me to return the favour, I'd be more than happy.'

'But you're so busy we hardly ever see you. Anyway, it's late now. Do you want me to pick up Eve tomorrow?'

'Could I message you if I do?'

'Of course, Eve is always so easy to be with, Maisie misses her a lot. They used to hang out together more often but less now I guess. Teenage girls, always so fickle, hey?'

'I guess so. Anyway, I'll let you go to sleep. Good night and thank you once again.'

He ended the call.

For a few minutes he stood in the hallway thinking what to do. Should he go upstairs now and confront her? Or leave it till tomorrow morning? Or not mention it at all?

Eve had lied to him. He couldn't leave it alone. Now was not the correct time to bring it up, tomorrow morning maybe, before his interview with Anita Forsyth, that's when he would have the chat.

What he needed now was a stiff drink. A large glass of something smoky and peaty, a glass of Lagavulin. He hadn't drunk anything in ages but tonight he needed something strong and then he would work.

He was sure there was something about the case he had missed. He couldn't put his finger on it, but there was something there.

Chapter FIFTY

'If we can't go to the police, now what?'

'You keep asking me. I don't know.' Robert Wallace buried his head in his hands.

'What did you do with Benjy?'

'Nothing.'

'You left him hanging there?'

'What was I supposed to do?'

'What if the kids see him? What do I tell them?'

'Okay, okay, OKAY.' He stood up. Clenching his fists with his arms by his side. 'I'll bury the damn thing, okay.'

'What shall I tell the kids?'

'Bloody hell, Martha. I've got some nutter who's demanding I kill myself and all you can worry about is what you have to tell the kids about the bloody dog.'

'But Robyn loves Benjy. We got him when she was two years old, remember?'

'I don't know what to tell them. Make something up. Tell them he's ill and we have to take him to the vet.'

'They'll want to go, too. They like Mr Williams, he gives them lollies.'

'For God's sake, Martha, think of something. Keep them busy while I bury him.'

'Where you going to put him?'

'I don't know. In the garden somewhere.'

'Right. I'll go upstairs and keep them busy.' She walked towards the door before stopping and turning back. 'We have to go to the police, Rob, it's our only option.'

The man put his finger across his lips and whispered. 'I think he's watching us.'

'How?'

'I don't know. But he knew exactly what we were talking about before. He knew we were talking about going to the police.'

She walked back to him and whispered in his ear. 'You think we're bugged?'

He nodded yes.

She whispered again. 'How? Where? How are we going to find it?'

He leant in close. 'You go upstairs and I'll search for the bug. Keep the kids occupied. Afterwards, I'll bury Benjy.'

'It's dark outside.'

'That's good. The kids won't see me.'

She nodded and left the room. He listened for her steps on the stairs before glancing around the room. Where would a bug be hidden?

He checked the Bang & Olufsen television, feeling around the edges for anything unusual.

Nothing.

He looked at the mantelpiece and the original painting by Arthur Delaney hanging above it.

Still nothing.

He checked the light fittings on the ceiling, the couch, the table, underneath the desk, even along the picture and dado rails.

Nothing.

What if the bug wasn't in this room but somewhere else? He couldn't search the whole house. And besides, they'd only discussed what was happening here. The bug must be somewhere nearby.

And then he spotted it. The thing was staring straight at him. A round eye inside the lamp with a view of the whole room. He launched himself at the lamp, picked it up and smashed it against the wall, grinding the small pieces into powder with the heel of his shoe.

'What's happening, Rob?' his wife shouted from upstairs.

'Nothing, dear, it's nothing, just knocked over the lamp.'

He had stopped the man from watching them; the bastard wouldn't know what they were doing any longer.

He sat down on the couch and put his head in his hands. The dog could wait until later to be buried. Right now, he had to think, had to work out a plan.

–

Back in Chorlton, he watched the man search the room. He had already foreseen this was going to happen. Already planned for the eventuality. The camera in the lamp was there for him to find. Once he had discovered it he would stop looking.

Knowledge is power and he knew everything they were doing and thinking. It had worked for him with the others and it was working now.

Robert Wallace would never find the bug hidden in his computer. Even if he did guess his laptop was watching and listening to him, it would still reactivate the next time he logged onto Signal.

That was the beauty of his plan.

Whatever they did, he was always going to be watching them. Always listening to them. Always in control.

Robert Wallace had just eighteen hours left to live.

Chapter FIFTY-ONE

Ridpath settled on the armchair with his large glass of whisky on the table to the left. Document by document, he went through all the files on both cases.

He listened to the dispatcher again and the call she received from Anita Forsyth. The young girl seemed calm – almost self-possessed, not like somebody reporting the death of her mother.

Why was she so calm? Perhaps he would find out tomorrow morning. The interview was at nine a.m. He would have to get there early to prepare as well as write out a list of questions. Any police officer, as Mrs Challinor had warned him, had to be extra careful when interviewing underage witnesses, particularly young girls. He should make sure Megan Muldowney attended the interview too.

He picked up his mobile and messaged her.

> I need you at the Anita Forsyth interview tomorrow. Please be there early at 8.30. Also can you bring your unit's camera and recording equipment? We'll need to tape the interview.

She replied almost immediately.

> Will do. HR finally came through with Jane
> Forsyth's details after you left. It merely
> confirmed everything Chief Inspector
> Howarth told Andy. Worked for three years
> with Tony Abbott as a civilian researcher. A
> good, steady worker, never missing a day.
> Left in December 2019. In the exit
> interview she gave 'another opportunity' as
> the reason. HR didn't follow up with her.

Andy Fletcher had been on the phone to Chief Inspector Howarth when Ridpath had re-entered the room after his phone call with Mrs Challinor. It seemed the HR files were consistent with the chief inspector's memories.

Ridpath messaged back.

> Have the case files they worked on come
> through yet?

> Not yet. Andy is ringing Howarth as we
> speak to hurry him along.

Meaning: Megan had just told Andy Fletcher to chase up the chief inspector. A few minutes later, she sent a follow-up.

Andy says they've just come through. Apparently Jane Forsyth and Tony Abbott worked together on 42 traffic cases over a three-year period from 2016 to 2019. Shall I forward the files? Some are over 100 pages long.

Ridpath thought for a moment. He would never be able to read all the cases before tomorrow morning. But somebody else could.

Get Andy to read them. He should look out for any anomalies, anything that doesn't feel right.

That's a pretty broad brief. What exactly is he looking for?

I don't know. Something that stands out.

Okay... I'll tell him.

How is he getting on with the BDSM group?

Spankingly. Apparently there isn't one in
Sale but there is one in Altrincham. He's
going to meet them tomorrow.

Good. It might not lead anywhere but the
fish hooks are another anomaly that
irritates me. Get a good night's sleep, we
have a busy day tomorrow.

See you at 8.30. BTW, Inspector
Pleasance wants a debrief immediately
after we interview the girl. He was insistent.

Right, let me handle him. You just get there
at 8.30.

Will do.

Ridpath could feel the uncertainty in her words as she
typed them. He could hear Andy Fletcher sitting next to
her saying, '*What the hell does he want? How am I supposed to
find "something that stands out" in nearly four thousand pages
of case files? I'm already meeting a gang of pervs because of him.*'

Ridpath knew he was being difficult, but coppers like
Fletcher annoyed the hell out of him. They always took
the path of least resistance, hitching themselves to a rising
star, hoping it would drag them ever upwards in their
career. The rising star in Fletcher's case was Ron Pleasance.

But Ridpath wasn't going to let him get away with it. It was time for him to be a copper, to use those instincts that made all the difference between being a time-server and being effective. As Charlie Whitworth had always said, 'It's time to get off the pot and shit. A copper is only as good as his last collar.'

God, he missed Charlie.

Ridpath put down his phone and picked up the witness statements from Alan Sagfield and the EMT, David Grayson. He scanned them quickly and they all looked kosher. There were a few anomalies that stood out: the timings and order of things were slightly off, but understandable in a high-pressure situation. It was the last remark in Grayson's statement that stopped him though.

> I am not certain whether the marks were caused by CPR activity before I arrived or they were made by the belt being placed around the neck.

Why had he written those words? Earlier in the statement, he said he had noticed the marks around the neck of Jane Forsyth and had pointed them out to Inspector Pleasance.

He picked up the pathologist's report on Jane Forsyth and this time read it through properly rather than simply reading the summary, as he had done earlier. The pathologist's work looked diligent and careful: it all seemed to indicate death by strangling. Even the toxicology indicated the presence of pentobarbital, which would have certainly immobilised the woman without killing her. She would have been unable to resist her daughter or anybody else as they strangled her.

He looked at the post-mortem photographs attached in a clear plastic file at the end. Jane Forsyth was lying on the stainless-steel bed of the laboratory, unmoving and strangely inhuman. The close-up of the woman's neck was clear. There was a large, bruised band, brown tinged with blue and yellow, circling it. Had a young girl really strangled her mother using a belt?

He stood up and walked over to the bureau in the corner of the room. Fishing in the bottom drawer he found what he was looking for: a magnifying glass.

He picked up another photograph, this time a close-up of the eyes of Jane Forsyth. They were a bright cornflower blue with the red dots of the petechiae across the sclera, the whites of the eyes. A classic physical example of a victim of strangulation.

He stared at the close-up of the neck again, looking at the bruising through the magnifying glass. It was clear and livid but weren't there other bruises just above the band? Had they been caused by the belt too? Or had they been made by the attempts at CPR, and that's why the EMT, David Grayson, had mentioned them in his witness statement?

Ridpath picked up his phone and dialled a number: he needed help on this.

'Dr Schofield, sorry for calling you so late. Is it a convenient time to talk?'

'I presume this is Inspector Ridpath.'

Ridpath felt foolish for not having introduced himself before talking. 'Sorry, Doctor, it is me. I need to ask you something, I hope it's okay to talk now.'

'I presume this is about work, Ridpath?'

'I'm afraid it is, Doctor.'

'Ask away.'

'I'm looking at a report from a Dr Lawson.'

'Mark Lawson? One of my colleagues, he is particularly detailed in his work.'

'The report is very thorough. I just wonder if, during CPR, is it necessary to touch somebody's neck?'

'An interesting question. It is not necessary but sometimes it happens in the heat of the moment. Probably not from a professional though. A member of the public or somebody not used to applying CPR may touch the neck or even apply too much pressure when looking for a pulse.'

'You've seen this before?'

'Not often, but it does happen, usually in stroke victims when a member of the public tries to help before the medical technicians arrive.'

'Okay, that might explain it then.'

'Explain what, Ridpath?'

'I'm looking at a post-mortem report of somebody who was allegedly strangled with a belt but I'm noticing other marks that look like the sort you see when somebody is manually strangled.'

'Well, the bruising could have happened when the ligature was removed or during CPR as I have suggested.'

'Okay, thank you for your time, Doctor.'

'No problem, Inspector. But can I suggest you go to bed. It is far too late to be looking at post-mortem photographs. They would give even me nightmares.'

Ridpath glanced at the time. 11.45 p.m. It *was* late and he needed to be sharp in the morning to handle Anita Forsyth, and his daughter: he mustn't forget Eve.

'You're right, Doctor,' he answered but still couldn't hang up the phone. Something about the picture was still nagging him. 'I wonder if...'

'You'd like a second opinion on the report?'

'Am I so transparent?'

'The answer is yes, Ridpath. Dr Lawson is an experienced and thorough pathologist. I'm reluctant to look over or criticise his work. It's a matter of professional courtesy.'

'Professional courtesy that might mean a young girl is incarcerated for the rest of her life for a murder she didn't commit.'

'That's unfair, Ridpath, beneath you.'

Ridpath closed his eyes, the doctor was right: he had been asking too much.

'But if it's so important to you, let me contact Dr Lawson tomorrow morning. If he agrees to me looking at his report, I will do it for you.'

'I can't ask any more.'

'No, you can't and you shouldn't.'

'Thank you.'

'Go to bed, Ridpath.'

The phone call ended. Ridpath glanced once more at the clock; he should have been in bed long ago.

He put all the photos back into the folder, placing it securely in his briefcase. The last thing Eve needed to see tomorrow morning were pictures of a post-mortem.

He stood up, stretched, yawned and began to climb the stairs to his bedroom. For a few seconds he stopped outside Eve's room and listened. No sounds were coming from inside, she must be fast asleep. He thought about opening the door and checking on her, but decided against it. She was too old for him to disturb her in her own room.

Instead, he stumbled across the landing to his bedroom. He opened the door and stared at the empty bed for a long time. Polly's picture lay on the bedside table staring directly at him.

God, he missed her.

Chapter FIFTY-TWO

Eve heard her father climbing the stairs. He seemed so slow and old. For a second, she stopped breathing as the sound of his footsteps stopped right outside her door.

Was he going to come in and check she was asleep like he used to do when she was a child?

Then the footsteps crossed the landing and she heard the familiar creak as his bedroom door opened. She waited for the door to close but it seemed to take years. What was he doing? Should she go and check on him?

She heard the click as the door finally shut and she breathed out, returning her gaze to her computer screen.

> **Rellik:** Are you still there?
> **Rellik:** Are you still there?

He must have been worried about her. That was why he had typed his message twice. She'd decided he was definitely a 'he' and definitely from Manchester. There was something in the phrasing and the solidity of his sentences.

> **HalfHalf:** Still here. Just listening to my dad go to bed. He sounds very tired this evening. Too much on his plate... including me.

Rellik: Stop that! You must stop seeing yourself as a problem, as something troubling your father. I'm sure he loves you and just wants you to be happy.

HalfHalf: I'm such a disappointment to him. Used to be top of my class, doing well at school. Now I can't be bothered, it's all so futile.

Rellik: You are not a disappointment. Whatever you do, he will still love you, it's the role of a parent; to give love without asking anything in return.

HalfHalf: We argued earlier. I lied to him and said I'd been at a friend's. I'm sure he knows. Just one more screw up in a long line of failures.

Rellik: Why did you lie?

Eve thought about what she should say to this man on the other end of the computer. Should she lie again? A lie to protect a lie?

She decided to tell the truth.

HalfHalf: I went out for a walk, I needed to get out of the house, away from the four walls, to be on my own to think. You see

She paused for a moment, working out how to phrase it correctly.

You see, I was attacked nearly a year ago and my attacker visited me at home this evening. Everything from that night has come back. I feel so vulnerable so exposed not even my dad can protect me.

Rellik: He can't if he doesn't know, can he?

Rellik: You are taking on all the troubles yourself. Share them with somebody, tell them how you feel.

HalfHalf: I can't tell my dad. He has so much on his plate already. He thinks I don't know about his work, but I always do. He leaves his briefcase lying around...

Rellik: The point of being a parent is to help your child with their burdens.

Rellik: Let me tell you about myself...

This was the first time Rellik had ever opened up about himself. She leaned closer to the computer.

Rellik: I was diagnosed as being on the spectrum when I was eight. My parents understood and took me out of school, and my mother home-schooled me. I took all the exams and passed them easily, but I couldn't go to university. I knew I couldn't handle it. I lived with them and my elder brother all my life in the same house. We were very happy. We didn't need anybody else, just each other. Six years ago tomorrow, both my parents were killed in a car accident by a drink-driver and I was hurt. The man who caused their deaths managed to escape justice and his crime was covered up. Meanwhile, I spent three months in a coma and nine more months in hospital. There were times when I felt I couldn't go on, I wanted to end it all.

HalfHalf: I'm so sorry for you. It's not fair.

Rellik: Thank you, but life isn't fair. It's how we deal with our setbacks that determines our happiness. After I came out of hospital, I decided to get a job helping people. Somehow, after the accident, I could function better in society, I also found a purpose for my life. We can let our fears, our demons, control us or we can act. I decided to do the latter.

273

HalfHalf: To help people?

Rellik: Partly, but also to bring the man who had murdered my parents and those who had covered up his crime to justice.

HalfHalf: You sound like my father, he has a strong sense of justice.

Rellik: If he has, he will understand why you lied. Tell him the truth, the whole truth. He will know what to do. Then find your own purpose in life.

Eve thought about what the unknown man in the chat group was telling her. She wanted to tell him more, explain everything.

Rellik: Sorry, I have a big day tomorrow. I must sign off now. Are you okay or would you like to talk to somebody else?

HalfHalf: I'm okay. Thanks for the chat, it's much clearer now.

Rellik: One last thing before I go. Have you seen or heard from Iceman123 recently?

HalfHalf: I saw him at school today. He looked happy and really focused. I'm glad he introduced me to you.

Rellik: So am I. Look after yourself and be honest with your father. He'll handle it.

HalfHalf: I will.

Rellik: Good, I'll sign off now.

Eve was intrigued, she quickly typed a message.

HalfHalf: Why is it such a big day tomorrow? And do you know your name is "killer" backwards?

Rellik: I know.

Eve tried to message him again but there was no answer, the man had already logged out. Perhaps she would find out more tomorrow night.

She logged off herself and padded over to her bed, slipping beneath the covers. She felt better tonight, better than she had in a long, long time.

She knew what to do now.

Chapter FIFTY-THREE

They lay together on the couch, her head resting on his shoulder. On their knees, each held a large pad and a thick pen. The dog had been buried beneath the magnolia tree an hour earlier when the kids had finally fallen asleep.

Outside the window the wind whistled through the trees and the yellow leaves swirled in a circle on the patio.

It was Martha Wallace who wrote the first line.

You're sure?

Her husband looked at her and scribbled a response.

> *No, but we can't take any chances. I found a bug but there may be more.*

Ok. What are we going to do?

> *We're going to the police.*

Are you sure?

> *It's the only thing we can do.*

They might not believe us.

> *I messaged a friend when I was in the garden earlier. He's sent me the private number of the head of the Major Investigation Team. They'll*

believe us, particularly when I tell them about the
Ashtons. We have to do it.

When?

After he gives us the final instructions tomorrow
morning. I'll screenshot them for proof.

The wind outside the house howled louder, rattling the glass in the window panes. A clump of leaves seemed to throw itself at the patio doors before swirling off into the dark.

What if he knows already? What if he's outside?
????????

He could be watching now.

All he'll see is us two writing messages to each
other. He won't know what's in the messages.

I'm scared, Rob. I don't want to die. I don't want
the kids to die.

The police will protect us.

What if they can't?

He stared at her as she began to cry, pulling her in towards him.

There was no need for messages any more.

Chapter FIFTY-FOUR

Detective Chief Inspector Steve Carruthers looked out through the glass of his goldfish bowl at the MIT floor. Most of the detectives were still there. Some were going through possible leads from the press conference and subsequent hotline. Others were checking up on offenders with a history of violence who lived in the north of England. Tomorrow, if they were still stalemated, he'd extend the search to the rest of the UK. Still more were ringing their confidential informants, seeing if there was any word – or words – on the street about the perp. The last lot, huddled in a corner on his left, were staring at hours and hours of CCTV footage gathered from the various doorbells, ATMs, shopfronts, ANPR cameras and buses who had filmed the area where the Ashton's lived in the days leading up to, and the day after, the invasion.

The meeting with Claire Trent had gone better than expected. Dennis Leahey had been there too on the principle that a pain shared is a pain halved. They'd been through every action on the case since they received the 999 call on Wednesday at seven thirty when the postie had seen a smear of blood on the Ashtons' downstairs window.

'Well, Steve, you seem to have covered every base. The analysis of the ANPR coverage was particularly good.'

'That was Helen Shipton,' said Leahey.

'Good, how's she working out?'

'Great, she's become a bit of a star with the audio-visual people. I reckon we got onto the Keppel Road address at least two days quicker than without her.'

'We should keep her there longer.'

Carruthers glanced at Dennis Leahey quickly.

'It's an idea, boss, but being inside staring at screens all day long can't be good for the soul. You just have to look at our audio-visual guys to work that one out.'

'Point taken. We'll rotate somebody else in there asap. How was the forensics on the van and the Keppel Road house?'

'We may have a partial on the lower bonnet of the van. We're not sure if it's our perp, though, it might be just some kid who'd leant against it.'

'When will you know?'

'We're running it through IDENT1 as we speak. The check will be over soon.'

'Let me know the results.'

'Don't worry, boss, you'll be the first to know if we get a hit.'

'Have you thought that it's Halloween tomorrow, does that have any bearing on the case?'

'We're looking into that, boss, but there doesn't seem to be any connection to October 31. We don't know when or where the killer will strike next. But I'm sure of one thing, he will strike again, I feel it in my water.'

'I hope you're wrong, Steve.'

'So do I.'

'Next steps?'

'Track the route of the van using ANPR, see if he stopped anywhere. Carry on searching for Ronnie Rellik through the local records, but Dennis feels he may have been born in Poland or Eastern Europe with a name like that. If there was no birth registration in the UK, we'll link up with Interpol liaison and get Europe to check their records. Finally, we have extra cars on the streets in order to respond rapidly if there is another incident.'

'I hope it doesn't come to that, Steve.'

'I hope so too, boss.'

The meeting was about to end when one of the new assistant chief constables barged in. 'What's happening with the raid?'

'The house was empty, sir.'

'Empty? You mean you missed him?'

'No sir, we believe the house had been empty since the day of the incident.'

'When are we going to catch him?'

'Just as soon as we can, sir, we have most of the MIT department working late into the night.'

'Get him and get him soon, is that clear? I want this sorted and off our books. Detective Superintendent Trent, I'd like to see you in my office, now.'

Claire Trent had openly rolled her eyes before following the man out of her office and down the corridor.

Steven Carruthers and Leahey were left in her office, twiddling their thumbs.

'Come on, Dennis, if Claire still wants us she'll come down to our floor. I have a feeling she won't be back for a while.'

That had been five hours ago. Since then, Carruthers had assigned all the teams something to look into or research. It was painstaking grunt work but it had to be done.

He ran his fingers through his hair and rubbed the back of his neck, trying to ease the tenseness in the muscles.

He'd finally come to a terrible conclusion: the only way they were going to catch this man was if he struck again.

The problem was they didn't know where or when or even how he would strike.

But they had to be ready to react. And having a half-knackered detective force wasn't likely to come up with the breakthrough that was needed, nor react properly if one came up.

It was time to tell them all to go home and come back tomorrow to start afresh.

Carruthers buried his face in his hands. Where would the man strike next?

The truth was that after a week of hard graft they hadn't got a clue.

A frisson of fear ran down Steve Carruthers' back. For the first time in a long time he was scared.

Very scared.

Thursday, October 31.

Chapter FIFTY-FIVE

Eve was already up and eating her toast when Ridpath made it into the kitchen the following morning at seven thirty.

'I made your coffee.'

Ridpath saw the cafetière of brown liquid standing on the counter, steam rising above the plunger. He grabbed a cup and filled it up, taking a long swallow. It was good: strong with enough kick to wake the dead.

'Great coffee.'

'Thanks, I used three spoons and let the water come off the boil before pouring it over. It's Sumatran, by the way...'

'It's good.' He took another sip, feeling the caffeine surge through his body and find his brain cells hidden behind a thin film of whisky. 'Sorry, I can't take you to school this morning, I have to interview somebody at nine.'

'For your case?'

He nodded. 'A young girl, never the easiest interview.'

'Younger than me?'

'About a year younger I think.'

'Are you going to charge her?'

Ridpath shrugged his shoulders. 'I'm not sure. I can't discuss this with you, Eve, you know that.'

She nodded. 'I know.' A long pause as she stared at her toast. 'Dad, about last night…'

'We need to talk about that, Eve.'

'I know, that's why I want to say sorry.'

'You didn't do anything wrong.'

'I did. I lied to you.' She took a deep breath. 'I didn't go to Maisie's last night. I went for a long walk; had to clear my head.'

Ridpath sat down at the table, placing his coffee cup carefully in front of him. 'I know, I rang Maisie's mum and she told me you hadn't been there. Why did you lie, Eve?'

It was her turn to shrug her shoulders. 'Lots of reasons. It seemed easier than telling the truth and I knew you'd be angry with me for leaving the house on my own. You can be a bit judgemental sometimes.'

'Only sometimes?'

She laughed. It was good to hear her laugh again.

'I asked you not to go out alone because it's not safe. Billy Diamond is out on bail pending his trial.'

'I know, that's one more thing I have to tell you.' Another long pause, this time she looked directly at her father. 'He came here.'

'What?' Ridpath shot out the chair.

'When I came home from school yesterday, he was waiting in the house.'

Ridpath pulled his phone out of his pocket. 'The little scrote, I'll have him back inside quicker than he can scratch his arse.'

She stood up and grabbed his arm. 'No, Dad, don't. He came here to apologise, to tell me he was sorry.'

'But how did he get in?'

She pointed to the living room. 'Through the window, he said you need to fix the latch.'

'Bastard, I'll show him.' He began dialling a number. 'He's out on bail. One of the conditions is that he not come within a mile of you or this house. The pillock has broken his bond and he'll be back in the nick by lunchtime.'

'No, Dad, I believed him, that he was sorry. I don't want him to go back inside.'

'He killed people, Eve, and he attempted to kill *you*. He should be locked away for a long, long time. It's only because the justice system is so screwed up that he's out at all.' He began to dial again.

'What are you doing?'

'I'm calling his custody officer. Then I'm going round to his place and making sure the bastard is put back in jail.'

'Dad, listen to me! Just this once, listen to me!' she shouted, tears forming in her eyes.

He stopped dialling and let his hand fall by his side.

'He was sorry and he won't come here again. Is there room in your world for forgiveness, Dad?'

He looked her in the eye. 'He broke the law, Eve, and now he's broken it again by breaking in here and contacting you. How can I leave you alone now? I'd be so worried he'd come back.'

'But he won't.'

'You don't know that.'

'I do. I'm sure he'll never come back here again.' She took his hands and forced him to sit opposite her. 'Weirdly, his visit made me think about what I've been doing. I had a chat with a friend last night.'

'Who?'

'It doesn't matter who. A friend. He told me I had to find my purpose in life. I've been so self-obsessed since Mum died and everything. I missed what was happening to you and to everybody else. I became so concerned with my own feelings, I denied them for others.'

'You lost your mum and you were attacked in a place that should have been a safe haven for you. It's no surprise you became anxious.'

'That's what the therapist always says. But there's more to life than myself. Billy's visit made me think. There's people like him, groomed since they were young to obey orders.'

'James Dalbey has a lot to answer for.'

'They have lost their lives. Billy will spend the rest of his in jail. And here I am worrying about my school and who I am and the latest music from Camp Ghost. I thought life was all so pointless, but I was wrong. There is a point.'

'And what's that?'

'This may sound a bit pompous and juvenile, but I think the point is to serve others, to help others.' She held her arms out wide. 'I'm not certain how yet or even why, but I know this is what I'm supposed to do. Does that make sense, Dad?'

'It makes a lot of sense. It takes some people a long time to find their purpose in life, you seem to have discovered it early.'

'Now, I just have to work out what it is in concrete terms. It's all a bit airy-fairy at the moment.'

'Talk to Margaret Challinor when you see her on Saturday. She found her purpose in life.'

'"To represent the dead in the land of the living."'

Ridpath looked at her quizzically.

'She talked with me before when I asked her what your job in the coroner's office really was. She said it wasn't about investigating or catching criminals, but it was about representing those who could no longer represent themselves. I understood then what drove you, and what drives her.'

Ridpath reached forward and gave his daughter a big hug, something he hadn't done for a long time.

From the depths of his arms came a muffled voice. 'I can't breathe, and you're going to be late for your interview.'

Chapter FIFTY-SIX

The camera was activated at exactly 7.32 a.m. by the noise of the family. Robert Wallace must have taken the laptop into the kitchen as he was making breakfast. The children sat at the island counter, eating their Coco Pops noisily. Martha Wallace was drinking coffee and Robert was munching on a bowl of muesli.

If he didn't know better, it looked like one of those happy families that appeared so often in cereal ads, all white, gleaming teeth and not a hair out of place.

The one difference from the happy family of ad-land was that at least one of these people would be dead by just after noon. Perhaps, all of them would be.

He decided to send his final message now rather than wait for nine a.m.

Rellik: Are you there?

He watched as Robert Wallace, hearing the beep from the laptop, suddenly became edgy. He put down his cereal bowl and slowly walked towards the computer. He could see the man in close-up as his hands tapped away on the machine.

PropMan76: I'm here.
Rellik: You have less than five hours left to live.

Robert Wallace turned away from the laptop. 'Robyn, James, take your cereal upstairs and eat it there. I have to make a call.'

'But Dad, you never let us eat in our rooms.'

'I am this time. Go on upstairs, now.'

Martha supported him. 'Come on upstairs, your dad has something to do.'

'Dad always has something to do,' moaned the youngest girl but she took the bowl and followed her brother out of shot.

Robert Wallace turned back to the laptop and began typing again.

> **PropMan76:** I don't want to do it, let me give you money instead. All my money, you'll be rich.
> **Rellik:** No. If you want to save your family, you must follow the instructions.
> **PropMan76:** I can't.
> **Rellik:** Then your family will die like your dog.
> **Rellik:** I am outside your house now.

He watched on the screen as Rob Wallace ran to the window and stared out. He flashed his car lights twice so Wallace would know it was him waiting there.

> **PropMan76:** What are you doing, I still have five hours left to live.
> **Rellik:** You have said you can't carry out my orders. Your family will die now.
> **Rellik:** Do not think about calling the police. It will take them at least fifteen minutes to get here. By then you and your family will be dead.
> **Rellik:** If you approach my car, they will die.

If you ring the police, they will die.
If you do not do as you have been instructed, they will die.
Are you going to kill yourself as you have been told?

He watched as Robert Wallace looked towards the window again, then he ran back to the laptop and began typing.

> **PropMan76:** Yes, I will do it.
> **Rellik:** There is one small change in your instructions. We will meet before your death. I will tell you where later.
> **Rellik:** Enjoy the rest of your life. You just have 270 minutes to live.

He logged off the app but continued to watch Rob Wallace on the laptop. For a long time, the man just stood there, his head in his hands, his chest slowly moving up and down as he sobbed silently.

Then Wallace picked up the bowl of muesli and flung it against the wall.

After all these years the man was finally suffering.

It gave him so much pleasure.

Chapter FIFTY-SEVEN

Ridpath parked outside the secure unit of Ford Avenue Children's Home at exactly 8.45 a.m., rushing into the main entrance. There he was greeted by a security guard who waved one of those plastic wands over his body to detect metal.

The thing beeped twice to find a bunch of change and Ridpath's keys. When he had signed in and been issued with a visitor's pass, he was told to wait while an officer came down to take him up to the interview room.

'Your DC has been here since eight a.m., setting up your recording equipment.'

It was exactly 8.55 when the officer appeared and the security guard unlocked the door to the inner sanctum.

The officer was a no-nonsense middle-aged child welfare social worker who Ridpath recognised immediately.

'My name is Ruby Grimes – I think we've worked together before DI Ridpath?'

'We have, Ms Grimes. I interviewed one of your previous... clients here. Daniel Carsley.'

'He was a juvenile too, so the same rules of engagement apply for today's interview with Anita. I've already told your DC what they are but I'll repeat them just for you.'

She talked as she escorted him up two flights of stairs. The home itself was impersonal and smelt of institutionalisation. Everything was sterile and clean, with that odour of suffering and unhappiness that enveloped these places in a cold hug.

'If Anita wants to stop the interview, it will cease immediately. Or if I feel that Anita is being put under too much pressure, I will call a halt. Understood?'

'Agreed. How has she been since coming here?'

'Nervous, on edge, frightened. You have to understand this young girl has just lost her mother and she blames herself for that death. Your previous interviews at the police station didn't help.'

'I didn't interview her.'

'It doesn't matter who interviewed her, it shouldn't have happened in the way it did.'

She stopped walking upstairs and turned to face him. He was forced to look up at her.

'Frankly, DI Ridpath, if I had my way, *this* interview wouldn't be happening at all. But as it's a murder investigation, my boss has ordered me to allow it. But I will stop it any time if I feel my client is becoming upset. Understand?'

'Perfectly, Ms Grimes. I thought the first interview was badly handled, too. I won't be making the same mistakes again.'

'Good. Who will be asking the questions?'

'I will, this time. My DC, Megan Muldowney, will be operating the equipment.'

She pointed off to a door on one side. 'You remember the room? I will bring Anita down in three minutes. Please make sure you are ready.'

She carried on climbing the stairs while Ridpath approached the room and knocked before entering. Megan stood in one corner next to a Sony camera on a tripod. In front of her a small table had a recording machine on the right-hand side and three chairs. One chair was for Ridpath and the others for the interviewee and the social worker.

'Sorry, I'm late, Megan.'

'No worries, I got here early to set up the equipment. I knew you'd want to be ready for nine a.m.'

Ridpath nodded his thanks and pulled out the chair he was supposed to be using, opposite the other two.

He took three deep breaths while Megan fiddled with the camera. He closed his eyes and tried to focus. This interview was important for him and for the young girl. Had she murdered her mother in cold blood by tying a belt round her neck after lacing a drink with pento-barbital? Or was she innocent and somebody else had committed the crime?

He went over the rules for interviewing juveniles and vulnerable adults in his head.

Establish rapport.

Make sure they know the difference between truth and lies.

Ask the interviewee to explain the event in their own words.

Drill down on the details.

Close the interview and explain the next steps.

Interviewing young people was always difficult. You had to be very conscious of the language you used and how the questions were asked.

He had wanted to be here much earlier this morning to prepare and ready himself for the interview, but Eve's need to talk had delayed him.

Never mind, it was worth it. He finally understood what she was going through. He thought again about ringing Billy Diamond's custody officer and reporting him for breaking his bail order but he remembered what his daughter had said: 'Is there room in your world for forgiveness, Dad?'

Was there? Did a copper have room for forgiveness or was upholding the law all that he should be doing?

He'd decide later but he knew if she found out Billy had been re-arrested, he would lose her. She would never trust him again.

His phone rang. Damn, he should have put it on airplane mode before the interview with the young girl. He was tempted to ignore the insistent sound but glanced at the screen. It was from Terri Landsman, the crime scene manager at the petrol station.

'Hiya, Terri. It's Ridpath. Listen I'm just about to go into a meeting, can I call you later?'

'I'll be quick, Ridpath. I examined the panel from Pump 8 this morning as Megan asked me. Unfortunately, it was scorched and burnt—'

'Thanks, Terri, but...'

'She said he'd written something on the panel before setting himself alight. It wasn't clear at first but then we put it under ultraviolet light. You see, the solvent in the ink—'

Ridpath leant forward in his chair. 'What did it say, Terri?' He interrupted the crime scene manager as she was in full chemistry teacher flow.

'That's the weird bit, Ridpath, it just said "I am guilty".'
Where had he heard those words before?

'"I am guilty"?'

'Just those three words, nothing else. I suppose it's a note of some sort but weird, huh?'

'And guilty of what?'

Ridpath was about to ask more but he heard a slight tap on the door, followed by Ms Grimes entering and encouraging somebody in the corridor to enter too.

'I have to go now, Terri. Thanks so much, I'll call you later.'

He ended the call.

Ruby Grimes was gesturing with her hand, reassuring the girl behind her.

Finally, a dark-haired girl stepped tentatively across the threshold. Anita Forsyth was younger looking and smaller than Ridpath expected. She looked closer to twelve than fourteen. Her eyes were darting from the camera to him to Megan Muldowney and back to the camera again, looking as if she wanted to turn and run.

Ridpath stood up and held out his hand. 'Hi Anita, my name is Thomas Ridpath and this is my colleague, Megan Muldowney. We're going to be chatting with you today.'

He pointed to the seat opposite his own and sat down. Anita glanced nervously at Ruby Grimes and stood still in the centre of the room.

Ridpath smiled at her. 'You can sit here and make yourself comfortable.'

Ruby Grimes indicated that Anita should sit.

Slowly, reluctantly, the girl sat opposite him.

'Hi, Anita, can I call you by your Christian name? What do your friends call you?'

'My friends call me Anita.'

The voice was weak and tentative, more a squeak than anything else, so different from the girl on tape in the first interview.

'Then I'll call you Anita, too. Both myself and Megan are here to represent the police. Our job is to find out the truth when things happen. It's only the truth we're interested in, nothing else. Do you think you can tell us the truth?'

'My mum always told me to tell the truth. She said lies get people in trouble.'

'Your mum was right. Do you know the difference between truth and lies?'

'Of course, everybody knows the difference.'

'Tell me.'

She turned to Ruby Grimes. 'What is this? School or something?'

'Just answer the question, please, Anita.'

The young girl pouted. 'Truth is what actually happens. Lies is what you make up.'

'So all I want to know today is the truth. I'm not interested in made-up stuff, just what happened. Okay?'

The girl shrugged her shoulders. 'Okay.'

Ridpath sat back and smiled, deliberately trying to lighten the mood. 'Did you know your mum used to work for the police?'

The girl nodded. 'She told me she worked for them for three years when I was younger. A civilian researcher, she said she was.' The girl's eyes moved up and to the left. 'She said it was the best job she ever had, she loved working there.'

'When your mum worked for the police, her job was to find out the truth about traffic accidents. Our job,' he pointed to Megan and himself, 'is to find out the truth when people pass away. Do you understand?'

She nodded, a little more animatedly. 'You want to find out the truth about Mum's death, don't you?'

'Yes, that's our job. I'm so glad you understand. You will tell us the truth, won't you?'

She nodded but didn't say anything, glancing towards the social worker instead.

'Now we've got to know each other, is it okay if I start the tape machine and record what you say? It's just so we get an accurate record and I can listen to you instead of taking notes.'

'That's what Miss Hargreaves, our English teacher says. "You can't take notes and listen properly at the same time."'

'It sounds like Miss Hargreaves is a good teacher. Do you like English?'

She nodded. 'I'm in the school play this year. We're doing *Macbeth* and I'm one of the witches.'

'Hubble, bubble, toil and trouble.'

'I thought you wanted the truth? They don't actually say that, you know. They actually say "Double, double, toil and trouble; Fire burn and cauldron bubble."'

Ridpath smiled. 'Thank you for putting me right. It's a long time since I read The Scottish Play.'

'You should read it again, it's very good on guilt and innocence and shame and ambition.'

For a second, Ridpath couldn't work out whether the girl was playing him or she was just enthusiastic about the play. It was time to find out.

'Is it okay if I start the tape now?'

Anita Forsyth nodded.

Ridpath pressed the record button. 'My name is DI Thomas Ridpath. With me is DC Megan Muldowney operating the video equipment. It is 9.10 a.m. on the morning of October 31 and we are in the secure wing of Ford Avenue Children's Home to interview Ms Anita Forsyth. Also present is Ms Ruby Grimes, a social worker with the Greater Manchester Children's Authority. There are no other people present.'

Ruby Grimes leant forward. 'Speaking for the record, I have instructed Anita that if, at any time, she feels uncomfortable or unhappy at any of the questions, she is to let me know and I will end this interview immediately. DI Ridpath has been made aware of these conditions.'

'Do you understand, Anita?' Ridpath asked. 'You can stop this chat at any time you want, okay? I will understand and will not hold it against you. All I want to do is to find out the truth of what happened last Saturday.'

'I understand,' said Anita.

There it was again, Ridpath thought, the self-assured voice. It was as if this person went from a frightened young girl to a self-assured woman in the blink of an eyelid.

'Before we start I'd just like to ask you if you'd like a solicitor present or any other legal professional to advise you?'

'No, why would I want anybody like that?'

'It is your right to have a solicitor present if you want one.'

'No, I'm happy to answer your questions.'

'Good. One more thing. You were already cautioned in Sale Police Station but I need to caution you formally again.'

'What do you mean "caution"?'

'Again, it's one of your rights. I must tell you that you do not have to say anything. But, it may harm your defence if you do not mention when questioned something which you later rely on in court. Anything you do say may be given in evidence.' He stopped reading from the card at the back of his notebook. 'I'll explain the caution to you. It means you do not have to answer my questions but if you forget to tell me something or do not tell the truth, it may be used against you if we ever go to court. Do you understand?'

'I do, DI Ridpath. I just want to tell the truth like you said earlier.'

'Great, that's all I want, Anita. Oh, and please call me Thomas.' He paused for a moment to gather his thoughts. 'I'd like you to cast your mind back to that morning, last Saturday: who got up first, you or your mum?'

'Me. I always get up first as mum likes a lie-in on a Saturday morning.'

'And last Saturday was like all other Saturdays?'

Anita's eyes went up and left again. 'I think so. Mum had been a bit down all week…'

'A bit down?'

'Not herself. She'd met somebody for lunch about a couple of days before and it had depressed her. It wasn't like Mum at all.'

'Who did she meet?'

'I dunno, she didn't tell me. But afterwards Mum was very quiet, like she was thinking. I remember telling her about my day last Thursday and five minutes later she asked me the same questions all over again. It was like she wasn't listening.'

'And this wasn't like your mum?'

'Mum was always so bright. There was just us two – she didn't have any friends of her own age really. She was more like a friend than a mum.'

'Wasn't she friends with Ms Docherty?'

'I don't think so, not really. They used to go to yoga together and I went to play with Debs occasionally but Mum didn't like Ms Docherty too much, said she was a gossip.'

'Okay... So your mum had lunch with somebody a couple of days before she died.' Ridpath waited for a reaction to the last word, when there was none, he carried on. 'Was it a man or a woman?'

'A man, I think. Yes, definitely a man. Mum said she was meeting "him", so it must have been a man.'

'She didn't tell you why she was upset after her lunch?'

'I wondered...'

'Go on,' encouraged Ridpath.

'I wondered if she was meeting my dad, but I asked her and she said it wasn't him.'

'You believed her?'

'Yes, my mum never lied. And besides, he lives in Scotland. I've met him a couple of times. He has a new partner now and I have a half-sister. I like her, she's cool.'

'So it wasn't your dad. Do you know who it was?'

'No, I was at school but I got the impression that he was something to do with the government.'

'The government? Why?'

'Because Mum dug out her old suit, the one she used to wear when she had to go to deal with the council or my teachers on parents' evening. She said she would have to diet if she wanted to wear it again.'

Ridpath frowned. A meeting with somebody from the government? This could be important or just a red herring. He could see Ruby Grimes checking her watch. It was time to move on.

'Okay, Anita, thanks for that, it was really useful. Now let's move to the day your mum died: tell me what happened from the time you woke up.'

'Like I told the other copper—'

'DC Fletcher?'

'Yeah, the ugly one in the cop shop. Like I said to him, I woke up at eight thirty. That's my usual time on a Saturday. Mum was already up and in the kitchen.'

'But you said earlier, your mum liked a lie-in on a Saturday?'

'Yeah, it was weird she was up, nearly freaked me out. She even made me breakfast. I always make my own breakfast on the weekends – Nutella on toast.'

'So this time she made it for you?'

'Scrambled eggs. I don't like them at all but Mum said it would be good for me. She said I needed building up.'

Looking across the table, Ridpath could see the girl was thin for her age, almost scrawny and undeveloped.

'So your mum made you breakfast, what happened next?'

'I watched cartoons for a while…'

'Which cartoons?'

'*The Simpsons*. I love *The Simpsons*.'

Ridpath quickly brought up the Freeview site on his mobile phone and checked the TV schedule. 'On Channel 4, you watched all the programmes? They start at 9.10 a.m.'

'Nah, I was bummed because I missed the first ten minutes. Mum wouldn't let me eat in the living room where the telly was. She wanted me to eat with her.'

'What happened next?'

'I was on my third *Simpsons* when Mum came into the room and switched off the telly.'

Ridpath checked the Freeview schedule again. 'So after 10.05?'

'Yeah, I'd watched about ten minutes if it. It's the one where Homer and Lisa get stuck in a cave, one of my favourites.'

'What happened then?'

'She switched off the telly and asked me to go back into the kitchen with her. Then she asked me to save her.'

'What were the exact words she used?'

Anita Forsyth paused for a moment and closed her eyes. 'She said, "I need to save you."'

Ridpath checked the transcript of the interview with Anita and Andy Fletcher. 'But in your statement, and just now, you said, "She asked me to help save her."'

For the first time, Anita Forsyth became agitated. 'That's not true, it's a lie – my mum never said that. She said, "I need to save you."'

Ruby Grimes glanced at Ridpath before putting her hand gently on the young girl's forearm.

The girl's words were on tape but Ridpath decided not to press the matter. 'No worries, Anita, let's move on, shall we? What happened next?'

'She gave me a whole box of these pills and told me to grind them into a powder and then put them in some hot milk. It was then she said, I needed to do it to save her.'

'Ah, I see. It was then she said it. How many pills were in the box?'

'Twenty, I think.'

'Had your mum ever asked you to do something like this before?'

'Never. She always kept her tablets in a cabinet in the bathroom and I wasn't allowed to open it. She said it was dangerous.'

'So what did you do next?'

'I thought that twenty pills were too many. So I pretended to grind them down but only did five instead.'

'What did you do with the other fifteen?'

'I put them in my pocket.'

Ridpath quickly checked the custody officer's report when Anita was taken to Sale. In her possession she had a Swatch watch, 15p in change, some sweet wrappers, a hair bobble and fifteen tablets of unknown origin wrapped up in a paper handkerchief. Fletcher hadn't even checked what the tablets were.

Ridpath tutted and shook his head. 'Sorry, Anita, please carry on. You ground down five tablets…'

'And I put some milk in a saucepan and boiled it up. My mum was upstairs lying down at this time.'

'When did she go upstairs?'

Anita stopped for a moment. 'I don't remember. She asked me to help save her and then she gave me the tablets and then she got a phone call and went upstairs.'

'She received a call?'

'Yeah.'

'Who from?'

'I dunno, but Mum went upstairs when he rang.'

'He?'

'It was a man on the other end of the line.'

'How do you know?'

'I heard Mum saying he couldn't do this to her.'

Why hadn't Anita mentioned the call before? Had Fletcher checked the calls into Ms Forsyth's phone? Ridpath hadn't seen any call logs in the folder. Come to think of it, there was no mention of the mobile phone at all. What happened to it?

'So you put the powder in the hot milk?'

'I then poured it into a mug for her and took it upstairs. She took it from me and began drinking it.' For the first time since the beginning of the interview, Anita's top lip began to tremble and her eyes flickered from Ruby Grimes to Ridpath and then back to the social worker again. 'I should have helped her properly. I should have done as she asked me. I should have put all the pills in the drink, not just five.'

Her eyes became moist and a large tear dribbled down the cheek. 'It's all my fault she died, I murdered her.'

Ruby Grimes raised her hand towards Ridpath.

Just then, his phone started to ring. He pulled it out of his jacket and glanced at the screen. 'Ms Grimes, I think it's time we took a break. I need to take this call.'

Ridpath stopped the recording machine and indicated to Megan to stop filming too. He got up from the table and went out into the corridor, leaving Ruby Grimes to console Anita Forsyth.

'Yes, Doctor, what is it?'

Chapter FIFTY-EIGHT

He sat out in the car, watching the house, listening to the noise inside. He hadn't eaten for at least twelve hours but didn't care. The work was nearly finished, he could wait a while longer to eat.

The couple were whispering now, hoping he couldn't hear what they were saying, but he could.

Every word.

Rob Wallace seemed reconciled to his fate, he knew he couldn't go to the police, he had no more options left. The only choice was to die.

He would watch Robert Wallace kill himself later. They would meet close to the location he had chosen for the man's death. There, he would give him the final instructions as he had all the others.

All of them had known they were going to die, but none of them knew how, not until the final minutes.

They all deserved it, every last one. What they did to his parents and brother and to him was unforgivable.

He remembered meeting Tony Abbott in the car park and telling him how he was going to die. As soon as he heard the news, the man was in a different world, as if he had taken a drug that had transported him there. His eyes were wild and unfocused, his speech disjointed, his movements jerky.

He had chosen the method of death in remembrance of his father. It was fitting that the man who had covered up his father's death should meet a similar end: to be consumed by fire.

To go through with it, all Tony Abbott needed was reassurance that his family would be safe if he went to the petrol station.

It was a promise he had been happy to give. He had no argument with the family; they were mere collateral damage in his plans.

He wished the Ashtons had listened to him. The man had all the attributes of a successful lawyer: arrogance and stupidity.

A deadly combination.

It was Ashton who had organised the whole thing in the first place. He had transferred the money. He had paid everybody off.

So he had to die first. The family was meant to live but, in his stupidity, Clive Ashton had refused to listen. He took no pleasure in killing the two young children. They bled so much, but it had to be done.

Only when he had finished killing them did Ashton realise he was a man of his word. The dawn of realisation on the man's face as he stared at his children bleeding out on the bed was priceless.

He'd let him live thirty minutes longer just so the knowledge would eat him up, devour him. Then he'd destroyed the parents' faces with the shotgun, just as his brother's face had been destroyed in the accident.

It was poetic justice, with him as the poet.

He hoped Robert Wallace would obey his instructions. He had no desire to kill the rest of the family, they were innocent. Or at least they were as innocent as anybody with a father like Robert Wallace could be.

The wife was speaking louder know, her words in his ear buds, clear and pleading.

'You have to do it, Rob, we have no choice.'

Robert Wallace had no choice, not any more. It was decided the minute he drove away from the accident and contacted Clive Ashton to arrange the cover-up.

His parents and brother had died in excruciating pain. He had spent over a year in hospital and a further eighteen months in rehab.

It was time for Mr Wallace to suffer the same pain, the same anguish, the same death.

He had just 148 minutes left to live.

Chapter FIFTY-NINE

'Have you found anything?' Ridpath asked breathlessly, making sure the door to the interview room was closed.

'Good morning, Ridpath, I do hope I haven't caught you at a difficult time.'

To Ridpath, the doctor's high voice reminded him of Anita Forsyth. It had exactly the same pitch and timbre.

'I'm interviewing the daughter of the woman who was murdered as we speak. At the moment, she is the prime suspect in the crime.'

'How old is she?'

'Fourteen years old but looks younger. I don't think she has been through puberty yet.'

'I think, and Dr Lawson concurs, that it is highly unlikely she is the perpetrator in this case.'

'What?'

'I said, it was highly unlikely—'

'I heard you the first time, Doctor, could you explain?'

'As we agreed last night, I rang Dr Lawson as soon as I got to the lab this morning at seven. He was already in and working. Early starts seem to be an occupational hazard for pathologists. You are on speakerphone at the moment and he is sitting next to me.'

'Good morning, Dr Lawson.'

'Good morning, DI Ridpath, I don't believe we have had the opportunity of working together yet. John speaks very highly of you.'

'I don't believe we have, Doctor. Why do you think Anita Forsyth couldn't have killed her mother?'

'I actually said I thought it was highly unlikely.'

Ridpath rolled his eyes. 'Why do you think it was "highly unlikely", Doctor?'

'Well, let me explain. Dr Lawson graciously went through his post-mortem report with me and I found his work as detailed and thorough as usual. His conclusions were based on the facts he had discovered in the post-mortem. But…'

At last, the words Ridpath had been waiting for. The phone went silent until he asked, 'But what, Doctor?'

'But when we actually re-examined the body of Jane Forsyth this morning, we noticed something.'

Ridpath felt like screaming down the phone but actually said quietly, 'You looked at her body?'

'It's still in one of the fridges in the mortuary. It hasn't been released to the family yet. A problem with finding a family member, I believe. Anyway, when we looked at the body, we found there were additional marks above the hyoid bone and around the back of the neck, on the posterior cervical area.'

'Additional marks?'

'Some bruises darken and become more visible after death, Ridpath. In this case, the bruises we have just seen were definitely caused before death, but have become more pronounced since the post-mortem.'

'What John means,' Dr Lawson interrupted, 'is that the bruises have not been caused by livor mortis, the post-mortem pooling of blood, but were created perimortem, around the time of death, and became more obvious in our recent examination.'

Ridpath was trying to understand what both doctors had just said. 'But you pointed out the bruising on the neck in your post-mortem, Doctor, I saw it in the photos.'

'But John told me this morning, the primary suspect for the case is a fourteen-year-old girl who strangled Jane Forsyth with a belt.'

'That's what the police believe.'

'Impossible, Ridpath. The marks of the neck indicate Jane Forsyth was manually strangled. The belt was used afterwards to cover up the manual strangulation.'

'You're certain, Doctor?'

'Absolutely, and there's more, Ridpath—'

'But before we tell you what it is, can you describe your suspect's hands to us?' interrupted John Schofield.

'Anita Forsyth's hands?'

'Exactly.'

'Just a moment.'

Ridpath opened the door to the interview room. Anita Forsyth was leaning into Ruby Grimes with her hands interlocked around her waist.

'How long is this call going to take, DI Ridpath?' asked the social worker. 'I don't think the interview can continue, Anita is too upset.'

'I won't be long, I promise. Anita…'

At the sound of her name, the young girl looked up and moved away from the social worker.

'Can you do me a favour? Could you show me your hands?'

'My hands?'

'What's this about, Ridpath?'

Anita frowned and moved back closer to the social worker.

'Just bear with me, Ruby. Please show me your hands, Anita.'

The girl raised her eyebrows but lifted her hands towards Ridpath, palms forward. He put the phone down and placed one of his palms against hers. It was almost twice the size. 'Thank you, Anita.'

He picked up the phone and went back out into the corridor, closing the door behind him. 'Anita Forsyth has small hands, Doctor Schofield, far smaller than my own. I would even say they are smaller than yours.'

'I'm surprised you noticed my hands, Ridpath.'

'Two days ago, when you pointed at the laptop screen during the post-mortem.'

'How observant of you? Then I think we can be certain your suspect did not murder Jane Forsyth.'

'How can you be so certain?'

'Because we have measured the fingermarks made by the murderer and the results show he is a man with unusually large hands and extremely strong fingers. Hand size is commonly measured in two ways: length and span. Span is the measurement from the tip of the little finger to the tip of the thumb when the hand is outstretched. Jane Forsyth was an obese woman with a large neck. We have measured the span of the fingermarks of the thumb and forefinger and it was 10.75 inches. Far wider than would be likely on a fourteen-year-old girl or even an adult female. You are looking for a male as the perpetrator of this murder, not a young female.'

'Thank you, doctors, for your work.'

'I'm only sorry I missed it the first time, DI Ridpath. But there's one more thing you should know.'

'What's that, Dr Lawson?'

'Studies have shown that hand size correlates well with height.'

'What does that mean?'

'You are looking for a tall man, unusually tall.'

Chapter SIXTY

Ridpath re-entered the interview room. Anita looked straight at him, her eyes ringed with tears. Megan was still at her position behind the Sony camera.

'I'm going to call a halt to this interview, Anita is too upset to continue.'

Ruby Grimes began to rise from her seat, pulling the young girl with her.

'Please, Ruby, just a few more questions. I promise I won't take more than five minutes of Anita's time. It's important…'

'I'm sorry, Ridpath, I have a duty of care to this child and it is obvious to me that she has had to relive the trauma of last Saturday here today. I cannot let it continue.'

Anita tugged the social worker's jacket. 'I don't mind them asking a few more questions. I'm here now, I want to get it over and done with. I don't want them to come back.'

Ridpath seized his chance and sat opposite Anita before the social worker could intervene, instructing Megan to start recording again. 'Thank you, just a few questions and I need to remind you that you remain under caution.'

The girl nodded and said. 'I remember.'

'On the morning of October 26, were yourself and your mother alone?'

The young girl frowned. 'Yes, there was just myself and my mum.'

'There was nobody else in the house? A man hadn't stayed the night?'

'Of course not, Mum didn't like men any more and nobody ever stayed. The house was just for us two, only the two of us.'

Her bottom lip quivered and her voice began to tremble.

Before the social worker could intervene, Ridpath asked another question quickly. 'When you rang 999, which emergency service arrived first, the police or the ambulance?'

Anita stared into the middle distance. 'The police I think, a tall woman PC and a man.'

'And what happened?'

'I told them about Mum. The man went upstairs and the woman stayed with me. She was nice, she asked if I wanted anything to drink or eat.'

'How long was the policeman upstairs with your mum?'

Anita frowned. 'I dunno, it felt like a long time but I didn't look at the clock. Then there was another knock on the door and the ambulance man came in.'

'He was alone?'

'Yes.'

'And what did he do?'

'You said just a few questions, Ridpath. This is more than a few, it's another interview. I'm stopping it now.'

'Just three more questions, Ruby, then I'm done, promise.'

The social worker looked at the young girl who said, 'I'm okay, I want to get it finished.'

'Just three more questions.'

'I'll ask again, Anita, what did the ambulance man do?'

'He talked with the woman police constable first and then he went upstairs to see Mum.'

'What happened next?'

'He was gone for a few minutes. I could hear sounds coming from upstairs but the woman from the police wouldn't let me go to see Mum. Then the male policeman came downstairs and asked if Mum had any allergies or if she had taken anything. I told him I had given my mum five tablets that morning in her milk. I showed him the box.' Anita became more agitated, her small hands grabbing the sleeve of the social worker. 'I didn't mean to kill her. I should have done what she told me and given her the whole pack, but I thought it was too much.'

'I'm ending this interview now, Ridpath. You're done. Turn off the camera.'

Megan looked across at Ridpath for confirmation.

He nodded.

'Come with me, Anita. I'll take you back to your room and we'll get you some orange juice or some hot sweet tea. Would you like that?'

The young girl was still crying. 'I didn't mean to kill her,' she said softly. 'I didn't mean it…'

Ruby Grimes wrapped her arms around Anita and almost lifted her off her chair. They staggered towards the door, Anita's head buried in the social worker's shoulder, still crying.

'I hope you are proud of this morning's work, Ridpath,' Ruby snarled.

The detective ignored her, speaking directly to the child. 'Anita, I said we wanted to find the truth this morning, didn't I?'

The girl stopped for a moment, staring at Ridpath through tear-sodden eyes.

'Thank you for your honesty. Please understand, you didn't kill your mother. Somebody else did. From what you told me, I think I know who it was.'

Chapter SIXTY-ONE

It was during the morning break that Eve finally decided what she was going to do. Her next class was history and Miss Wellacre was always so easy-going.

They had just sat down when Eve pretended to bend over double, clutching her stomach.

'Are you okay, Eve?' the teacher asked.

'Sorry, Miss Wellacre, I'm not feeling so good. Cramps and I want to throw up.'

The teacher looked concerned. 'Is it that time, Eve?'

Ridpath's daughter nodded, leaning on her desk as though her cramps were worsening.

'Okay, you'd better go home. No point in keeping you here today.'

Eve smiled inwardly. *It was easy, so easy. I should have thought of this earlier.*

'But on your way out, check in with Mr Fellowes and make sure you get an absence pass from him. We wouldn't want the truancy officers picking you up on your way home, would we?'

'I'll do that, thank you, Miss Wellacre.'

'Maisie, help Eve to the office, will you?'

Maisie came around and offered Eve her arm and picked up her backpack. Together, they walked out of the history class and down the corridor.

'Are you really ill?'

'Why?'

'It's just you were fine this morning and you've been acting so strangely recently.'

'I'm ill, Maisie, obviously. It's that time of the month.'

Maisie counted on her fingers. 'But you're the same as me and I'm not due for another two weeks.'

'It's early.'

They arrived at the school office. Eve pretended she was in pain once more, sinking down to her knees.

'What's up, Eve?'

Mr Fellowes, the deputy head, was standing over her.

'Not feeling so good, have to go home,' she mumbled.

'Do you want me to call a doctor?'

She shook her head vigorously. 'No, it's that time of the month.'

The deputy head visibly reddened. 'I'll give you an absence pass,' he stammered, 'let me ring your father first to see if he can pick you up.'

Eve actually felt a pain in her stomach. 'It's not necessary, I—'

'Sorry, school protocol if a student is taken ill.' He went back to the computer and checked the number on her school profile, dialling it on one of the landlines. 'Won't be a minute, Eve,' he said reassuringly.

She closed her eyes. *If Dad answers I'm going to die, what do I tell him?*

'It seems to have gone to voicemail. I'll leave a message. "Hello, Mr Ridpath, this is Eve's school, she's not feeling well so we've sent her home. It doesn't seem to be anything serious, but you might want to call at home to check. I'll ring your other emergency contact now. Bye."'

The deputy head checked his list and rang the number. 'Hello, Mrs Knight, this is the school—'

'Is something wrong with Maisie?' The volume was so high, they could hear her responses.

'No, it's Eve, you're down as her emergency contact as well as her father.'

'Is she okay?'

'We don't think it's serious but she needs to go home. Could you come and pick her up? We've tried her father but he's not answering his phone.'

'Ridpath is probably busy. It's not a problem – I'll be there in twenty minutes.'

'Great, we'll keep her in the school office till you arrive.'

The deputy head quickly put down the phone and scribbled an absence pass for her. 'Make sure you keep this safe, Eve. Please wait for Mrs Knight to take you home.'

Eve took the absence pass, folded it carefully and placed it on the inside pocket of her uniform.

–

Mrs Knight, Maisie's mum, arrived twenty-five minutes later.

'How are you feeling, Eve?'

'It's just bad cramps, Mrs Knight, nothing too bad, but I feel like I want to be sick.' Eve pretended to retch again.

'Do you want me to take you to the doctor?'

'No,' Eve said quickly, 'I just want to go to bed with a hot water bottle. I'll be fine later on.'

'Okay, let me take you home.' She turned to her own daughter. 'Don't you have classes, Maisie?'

'I thought I'd come home with Eve, too?'

'No, you don't little lady, back to classes for you,' she said firmly. She put her arm round Eve, helping her to her feet. 'Come with me and I'll drive you back.' She stared back at her daughter over her shoulder. 'Maisie, back to your classes.'

'I'll let you know if there's any history homework, Eve.'

Mrs Knight picked up Eve's backpack and helped her to hobble out of the school.

The drive back home was quiet with Eve lying across the back seat, pretending to dry heave every few minutes. Mrs Knight stopped outside the front door of Eve's house, and helped her up the garden path.

'Are you sure you'll be okay? I know how bad menstrual cramps can be. I suffered myself when I was your age.'

'I'm okay, really, Mrs Knight.' She put the key in the lock and opened the door. 'Thank you once again, Mrs Knight, you're a star. Thank you so much.'

She then went inside closing the door behind her, leaving Maisie's mum standing on the garden path.

Eve leant against the door and breathed a sigh of relief. The first part of her plan worked, now to implement the rest of it.

She straightened up and ran up the stairs.

She needed to change out of her uniform, pick up a few things and check her father's laptop for the address. Then she would do what she had been planning since last night.

It was time to see Billy Diamond again.

Chapter SIXTY-TWO

Megan Muldowney waited exactly thirty seconds before she spoke. Enough time for the social worker and Anita Forsyth to be well away from the room. All the time, Ridpath just sat there staring into mid-air, thinking.

'What did you mean, Ridpath? You know who killed her mother?'

Ridpath scratched his head. 'I think I do, but give me a few moments. I just need to work it all out in my head.'

He closed his eyes and replayed the events of the last three days in his mind while Megan remained dutifully quiet.

At first it was cloudy and unclear. The testimony of the witness, Paul Dacre, about Tony Abbott walking up to the petrol station. Mrs Challinor voicing her worries about the investigation into the death of Jane Forsyth. Ridpath's attendance at the weekly MIT work-in-progress meeting. Being briefed by Steve Carruthers. Eve being anxious and upset. Ron Pleasance hurrying to solve the murder and the suicide, rushing to the wrong conclusions. Why were they all wrong?

And then it came back to him. Carruthers' words at the meeting, what were they? It was about the home invasion in Saddleworth, the crime they were all investigating. Something written on the mirror. 'I am guilty', that was it. Nobody understood why the killer had used those words.

But this morning Terri had told him Tony Abbott had written exactly the same words on Pump 8 before he died.

A coincidence?

You don't believe in coincidences, remember? 'Ridpath, what are you doing?' Megan's voice intruded on his thoughts. 'Shouldn't we go back to the station now? Inspector Pleasance wants a report on our interview with Anita Forsyth this morning.'

He put his finger up to stop her speaking. He was close now, he could feel it. How did the death of Jane Forsyth fit in with all this? A murder committed not by a fourteen-year-old girl but by a tall man with large hands.

How did it all fit together? Were the deaths all linked, including the murders of the family in Saddleworth?

But how did Tony Abbott's flat being trashed come into all this and why was he wearing hooks in his skin when he died?

Why didn't the pieces fit together? There seemed to be too many and they were all different sizes, like a jigsaw puzzle made by a madman.

One piece was missing and, if he was right, he knew where to find it. If it was there, it would prove it wasn't a coincidence. It would prove the deaths of Jane Forsyth, Tony Abbott and the Ashton family were all linked. The same tall man with large hands had killed all six people either directly or by forcing them to kill themselves.

He opened his eyes. 'Megan, call Andy Fletcher. Tell him to meet us at 26 Handley Road as soon as he can. Make sure he brings all the files from Tony Abbott's cases with him and the keys for the house.'

'What about Inspector Pleasance? He's going to be really pissed off with us. Remember he said to brief him as soon as we'd finished interviewing the girl?'

'This is more important than Ron Pleasance.'

Ridpath's phone rang again. He checked the screen, but didn't recognise the number. He'd let it go to voicemail and answer it later.

'But you told me covering your arse with your boss was one of the most important jobs for any junior officer.'

'Sometimes, you have to ignore what I say. This is more important, make the call to Andy Fletcher.'

'Okay, you're the boss.' She pulled out her mobile phone.

'One last question before you make the call. Do you know a Sale police constable, Alan Sagfield?'

'Yeah, I've seen him around the station.'

'How tall is he?'

'What?'

'How tall is he?'

'Are you serious?'

'I've never been more serious, Megan. I'll ask again, how tall is he?'

'A lot shorter than you. I'd say five foot eight inches, give or take an inch.'

Ridpath closed his eyes. He knew who the killer was. Now, he just had to prove it.

Chapter SIXTY-THREE

He sat outside their house in Hale, watching and listening to Robert Wallace's last moments with his family.

'I have to go now. Be good to your mother.'

He bent down in front of his son and gave him a hug. 'You're going to be the man of the house from now on, James. You need to be strong. Your mother will need your help.'

'Where are you going, Dad?'

The man glanced at his wife. 'Just away for a while.'

'When will you be coming back?' the boy asked.

The father didn't answer but moved along to his young daughter. 'Robyn, you're nearly ten now. You have your exams this year. Make sure you do well – make your father proud.'

'They're easy, Dad. My school says I'm sure to pass.'

'You're going to be late, Robert.'

The man glared at his wife. 'I'm saying goodbye to the kids, Martha, I know the time.' He turned back to his children. 'Now come together and give me a big hug.'

Looking at the scene on his iPad, the man found it almost touching, like something from that old Seventies TV series, *The Waltons*.

'Why are you crying, Daddy?' the young girl asked.

'I'm not crying, Robyn, just have something in my eye.'

'If you don't leave now, you're going to be late. He might get angry.'

The man released his children and knelt on the floor his head bowed and his hands on his knees.

After what seemed like an age, he nodded once and then slowly, painfully, clambered to his feet. He went out into the hallway where the man couldn't see him, returning thirty seconds later wearing a coat and a scarf.

How charming, the man thought, *he's on his way to die and yet he still remembered to wrap up well. Tony Abbott didn't bother. He just walked out into the late autumn night in his T-shirt and jeans.*

The wife adjusted his scarf. 'You'd better leave now. Try to offer him money again. We'll sell everything, including the house and the business, and give it all to him.'

'He's not interested in money.'

'Try anyway. Don't give up, keep trying.'

'That's what you said to me when I was playing football, Daddy, "never give up",' his daughter said.

Robert Wallace stared at his daughter, his eyes filling with tears.

'You'd better leave now.' His wife put his arm around his shoulders and ushered him out of the living room, before rushing back five seconds later. 'Don't forget to take your laptop. He said to bring it with you and you'd better keep it open in case he messages you.'

The camera on the laptop shook for a few moments as it was handed across to Robert Wallace.

'Bye,' was all Rob Wallace said and he walked out of the house.

The man lifted his head from the iPad and looked through the windscreen. Robert Wallace walked from his front door to the car, placing the laptop carefully on the passenger seat facing him. He then walked round the back of the car, opened the driver's door and climbed in.

The man returned to watching his iPad. Robert Wallace just sat there staring out of the windscreen, his eyes glazed and filmed with tears.

For a second, the man watching thought he was going to walk back into the house, not carry out the instructions.

Then Robert Wallace banged on the steering wheel once and started the engine, pulling out onto the main road through the open iron gates without looking back.

The man smiled. He had started on his journey.

It would only end one way: with Robert Wallace's death.

He started his own engine and followed the car. In sixty minutes, it would all be over. The man who had killed his parents would be dead.

Was he going to join Robert Wallace or was he going to leave England completely, go somewhere interesting like Thailand or Bali? Find a new life, become another person?

He didn't know yet, he would decide after his target died.

It was the only part of his plan that was still up in the air.

Chapter SIXTY-FOUR

Eve rushed upstairs and immediately changed out of her uniform. Standing in front of her closet, she realised that everything inside was black. Black dresses. Black shirts. Black jumpers. What had happened to all the bright colours she used to wear when her mum was alive?

Memories of her mother wormed their way into her brain. Her smell: a hint of lavender mixed with the softest aroma of almond. Her touch: too gentle, almost tentative as if her mother were afraid of breaking her. Her sound: a voice soft and generous and warm, not like a teacher's at all. Her face: vague now becoming vaguer. Why was it so difficult to remember what her mum looked like?

She walked into her dad's bedroom. The picture of her mum still in its frame beside his bed. A shrine to her memory. It was almost as if her dad had placed incense and a bowl of fruit on it like the little temple to their ancestors found in her grandparents' home.

She picked up the picture. It didn't look like the mum she remembered. Yes, it was a version of her taken at that particular time, but it didn't capture her mum's vivacity, her life, her green hair at Christmas, her love of dim sum, her laugh…

Enough.

She put the picture down and went back into her room. It was time to move on in so many ways today. To look forward, not back. She chose a pair of black jeans and a simple black jumper. She wanted to look as unobtrusive as possible before she met Billy.

Downstairs, she slipped on her shoes and went into the kitchen. She thought about grabbing something to eat before she left but she wanted to get this over with. Instead, she took a glass of milk from the fridge. Why was she drinking so much milk these days?

Another phase she was going through. Her body must need calcium.

Taking the glass of milk into the living room, she sat down behind her dad's laptop. He was always cagey about logging onto his computer in front of her but she had still managed to see his password. He was one of those tech illiterates who used the same password for everything. Holding more than two in your head at any one time was impossible once you were over forty, apparently.

She typed the password into the laptop.

POLLY.

Pretty predictable, Dad, but still nice. One day, he would have to move on, too.

The screen flashed up and she clicked the GMP icon that would lead to his police account. Now was the harder part: she didn't know what the password to enter this was but Dad had written it down in his desk diary under his home details. She guessed that was in case he forgot it.

She entered the twelve numbers and letters. GMP hadn't got around to creating two-step security like a messaged password yet, luckily for her.

She ignored all the files arrayed in a straight line down the left-hand side and honed in on one titled Billy Diamond. She clicked it and Billy's details came up. Apparently, he had been released on bail into the care of an aunt who lived in Didsbury. Not too far away but it would still take some time to get there.

She copied the address down on her hand and closed the laptop, remembering to log off before she did. There would be a record that somebody had accessed his files, but she hoped Dad wouldn't check.

Perhaps she would tell him what she had done.

Perhaps.

She went back into the hallway and checked the address one more time. She knew roughly where it was. Glancing at the clock, she put on her coat, pulling it tight around her body.

In the kitchen, she opened the cutlery drawer and took out a knife, a small one that would perfectly fit in her pocket; nobody would be able to see it.

Back in the hallway, she took one last look around the house.

She had spent so much time here, both happy and sad.

She tried to concentrate on the happy times but the sad ones kept intruding.

Life was like that, she thought, people always remembered the bad stuff never the good.

Chapter SIXTY-FIVE

'Where is he?'

Ridpath checked his watch again. 10.50 a.m. Traffic had been heavy getting to Sale from Ford Avenue, the usual road works. He'd expected Andy Fletcher to already be at the house waiting for them when they arrived but he was nowhere to be seen.

'Call him, Megan, find out where he is.'

She made the call, Ridpath listening in to one side of the conversation.

'Where are you? … On the way? You should have been here twenty minutes ago. … What? Inspector Pleasance did that?' She frowned and bowed her head. 'Get here as soon as you can, Andy. We're waiting outside the house on Handley Road.'

She ended the call but didn't say anything.

'Well?'

'He was about to leave when Pleasance called him into his office and wanted to know everything about the investigation. Apparently you're going to be taken off it by this afternoon and Pleasance put back in charge. Your boss, Claire Trent, was told by the assistant chief constable yesterday evening. Pleasance is just waiting for the email to come through before he removes you.'

Ridpath smiled. 'He'll have to find me first.' He switched his phone to airplane mode.

'Shouldn't we go back to the station? At least you can brief Pleasance before he takes over.'

'We're going nowhere near Sale nick, Megan, not for as long as we can. We're this close to working out what happened.' Ridpath held his index finger and his thumb millimetres apart. 'I just need one final confirmation that the cases are linked.'

'Which cases are linked? I don't get it...'

'Is that his car?' Ridpath pointed as a blue Vauxhall turned the corner at the top of the road at too high a speed.

'It looks like Andy's driving. And you still haven't answered my question.'

'Give me a few more minutes and I'll know. Please?' he added at the last second.

'Okay, just ten more minutes and then we go back to the station. You might be at the end of your career but I'm just starting mine. I can't afford to piss off people like Pleasance or else I'll end up handing out parking tickets for the rest of my life.'

The blue Vauxhall parked behind them and Andy Fletcher stepped out of the car. Ridpath and Megan went to meet him. The young detective was breathless.

'I had to sneak out the back way. Pleasance told me not to come here, said he was taking over. Melissa is covering for me, she'll tell him I'm having an early lunch.'

'Thanks, Andy, do you have the keys?'

'I had to nick them from the evidence store. Pleasance is going to kill me.'

'But you still did it.'

Fletcher shook his head. 'I don't know why – I'm a bloody fool.'

'You might make a good detective yet, Andy.'

They walked up the driveway and Fletcher opened the front door to the house, clearing the police tape out of the way.

The house smelt dusty and unlived in, the whole atmosphere cold and unloved. Ridpath could smell the acrid tang of fingerprint powder and acetone in the air. The traces the forensics teams always left behind.

'Why are we here?' asked Megan.

'I want you to search the house. You two take downstairs while I take upstairs.'

'What are we looking for?'

'Writing, a message somewhere. Remember to wear gloves, we don't want to contaminate the scene any more than it's already been messed with.'

'What message?'

'You'll know when you see it,' Ridpath said over his shoulder as he strode up the stairs.

At the top, he looked for the master bedroom and found it on the right. Inside was completely normal except that the bed itself had been stripped of its sheets and mattress, leaving only the bed frame.

This was where Jane Forsyth had lain down, where PC Sagfield and the EMT, David Grayson, had tried to resuscitate her with CPR. Where somebody, not her daughter, had strangled her with their bare hands and then covered up the murder by tying a belt around her neck, pulling it tight, and then taking it off, leaving it next to her.

Ridpath put on his gloves and opened the right side of the wardrobe door. Inside were some women's clothes, nothing fancy just coats, shirts and dresses hanging up. The other side had a row of drawers. He opened the top one and saw underwear, the next one down had bras, the third socks and the fourth a few belts. Jane Forsyth was as obviously neat and organised as HR had reported.

The belt drawer looked like something was missing to Ridpath's eyes. Had the killer taken the belt from here and left it on the bed to cover up his murder?

Probably.

He scanned the walls, there were no messages written on them, certainly not what he was looking for. Had he got it all wrong? Had he not understood? Jumped to conclusions too quickly, not tracked the evidence properly?

Andy shouted from downstairs, 'I think you'd better come and see this, Ridpath.'

Chapter SIXTY-SIX

The killer stayed three cars behind Robert Wallace as he followed the route in his instructions. From Hale he went up the A560, turning onto Princess Parkway just after Baguley and leaving it at the junction with Barlow Moor Road. It was not the most direct path from Hale to the roundabout near the M60 in Carrington, but there was a reason for that.

He wanted Wallace to drive past his parents in Southern Cemetery, to honour them for a few seconds as he drove to his death.

When he turned left at Wilmslow Road, Wallace would pick up the same route taken by his parents on this day six years ago. The man was about ten minutes ahead of schedule but that was allowed… just.

As he drove behind Wallace, the memories flooded back again. His dad driving. His brother with the map on his knees. His mother already getting the travel Scrabble out of its bag and the clack clack clack as she mixed up the tiles.

Driving down the road, merging with Edge Lane, past Turn Moss playing fields where he and his dad and his brother used to walk the dog even on the coldest days, over to the banks of the Mersey to hear the rushing, trilling sound of the river in full spate, the dog barking, his dad saying, 'Keep up, David, Keep up.'

Memories.

Even when his family was gone, their memories still remained like stains on a wall.

Unchangeable.

Fixed.

Immoveable.

Wallace turned left on Chester Road and filtered onto the correct lane for the M60. It was while they were waiting at the lights to turn onto the ring road that Mum had remembered she'd forgotten the butter.

It was all flooding back now, every sound, every breath, every nuance of feeling. Time was standing still for him, the cars moving as if they were driving through glue.

He followed Wallace as he kept in the left lane, indicating left at the Carrington turn-off. As instructed, he took the correct first exit off the roundabout and immediately pulled his car over.

He drove past him and parked at a lay-by approximately 100 yards ahead, looking back through the rear-view mirror at Wallace's Volvo as it parked on the road.

He checked the image on the iPad. The man was doing exactly as instructed, sitting in his car waiting for his orders. The only sign of nervousness a never-ending tapping of the steering wheel with his fingers.

Should he end it now? Tell him how he should kill himself?

No.

He'd waited this long and he could wait fifteen minutes more. There was a certain beauty in making the man commit the act at exactly the same time his parents and brother had died six years ago.

12.02 p.m. on October 31, 2018.

He checked his wrist. The watch he had been wearing that day was covered by his sleeve. He pulled back the cuff to see the cracked glass and the time frozen forever.

12.02.

He typed a message on the keyboard.

> **Rellik:** Wait fifteen minutes. Your final instructions on how to kill yourself will be delivered then.

He logged out of Signal. The last thing he wanted now was to engage in conversation with Robert Wallace. Not yet anyway.

On the screen, the man was checking his laptop.

His face filled with pain.

David Grayson smiled. He could feel the presence of his mother, father and brother in the car with him.

They were smiling too.

Chapter SIXTY-SEVEN

She stood outside the house in Didsbury where Billy Diamond was staying, according to her father's records. It was strangely designed, with a portal-like window of a ship halfway up the right-hand wall.

Off to her left, the Mersey meandered through the suburbs of Manchester, eventually making its way around to Stretford Cemetery where her mum was buried. As ever, it seemed like everything was connected in this and every other world.

Her mum, her dad, herself and Billy.

She'd read somewhere about the butterfly effect. It came from chaos theory, where a tiny change in one part of a system can cause a huge, non-linear effect elsewhere. The flapping of a butterfly's wings in the Amazon could cause major storms over Manchester. Perhaps that was why there was so much rain. She laughed to herself. 'Bloody butterflies, stop flapping your wings.'

But she knew she was just deflecting again. Making everything an academic exercise rather than dealing with the emotions of the here and now. Her therapist said there was nothing wrong with it; it was her way of dealing with the world and her life. A way of distancing herself from the depth of her feelings and the unpredictability, the chaos of emotions.

She wished she didn't do it, though. She wished she was more like her dad, who confronted people and forced them to admit their guilt.

Perhaps that's what she had inherited from her mum: the ability to distance oneself. She remembered when her dad was ill with cancer, it was her mum who had been able to carry on as normal, to keep the family together. Her father had given himself over to depression, watching so many endless hours of daytime television, he could almost be an antiques expert or a property agent.

Her mum had been the steel that had kept him going, kept him fighting.

Enough.

She had put this off too long. It was time to face up to Billy Diamond and confront her fears. She couldn't let him rule her for the rest of her life.

She felt the sharp edge of the blade in her pocket as she opened the gate of the house where Billy was staying.

She marched up to the front door and hesitated, her hand poised in front of the bell.

Could she do this?

Should she do this?

She took a deep breath, stood up straighter and pressed the button.

Inside, she could hear a male voice.

The door opened.

Chapter SIXTY-EIGHT

Ridpath ran downstairs as quickly as he could. Andy Fletcher was standing next to a door in the kitchen with Megan beside him.

'There's a downstairs bathroom and I saw something written on the mirror.' He led Ridpath into a small room with a toilet and sink in one corner and a washing machine and drier stacked in the other. There wasn't much room for anything else.

Fletcher pointed to a mirror above the sink. 'Is this what you were looking for?'

On the mirror, written in red felt pen, the words 'I am guilty' were clearly visible. The killer in the Ashton home invasion had also written on a mirror.

Ridpath moved closer to the sink to examine the words carefully. As he did, he realised he could see his own reflection through the words. Was this what the killer was saying about his murders or was he saying it about the victims?

Or was it both?

'That's it, Andy.' He took a picture of the mirror using his mobile phone, took his phone off airplane mode and sent it to Steve Carruthers along with a message, *I need to talk to you.*

'Is this the connection you were looking for, Ridpath?' asked Megan.

He nodded. 'Terri told me this morning that Tony Abbott had written the same words on the panel of Pump 8. If the words were also in this house, the deaths are connected. Even more, it's linked to the home invasion in Saddleworth, too. Andy, I need you to go through Tony Abbott's case files. Were there any cases where Tony, Jane Forsyth and a solicitor called Clive Ashton were involved in some way?'

'I don't remember but I can check it out on my laptop.'

'Do it and quickly. Megan, I want—'

Ridpath was interrupted by the sound of his mobile ringing.

'Boss,' he answered. It was Carruthers.

'This better be good, Ridpath. I'm in the middle of a meeting with the assistant chief constable who's presently dragging me over a pit of coals backwards and, guess what, your name has come up more than once. If that photo is your idea of a joke, I'm going to have your balls for a paperweight.'

Ridpath took a deep breath. 'It's not a joke, boss. Remember you asked me to look into the case of a woman who was killed by her fourteen-year-old daughter? Well, I'm at the house now and "I was guilty" was written on a mirror...'

'The same as our home invasion?'

'Exactly.'

'But why wasn't it picked up by the CSIs? I would have been told immediately if those words appeared anywhere.'

'I think he came back to the house after the CSIs had finished. He probably couldn't do it at the time, too many people around. Anyway, I believe he came back afterwards and finished the job.'

'By writing on the mirror?'

'Right, but that's not all. I was also looking into a man who killed himself in a petrol station. Get this, the woman who was murdered worked for him in the Road Policing Unit. I asked Terri Landsman to check something he had written on the panel of a pump before he died. He also wrote, "I am guilty".'

There was silence at the other end of the phone. 'I don't get it, Ridpath. Are you telling me the murder of a family in Saddleworth, another murder of a woman in Sale and the suicide of a man in a petrol station are all connected?'

'Yes, sir.'

'How? Why? When?'

'Just a minute, boss. Andy have you found any cases that link the three people?'

'I think so.' Andy Fletcher came into the bathroom with his open laptop. 'There's just one case when a solicitor called Clive Ashton represented somebody involved in a traffic accident. The weird thing is this is the shortest case in Tony Abbott's files. Despite three people dying, the investigation seemed to reach its conclusions quickly.' Fletcher scanned the report. 'It was driver error with no other vehicle involved apparently. The documentation for that conclusion seems a little lacking. No witnesses and no interviews with any of the occupants of the car. Also, some of the documentation seems to have vanished.'

'What?'

'See, it says there should be thirty-seven pages but there are only eleven in the case file.'

A tinny voice came from the loudspeaker of the phone. 'What's going on Ridpath? Ridpath!'

'Sorry, boss, I think we've found the link between the victims. There was a traffic accident and three of our victims were involved in the investigation afterwards.'

'What accident?'

Ridpath scanned the initial accident report. 'Three members of a family died in an accident on October 31, 2018 with one person surviving. The name of the family was… Oh shit.'

Chapter SIXTY-NINE

David Grayson stepped out of his car and walked towards the area where Robert Wallace was parked.

He adjusted the bright green jacket of his uniform so it kept out the wind. He always found it useful to wear his uniform during the day even when he wasn't working. People naturally assumed you were just going to work or coming off shift. And anyway, he was proud of the work he did.

Robert Wallace ignored him when he knocked on the window. He knocked again and the window wound down.

'Sorry for parking here – I won't be long. I'm just waiting for something.'

'You're waiting for me.'

Wallace looked at the uniform and his mouth dropped open. 'What?'

'I'm here to give you the final instructions.'

'It's you?'

'It's always been me.'

'You killed Clive Ashton and his family?'

He nodded. 'I wanted all of you to kill yourselves, but he thought he was too clever. He was going to go to the police the following morning so I had to kill him that evening. The kids bled everywhere. Very messy. Of course, I shattered the heads of Clive and his wife with a shotgun. You see my brother died in the same way. His head was smashed too. That's what happens when human flesh hits the hard edge of a glass windscreen. But you know all this, you were there. You caused the accident.'

'I didn't mean to. It wasn't my fault.'

'That's not what Clive told me before he died. He said you'd been drinking and hadn't stopped at the roundabout so you crashed into my dad's car. I knew you paid everybody off, the investigators Tony Abbott and Jane Forsyth received 100,000 quid each from you. Is that the cost of three human lives these days? 100,000 pounds?' He whistled. 'A bargain, I think.'

'I panicked, I didn't know what to do... You killed them all?'

'Jane screwed up her death. I made sure I was on call in that area on the day just in case. She was supposed to die like my mother: pumped full of drugs and impervious to the world. But she messed it up so I had to finish her off. I quite enjoyed strangling that fat neck while the police were just yards away downstairs. She was too far gone to resist. Tony Abbott was far more stoical. I suspect he was looking forward to dying, his guilt was such a burden to him.'

'You're a monster...'

'I'm the monster? I didn't pay people money to cover up deaths, did I?'

'It was an accident...'

'An accident. That's the way you're going to die today. Here are your final instructions. You are to walk back to the bridge over the M60. When you reach the middle, you are to stand on the parapet, shout out "I am guilty" and then you are going to jump. The beauty is that you probably won't be killed by the fall but by the cars rushing along the highway at over seventy miles an hour, crashing into your prone body. It's going to be another traffic accident. You won't feel a thing by the way, not after the first car hits you.'

'I'm not going to do it, I refuse.'

He brought up the iPad so Robert Wallace could see it, showing a picture of the outside of his house. He'd left a camera there to make sure the wife did as she was told and stayed in the house.

'I just need to contact my associate who is outside your house.' He checked the time on the screen. 'Unless you walk to the bridge and jump from it in exactly eight minutes and thirty-six seconds, I will send him a message to kill your family. He will make certain the children die first and painfully.'

'But you can't do this… I can't…'

'You have your instructions. I am going to walk back to my car and watch as you carry them out.' He checked the iPad again. 'You now have eight minutes and twenty-eight seconds.'

David Grayson walked away from the car knowing that Robert Wallace was watching him. There was no accomplice watching the house ready to kill the family but Wallace didn't know that. If the man didn't do it in the next eight minutes he would keep his promise though.

He would kill Wallace now and the family later. It wouldn't be as fitting as the man killing himself. But he would die nonetheless and that's all that mattered.

He reached the car and turned back.

Wallace was watching him. He held the iPad up.

Seven minutes and ten seconds to go.

Chapter SEVENTY

Ridpath stared at the name of the family on the accident report.

Grayson.

There was his proof. He had already worked out that only two people had the means and opportunity to kill Jane Forsyth: the copper who had gone upstairs to perform CPR and the EMT who had come to the house in answer to the 999 call. If the doctors were right, Alan Sagfield wasn't tall enough, nor were his hands large enough, to strangle Jane Forsyth.

That only left David Grayson.

Looking at the traffic report, Grayson now had a motive too. His whole family died in an accident, but who had killed them?

It was obvious that Tony Abbott and Jane Forsyth were involved in the cover-up. Their sudden ability to buy expensive houses suggested a new source of wealth. The solicitor, Clive Ashton, had probably organised it all, bribing the officers to cover up for the man who had caused the accident in the first place.

But who was he?

Ridpath scanned the report looking for a name, any name.

Nothing there.

'Ridpath… Ridpath…' Steve Carruthers' voice was coming from his phone. 'What's going on?'

'Boss, I think your killer is an EMT called David Grayson. That's spelt G-R-A-Y-S-O-N. See if they can track where he is right now.'

'Got it, Ridpath. Are you sure it's him?'

'Definite, boss. Motive, means and opportunity to kill Jane Fletcher and I remember EMTs being present at the death of Tony Abbott. I'll bet he was there too. I have no description of him other than he is a tall man…'

'Tall?'

'Extraordinarily tall according to the doctors.'

'No worries, I'll get a current picture from the ambulance service.'

'Great, boss.' Ridpath continued to scan the accident report. 'Somebody called the accident in to the call centre at 12.02 p.m. on October 31, 2018 but that person had already left the scene by the time the police and ambulances responded.'

'Good work, Ridpath.'

Ridpath continued to read the report, something about it was nagging away inside his head. What was it?

And then it hit him like a two-ton piledriver.

'Shit,' was his only response.

'What is it, Ridpath?'

'The accident, it happened on this day six years ago, boss. If David Grayson has been killing all the people involved in the cover up of his family's death, wouldn't he kill the person who actually caused it?'

'What are you on about, Ridpath?'

The detective checked the time on his phone. 11.55 a.m.

'Boss, the next victim is going to die in exactly seven minutes…'

'What? Who?'

'I don't know who but I think I know where. We've just got seven minutes to get there.'

Chapter SEVENTY-ONE

David Grayson moved his gaze from the Volvo just one hundred yards away to the iPad with its image of Robert Wallace sitting behind the wheel of the car.

The man had his head in his hands, his chest heaving, as he wept for himself.

For a second, Grayson's attention was diverted from the car to the ditch that ran beside it. There were no scorch marks any more and the burnt-out carcass of their old Rover had long since been dragged away to the scrapyard.

He remembered lying in that ditch reaching up to Wallace staring down at him. Reaching out for him and the man simply running away, leaving him there to die.

Once again, the image of his father's face being eaten by the flames erupting inside the car came back to him. He was sure he could hear his father's screams even now. A high-pitched yell that cut through his body like a hot knife through butter.

And then there was silence.

And the smell of burning rubber and petrol.

And then blackness.

Grayson came back to the present. Wallace was still sitting in the car, crying. Was he going to kill himself or would he run away from this task, too?

He reached into the back seat and pulled out the shotgun from its fabric case. He broke it open, checking that the two shells were still loaded inside. Then he locked the barrel and placed it carefully on the passenger seat. He picked up the iPad, checked the time and sent a message to Wallace.

> **Rellik:** Five minutes and twenty-two seconds to go. Are you going to do it or will I message my associate to kill your wife and family? He will kill the children first and force your wife to watch. Is this what you want to happen?

The answer when it came back was blunt.

> **PropMan76:** No.
> **Rellik:** No, you won't do it or no, don't kill my children?
> **PropMan76:** Don't kill my children.
> **Rellik:** Then do it.
> **Rellik:** You have four minutes and twelve seconds left.

Chapter SEVENTY-TWO

The door opened as Eve reached up to press the bell one more time. An older woman with a kindly-looking face answered.

'Can I help you?'

'I'm looking for Billy, is he here?'

'He is, but he's not supposed to see people. He has to stay in the house and I can't let you in.'

'I don't want to come in – I just want to talk to him.'

The woman's eyes narrowed and her voice became sharper. 'How do you know Billy? Did you used to work with him in the care home?'

Eve's eyes darted left and right and she tried to think of an answer. She could hardly say, *I know him because he once tried to kill me.*

'I met him at school...' she blurted out.

'School? But he stopped going to school at fourteen, his father...'

'His father controlled him. I know, he told me. Look, I won't be long, I promise. I just want to speak with him.'

The woman seemed to think about this for hours, before finally shouting over her shoulder. 'Billy, it's for you, someone to see you.'

She then turned back to Eve. 'He's different now, a very different person away from the influence of his father and that awful man, Lardner. He's changed.' She then shouted upstairs again. 'Billy, there's somebody to see you. I have to go now and check on my potatoes but don't be too long, dear. I'm sorry I can't let you into the house,' she said directly to Eve.

'I'll stay here, promise.'

She walked away, leaving Eve standing outside. Her hand was in her pocket, feeling the sharp edge of the blade against the ball of her thumb.

A dark shadow appeared at the door followed by the body and head of Billy.

When he saw it was Eve, his mouth opened wide and he took a step backwards. 'You... What are you...' he mumbled.

Eve felt the edge of the knife in her pocket. 'Surprised to see me, Billy?'

'How did you find this address, *my* address?'

She ignored the question. 'It was about a year ago, you were standing on my doorstep, looking up at me. You wanted to come inside, remember?'

'I didn't mean it, I was...'

Billy didn't finish his sentence.

'You wanted to kill me. You broke down my front door, chased me up the stairs and tried to break down my bedroom door while I was cowering inside. I was so scared, Billy.'

Tears began to run down her cheeks as she fought to control her emotions and finally get the words out that had been bottled up inside her for a year.

'I'm sorry, Eve, I really am sorry. I came to your house to tell you.'

'You wanted to kill me, Billy. You think just saying you're sorry makes up for all the pain and fear and anguish

I've been through?' She felt the knife in her pocket, gripping the handle. 'For the last year, I've lived in fear. At night, I lie in bed and I hear your grunts as you tried to break down my door. I hear the splintering of the wood as you hit it. Every single minute of every hour of every day, I hear your snarl as you charged towards me. Your eyes, I'll always remember your eyes, filled with hate and loathing and anger.'

Billy took another step backwards, holding his hands up. 'I'm so sorry, Eve—'

She stopped him from talking with her hand. 'And you know what's the worst? You filled me with your anger that night. You left all that hate inside me. I've had to live with that for one whole year. But not any longer…'

She let go of the knife in her pocket and held up both arms in front of him.

'I forgive you, Billy. I forgive you for everything you did to me that night.'

As she said the words, it felt like a heavy weight had been lifted from her shoulders, that she was no longer weighed down, her back bent double with anger and loathing and hate.

'I forgive you, Billy Diamond,' she repeated before turning her back and striding down the path and onto the streets of Didsbury, leaving Billy standing at the door, tears running down his cheeks.

For the first time since her mother had died, Eve felt that she was free.

Chapter SEVENTY-THREE

Ridpath accelerated down the wrong side of the A56, barely avoiding the traffic island and a zebra crossing.

Beside him Megan hung onto the strap above the passenger door for dear life. In the back of the car, Andy Fletcher was on the phone to Steve Carruthers and, at the same time, being swung from side to side as the car slalomed down the road.

The blue lights on the grill in the windscreen were flashing while the noise from the klaxon was so powerful it was even drowning out the roar from the engine.

'We're on the way to Carrington Spur, sir,' Fletcher shouted. 'Sorry, I can't hear you sir. Why? I don't know. Why are we—?'

'Because that's where the next murder will take place.' Ridpath narrowly avoided an old lady as she crossed the road illegally outside the M&S Simply Food. 'We've got to get there before noon.'

He carried on driving down the middle of the road, the cars in front seeing his lights, dutifully pulling to the side of the road. The traffic lights on School Road were red but that didn't stop him. He slowed slightly, passing the traffic in the outside lane and, checking the crossing traffic was stopping, accelerated across the broad junction.

The road was clear ahead and he stomped even harder on the accelerator. The car surged forward like a thoroughbred given its head.

'DCI Carruthers has also dispatched cars from Stretford, Ridpath. Their ETA is 12.08.'

'Too late.'

He surged past the red lights at Cross Street, coming to a stop as an old biddy was trying to turn right into Chapel Road. Could he squeeze through the gap on the left before the lorry reached him? Megan let out a scream and covered her head with her arm.

He swung the wheel left as the truck braked hard, just missing the rear of the old woman's Toyota.

Once again, he pressed his foot as hard as he could against the accelerator.

'I'd like to get to this place in one piece, Ridpath. No, more than that. I'd love to get there alive.'

The clock on the dashboard said 11.58. Ridpath glanced down at his speedometer. 78 mph. Perhaps he could go a little faster.

'Hang on, Megan.'

He pressed once more on the accelerator. Would they get there on time?

'Andy, have they found David Grayson yet?'

Fletcher relayed the message on his phone, all the time staring out through the windscreen as the buildings, banks and supermarkets of Sale raced past them in a blur.

'Not yet,' he answered. 'Grayson isn't answering his phone and he's not on duty until two p.m.'

'Shit, he's already there.'

Chapter SEVENTY-FOUR

David Grayson glanced at the time on his iPad once more.

11.59.30.

Robert Wallace hadn't moved for the last three minutes. He'd just sat there, staring out through the windscreen, his eyes fixed at some long-lost point on the horizon.

Should he send him one last reminder?

He typed in the words.

> **Rellik:** You have 150 seconds left to make your decision.

He watched as Robert Wallace heard the noise from the message app and stared at his computer screen.

Still he did not move.

> **Rellik:** 100 seconds left

Still no movement.

He checked his watch now. The old cracked one with the time frozen at 12.02. A moment stuck in time.

> **Rellik:** 70 seconds left.
> **Rellik:** If you do not move now, I will send the message to my associate. Your wife and children will be killed.
> **Rellik:** I will kill *you* myself.

Robert Wallace glanced at the computer screen. Still, he sat there behind the wheel of his car, unmoving, showing no emotion, almost catatonic.

This was the moment of most danger in Grayson's plan. If Wallace decided to do a runner now, he'd have to follow him through the streets of Manchester, waiting for a red light to take a shot. Or he could use Plan C; walk over to the car and just kill him before he drove away.

He decided the latter was the best course of action. David Grayson lifted the shotgun from the passenger seat and opened his driver side door.

Fifty seconds.

What a shame. Now he would have to kill the wife and children, too. He didn't really want to, but Wallace had not completed his end of the bargain and such duplicitousness could never be forgiven.

Forty seconds.

He stepped out of the car, holding the shotgun in his right hand.

For the first time, Wallace seemed to come out of his trance. He opened his own passenger door, and leaving it wide open, began to walk towards the bridge over the M60 at Carrington Interchange.

Thirty seconds.

He stood in front of the parapet of the bridge, staring down at the traffic below as it raced past beneath him.

Drivers hurrying to their next meeting. Mothers going home to see their children. Truck drivers trying to make the last delivery before their lunch. None of them noticed the man standing beside the bridge looking down on them. Even if they had noticed, most wouldn't have cared.

Twenty-five seconds.

Grayson watched as the man raised his right leg, placing his knee on the top of the parapet. He levered himself up until he was kneeling on top of the bridge over the thousands of cars rushing beneath.

Fifteen seconds.

Slowly, he raised himself up until he was standing upright on the bridge. He raised his hands in the air as if appealing to some God in the skies above his head, and yelled out.

Ten seconds.

'Do it,' shouted Grayson. 'Jump.'

The man bent his knees.

Five seconds.

Out of nowhere a car, its lights flashing and klaxon blaring, came racing around the roundabout, sliding to a halt near the man on the wrong side of the road.

A man jumped out the car and immediately stopped, holding his hands down and saying something to Robert Wallace. The man advanced slowly to where Wallace stood, talking all the time, holding his hands out.

'Jump, you bastard. Jump,' he shouted.

Wallace and the detective looked back at him.

He had to go.

It was time for Wallace's wife and children to die.

Chapter SEVENTY-FIVE

Ridpath opened the door and jumped out. He saw the man standing on the edge of the bridge. Beneath him the cars rushed past on the M60.

Ridpath stopped.

The man's knees were trembling, his feet near the edge of the drop onto the road below.

'You don't have to do this, we know who he is.'

He took two steps forward and stopped again, his hands held low. Behind him, he could hear the sound of the klaxon and see the reflections of the flashing red and blue lights on the road.

'Turn that bloody noise off,' he shouted over his shoulder.

The sound stopped instantly as Megan shut it off. All that remained now was the roar of traffic beneath their feet.

'Did you hear me? You don't have to do this any more, we know it's David Grayson. He's been killing people in revenge for the deaths of his family six years ago.'

He took one step forward.

'What's your name?'

The man's eyes jerked left and right, finally noticing somebody shouting a hundred yards away and then placing something on the front seat.

An ambulance. What was an ambulance doing here?

And then it struck Ridpath. Was that Grayson? Was he watching?

The ambulance quickly U-turned and sped away from the scene.

Ridpath turned back to the man on the bridge, he'd deal with Grayson later. Right now, he had to solve the problem in front of him. 'What's your name?' he asked gently.

'Wallace… Robert Wallace.'

'You drove the car, didn't you?'

The man nodded, glancing across to his right at the ambulance leaving the scene.

'My wife and children, he's going to kill them.'

Ridpath advanced one more step, holding out his hand. The man's knees were trembling even more now. At any moment, they might give way and he would fall thirty feet onto the road below.

'Come on, get down, it's all finished.'

'Don't you understand, it's *not* finished.'

In the distance, Ridpath could hear the cars from Stretford station approaching. They had made good time.

'Come down and tell me about it.'

'He's going to kill them.'

'Who's going to kill them?'

'Him.' Robert Wallace pointed to the ambulance that was driving away from the scene, disappearing round a bend on Carrington Road.

Ridpath took one step closer. He was close enough to grab the man, stop him from falling, but that was a last resort. He tried one last time to talk him down.

'Take my hand.'

The man stared at it for a long time before finally grasping hold and shuffling away from the edge of the parapet.

When he was safely on the pavement, Megan and Andy Fletcher rushed forward to wrap Robert Wallace in their arms and ease him towards their vehicle. The squad cars from Stretford had reached the roundabout and were racing around it to where they were.

The man suddenly began resisting. 'You don't understand – he's going to kill my wife and children. I have to go and save them.'

Ridpath glanced back in the direction of the ambulance. It had vanished out of sight now. 'You're sure Grayson was in that car?'

'He's going to kill my family. He said he has an associate too. They might already be dead.'

Ridpath took him by his shoulders. 'Where is your family?'

The man's eyes glazed over as if the question was too difficult to answer.

'Where is your family?' Ridpath repeated.

Suddenly, the man's eyes focused. 'Hale – 27 Bridge Street.'

Ridpath let him go and jumped in the car. 'Megan, you stay here with him,' he shouted through the open window. 'Get the squad cars to follow me.'

Ridpath leapt into the car, seeing in the rear-view mirror that Robert Wallace was being looked after by Andy Fletcher on the bridge. The passenger side door opened and Megan slid into the passenger seat.

'No copper chases after a suspect on his own. Those are the rules, Ridpath.'

He stared at her. 'While you're here you'd better make yourself useful. Put the address in the satnav. 27 Bridge Street, Hale. And make sure we have backup.'

Without waiting for a reply, he stepped on the accelerator. The car stayed still for a second before the tyres eventually gripped and it fish-tailed before surging forward.

Ridpath flicked the switch on the dashboard. The loud whining noise of the klaxon reverberated through the car once more.

Chapter *SEVENTY-SIX*

Who was the copper? What was he doing there? He had no right to intervene. Robert Wallace was about to jump from the bridge. His body would have been smashed by the cars on the M60 and his nightmare would have been over.

Six years of planning, six years of dreaming, destroyed by some interfering copper.

Bastard.

He banged the steering wheel with his fist.

Bastard.

Now was the time for Plan B. Time to kill Martha Wallace and her children. Time for Robert Wallace to suffer for not obeying his instructions.

Where had he gone wrong?

Had the wife rung the police? Impossible, he hadn't revealed the final destination until after Wallace had left the house.

Had Wallace called the police? Again, impossible. He had been watching him the whole time on the computer. The man had neither made nor received any phone calls.

Perhaps he had messaged his wife and she had called the police?

Bastard.

They would pay for their treachery now. He switched the klaxon on his ambulance on and the vehicle filled with sound. Ahead of him, cars began to pull to the side of the road, making way for the ambulance.

The training facilities of Sale Sharks were on his left. It would only take him twelve more minutes to get to the Wallace's house using this back route through Carrington.

He patted the shotgun on the passenger seat beside him. He'd blow the wife's head off and cut the children's throats. That would teach Wallace for his treachery. Then he would start planning to find Wallace and kill him too.

The police couldn't keep him in witness protection forever. One day, he would come out and David Grayson would be ready.

He wouldn't survive long.

This wasn't the end of his quest, it was simply a postponement.

Wallace and his family would pay for what they had done to his mother, father and brother.

The wife and kids today.

Wallace in the future.

Grayson accelerated and the car raced past Carrington Power Station. In just nine more minutes he would be there.

And they would be dead.

Chapter SEVENTY-SEVEN

Without waiting for the satnav to calculate their route, Ridpath accelerated after David Grayson down Carrington Spur with his lights flashing and siren blaring.

Next to him, Megan Muldowney was on her mobile. 'Control, this is 4762 DC Megan Muldowney. We are requesting backup immediately, Code 1. We are currently in pursuit of an emergency ambulance along Carrington Spur...' She held her phone over the mouthpiece. 'Did you get the licence number of Grayson's vehicle?'

Ridpath stared at the road ahead as he accelerated past some lights in the wrong lane, overtaking two articulated lorries and a school bus. 'No,' he answered.

'Vehicle number unknown. The occupant is an IC1 male, David Grayson, wanted in connection with a home invasion in Saddleworth in October. He is probably armed and dangerous. His destination is 27 Bridge St, Hale. Over.'

'Control here, 4762, immediate assistance acknowledged. All units converging on Carrington Spur and surrounding roads. A unit dispatched to 27 Bridge St, ETA eleven minutes.'

'Tell them not to approach the perp,' shouted Ridpath, as he swerved around another lorry as it hogged the outside lane.

'Control. Responding officers do not approach. Repeat. Do not approach. Suspect armed and dangerous. Over.'

'Instruction received, 4762. Do not approach, suspect armed and dangerous. Standby tactical unit alerted and responding. ETA fourteen minutes. Police helicopter overhead and tracking. What is make and model of the car you are following?'

A quick image flashed in Ridpath's head of the white and green rear of a car vanishing around the corner of the road.

'It's an emergency response ambulance. Don't know the make or model.'

Megan repeated the information to the control officer. 'He's probably got his siren on too and driving quickly.'

'Did you get that control? Over.'

'Understood, 4762. An emergency response vehicle on Carrington Road. Helicopter H4 in the air. ETA three minutes. Over.'

Megan put down her phone and flinched as Ridpath accelerated through a red light and across a road junction, forcing drivers to stamp on their brakes.

'He'll be using his lights, too. All the cars will pull out of his way. We need to move quicker.'

'Take the next left, Ridpath, down Isherwood Road and past United's training ground.'

Ridpath swung the car left without braking, throwing Megan heavily against her safety belt. 'We need to arrive there in one piece.'

'No, we need to arrive there quickly.'

She concentrated on the satnav, deliberately avoiding looking through the windscreen at the blur of hedges and cars rushing past on the narrow country road. 'Once past

United's training ground turn left at the T-junction onto Sinderland Road.'

'No, we need to avoid the centre of Altrincham, we'll get stuck there. I know a quicker way.'

He turned right at Sinderland Road and then almost immediately left, accelerating once more.

'I don't believe this, Ridpath, you're taking us past the crematorium.'

'The dead centre of Manchester, Megan. But it's the quickest route. We'll go down School Lane and then left along Charcoal Lane through Dunham Massey. The roads are narrow but we'll make good time. Langham Road will take us into the heart of Hale through the back way.'

'The satnav is saying we should U-turn, Ridpath.'

'Bugger the satnav. Trust me, this is the quickest way.'

He accelerated once more, focusing totally on the narrow country lane ahead. Dunham Park flashed by on the right-hand side, its red brick walls protecting the country house and the deer from the prying eyes of strangers.

They slowed as they reached a line of traffic queueing at traffic lights to cross the A56.

'Bugger this,' shouted Ridpath, accelerating out into the opposite side of the road, forcing the oncoming traffic to pull to the left. He slowed slightly for the traffic lights on red, before shooting across the road, narrowly missing an oncoming Amazon delivery van.

Megan closed her eyes and gripped the dashboard with her fingers.

Above their heads, they could hear the sound of the helicopter.

'4762, over.'

Megan picked up her radio. 'Here, control, over.'

'Helicopter is tracking you. Support vehicles on their way but stuck in Altrincham. New ETA is 12.34. Over.'

'Roger that, control. Over.'

Ridpath swung right along South Downs Road. 'Bridge Street is on the right, just off Bankhall Lane.'

The large houses and well-manicured gardens of Bowdon and Hale rushed past outside their vehicle.

'There he is,' shouted Ridpath.

Up ahead, the green and white rear of an emergency response ambulance was turning right with its lights flashing. A car stopped to let it cross in front of him and the ambulance raced down Bridge Street.

Ridpath went even faster, the engine roaring in response.

The car which had stopped for the ambulance now moved forward, saw Ridpath coming straight for him and stalled, blocking the right turn.

'Get out the way, man!' shouted Ridpath.

The elderly driver was panicking as he tried to find the right gear on his car.

'GET OUT OF THE WAY!'

Finally, the old man found it and reversed backwards into the car behind him.

Ridpath swung right, narrowly avoiding the bonnet of the old man's car and raced down Bridge Street.

At number 27, an emergency response ambulance was parked haphazardly across the road.

There was nobody inside.

Ridpath stamped on his brakes, sending his car into a long slide. Megan covered her face as the rear of the emergency ambulance came ever closer.

They stopped inches away from a sign in bright neon-green letters. *Ambulance.*

Ridpath flung the door open and ran towards the open gate of number 27.

Behind him, he could hear Megan's footsteps as she raced to keep up.

He ran past the metal gate and up the steeply sloping path, bordered by elegantly clipped hedges.

Then he heard the loud blast of a shotgun.

Three weeks later

Chapter SEVENTY-EIGHT

Mrs Challinor placed the *Evening News* down in front of Ridpath. The headline in big, black bold type on the front cover screamed, 'KILLER TARGETED FAMILY IN REVENGE ATTACK.'

They were sitting in the warm kitchen of her cottage in Little Bollington, with the delightful aroma of roast pork coming from the AGA. Ridpath and Eve had started coming here for lunch on Saturdays. His daughter loved chatting with Mrs Challinor and had become firm friends with Sarah, her daughter. They had gone out for a walk with the dog, leaving Ridpath and Mrs Challinor alone.

He picked up the paper. 'It's pretty much all there. I think GMP's communication people must have briefed the reporter.'

'All of it?'

'Well, not all of it obviously. But certainly the spin that GMP wants to put on the case is front and centre.'

Mrs Challinor checked the roast potatoes were browning nicely. 'So what really happened?'

'It seems David Grayson was taking revenge for the death of his parents and brother in a car accident six years ago. He'd spent time planning it and everything was plotted out to the nth degree. They found all the details in the attic room of his house in Chorlton. They were a strange family, very insular, the kids still living with their parents.'

'Pretty common these days.'

'Not when they're in their forties, surely?'

'I don't know, what with house prices these days.'

Ridpath sighed, thinking of Eve's future. 'Anyway, he killed the Ashton family in Saddleworth, Jane Forsyth in Sale and managed to persuade Tony Abbott to kill himself.'

'I've passed the inquest onto Helen to handle. I feel it wouldn't be correct for me to chair it.'

'Probably the right decision. This is what's not stated in the article: Robert Wallace bribed the accident invest-igators, Abbott and Forsyth, to kill the investigation. The payments were made through his solicitor Clive Ashton.'

'Is he going to be charged?'

'I think so, after all he killed three people and bribed serving police officers to escape conviction. The least he should get is a custodial sentence.'

'Mrs Wallace shot David Grayson?'

'Accidentally according to her. Apparently, she thought her husband couldn't go through with killing himself so she locked up the house and told the children to hide. When Grayson arrived she checked the video doorbell and saw a man dressed in a medic's uniform standing outside. Naturally, she opened the door thinking the EMT was there to tell her of her husband's death. She let him in and when he produced a shotgun, she grabbed it, twisted it upwards and it went off.'

'That's when you arrived?'

'I found her standing over him with the shotgun. He was lying on the ground with half his face shot off while she was screaming at the top of her voice.'

'You should never mess with a woman defending her children.'

'Anyway, I took the gun off her and called the emergency services.'

'You make that sound so nonchalant, Ridpath. "I took the gun off her." Was it as easy as that?'

'Not really, but I had help. Megan Muldowney, the DC, was brilliant. She talked the woman down and unloaded the shotgun after I'd taken it off Martha Wallace.'

Mrs Challinor shook her head. 'You'd better keep this knowledge from Eve. I don't think she'd understand how much danger you were in.'

'I know. I didn't think about it either until it was all over. What would have happened if Martha Wallace had used the gun on me too? She wasn't really in control of herself or her actions.'

The door opened and Ridpath quickly removed the newspaper from the kitchen table.

A dog entered, shook itself violently and went straight to its bowl beside the dresser. It was followed by Eve and Sarah, both of whom were laughing.

'And what did he do next?'

'Well, Sarah, the teacher just stood there for a long time and then said, "I think you should see the deputy head about that, Fulford."'

They both collapsed in gales of laughter, leaving Mrs Challinor and Ridpath to watch them.

'Is it cold outside?' asked Mrs Challinor.

Eve's nose was bright red. She took off her bobble hat and said, 'Freezing but it was a lovely walk in the Bollin Valley. Rufus had a great time.'

The dog, hearing his name, left his now-empty bowl and wandered over to Eve, pushing his head against her leg as she kicked off her wellies.

'I'm starving, Mum, is lunch ready?' said Sarah.

'It'll be five minutes. Are you going to wash your hands first?'

'I'm in my mid-thirties, Ridpath, with a kid, and she still treats me like I was ten years old.'

'I'm sure it will never change, Sarah.'

'Too right,' said Mrs Challinor.

'Come on, Eve, I'll show you the bathroom and you can get changed in my bedroom if you want.'

'Thanks, Sarah.'

They both ran upstairs, making so much noise it felt like the floor of the cottage would collapse.

When it was obvious they could no longer hear, Mrs Challinor asked, 'What happened to the young girl?'

'Anita Forsyth?'

Mrs Challinor nodded her head.

'She was released from the children's home and has gone to live with her dad in Scotland. She'll be given counselling of course, plus it wouldn't surprise me if she's contacted by an ambulance-chasing lawyer soon...'

'One of the no-win, no-fee, people?'

'Exactly. GMP cocked up her initial interview and didn't follow procedures for dealing with a young child. Ron Pleasance has received a black mark on his record and the force is just waiting for the lawsuit.'

'Couldn't happen to a nicer man.'

'And Claire Trent?'

'Her leaving do was last night.'

'Did you go?'

'For five minutes, but the boss knows I have to be back for Eve so she understood. I'll miss her...'

Mrs Challinor sighed. 'I will too.' A long pause. 'I have some news of my own, Ridpath.'

He looked up.

'I think I'm going to retire. After the attack, I haven't felt at my best. I'm not sure I can handle the work any more. I keep losing my temper with the staff, blowing my top for no reason at all. I talked with the neurosurgeon, Mr Pereira, and he says sometimes it's one of the after-effects of a traumatic brain injury – an inability to control the emotions.' She laughed. 'I even found myself crying during an episode of *Strictly* last week. Tears running down my cheeks. What if that happened in court?'

'I understand, Mrs Challinor.'

'I'm sorry, Ridpath.'

He stood up and walked over to her. 'Whatever is right for you, Coroner, you know you'll always have my support.'

'Thank you, Ridpath. I'm so glad you understand.'

'When are you planning to leave?'

'About six months from now. It'll take them that long to find my replacement. But until then, we still have lots to do.'

'We still have time to represent the dead in the land of the living.'

'Exactly, Ridpath. A lot more causes to fight, and wrongs to make right.'

'I'll miss you, Coroner.'

'I'll miss you too, Ridpath, but I hope we'll still have our Saturday lunches with Eve.'

'I hope so, too.'

The coroner brushed her long curly hair away from her face. 'Talking of your daughter, she's told me what she wants to do.'

'She's been hinting to me, too. She wants to be a barrister, doesn't she?'

'Not only that, a barrister specialising in human rights.'

He shook his head. 'At least that's a long time in the future.'

'I wouldn't take her dreams too lightly, Ridpath. Once your daughter sets her mind on something, nothing will get in her way. A bit like her dad really.'

Ridpath smiled but inside he was thinking. *What does the future hold?*

And, for the first time since Polly died, he didn't have a clue.

ⓒ CANELOCRIME